Somebody Killed
His Editor

For sixteen years reclusive mystery writer
Christopher (Kit) Holmes enjoyed
a very successful career, thanks to the popularity
of elderly spinster sleuth, Miss Butterwith,
and her ingenious cat, Mr. Pinkerton.
But sales are down in everything but chick lit,
and Christopher's new editor doesn't like geriatric
gumshoes. It's a pink, pink world for Mr. Holmes.

At the urging of his agent, Kit reluctantly
agrees to attend a mystery writers' conference
at a remote Northern California winery.
But no sooner does he arrive than he discovers
the pajama-clad body of a woman in the woods.
If nearly two decades of mystery-writing
are anything to go by,
the woman doesn't appear to have died
a natural death.

Somebody Killed His Editor

Holmes & Moriarity I

Josh Lanyon

VELLICHOR BOOKS

An imprint of JustJoshin Publishing, Inc.

SOMEBODY KILLED HIS EDITOR

Holmes & Moriarity I

June 2019

Revised edition, August 2016

Copyright (c) 2016 by Josh Lanyon

Cover by L.C. Chase

Book design by Kevin Burton Smith.

Edited by Sasha Knight

Additional edits by Keren Reed

ISBN: 978-1-945802-86-7

Published in the United States of America

JustJoshin Publishing, Inc.

3053 Rancho Vista Blvd.

Suite 116

Palmdale, CA 93551

www.joshlanyon.com

This is a work of fiction. Any resemblance to persons living or dead is entirely coincidental.

CHAPTER ONE

I can understand suffering for one's art—but dying? Not really my style.

But death did appear to be on the day's program judging by the groaning sounds from the bridge beneath me. I grabbed for the rain-slick wood railing with my free hand and stared down. A churning brown froth of mud, rocks, and tree branches battered against the sagging pilings. I made groaning sounds of my own.

My disabled silver Lexus sat on the opposite side of the swaying bridge—too far to turn back now. I clung to the rail as the bridge heaved. Rain came down in glinting needles. I squinted, trying to make out the opposite bank. I couldn't see it.

As I hesitated, the decision was made for me. The bridge shuddered and then ripped partially away from its moorings. I had no choice but to race for the other side, clunk, clunk, clunking unevenly along in impractical Bruno Magli boots, and trying not to trip as my obscenely heavy suitcase banged against my knee, my bulging carryall bouncing from my hip to my butt.

I could hear the voice of Rachel, my agent, ringing in my ears. "It won't kill you to dress up for once."

Famous last words. Me and my career, both dead in one week.

Clunkclunk, clunkclunk, clunkclunk...

Over the roar of the flood I could hear the shriek of joints giving way (luckily not my own) and splintering wood. The slats beneath my feet seemed to fall away. I pictured myself as one of those cartoon characters, legs bicycling in empty air for a few seconds before gravity kicks in. I ran harder—like the cartoon characters always do.

I'd known this weekend was a mistake from the moment Rachel had suggested it. I'd known, but I had ignored my instincts. And now I was well in the lead for this year's Darwin Award.

The bridge returned, rippling beneath my clattering feet.

Clunkclunkclunkclunkclunkclunkclunk... My boots telegraphed panic.

Nobody was going to believe this. Hopefully. Hopefully nobody would believe that I was this stupid. Well, first off, nobody was going to believe I'd voluntarily gone to a writers' retreat. I was going to wind up as an episode in *Unsolved Mysteries*.

I could practically hear Robert Stack now, solemnly spelling it out for the at-home viewers.

"But questions remain. Why would Christopher Holmes choose to cross a rickety old half-flooded bridge on foot after deeming it unsafe to drive across? Why would the forty—er—thirty-nine-year-old author of numerous award-winning mysteries have agreed to visit a remote writers' retreat in California wine country when friends and family agree Christopher loathed writers' conferences and red wine always gave him a headache? And why would this reasonably intelligent and supposedly sane man have spent SO GODDAMNED MUCH MONEY ON A PAIR OF BOOTS THAT WERE PROBABLY GOING TO PROVE THE DEATH OF HIM?"

Robert Stack's God-like voice had to shout to be heard over the boom of water and eroding earth. I lumbered along like a drunken pack mule, listing from side to side under the weight of my luggage, and to my own astonishment I felt the wooden planks give way to…mud. Mud and grass. My toes sank into the turf like rock-climbing crampons holding my wildly teetering self safely in place.

I was on the other side.

I was alive.

I clambered up the uneven slope and turned back to see the wooden bridge that connected Blue Heron Lodge to the outside world half-submerged beneath the flooded creek. Brush, boulders, and bedraggled saplings rammed against the fallen structure and spun away to be washed downstream.

My legs gave out, and I collapsed on top of my bags. Shock, I guess. Not to mention more exercise than I'd had in the past five years. Cold rain peppered my head and face. I clutched my bags as though they contained all my worldly possessions, which to all intents and purposes they did. Fortunately there were enough extra clothes stuffed in there to make shelters for a dozen refugees, which is what I felt like.

I checked my watch. Four o'clock. It seemed later thanks to the lousy weather. One thing for sure: I didn't want to be wandering around here in the dark. I hauled myself to my feet. Why the hell hadn't I thought to grab the map when I bailed out of the car?

The lodge was nowhere to be seen. That would have been too easy. I mean, why would anyone want to house writers within walking distance—or even sight—of a main road? You might have scribes going AWOL, fleeing rubber round steak and limp lettuce for local fast-food joints—or bars—skipping out on workshops given by equally desperate colleagues, or, God forbid, deciding that their time would be better spent writing rather than paying money to talk about writing.

A crooked dirt road led up and over a small pine-covered hill that seemed to vanish into the low, sullen skies.

I picked up my suitcases and hobbled toward the hill. The distant tang of the sea and the smell of woodsmoke hung in the air.

After a few yards of my Long-John-Silver-on-a-Bender routine, it occurred to me that quite possibly I was carrying appropriate footwear in my suitcase. I abandoned the road, evading the branches of the pine trees. The canopy provided scant protection from the downpour, deadening the sound of the rain. Kneeling in a nest of pine needles, I snapped open the locks on my suitcase, fishing around inside a pile of clothes I didn't recognize.

I didn't recognize them because they were brand new and had been selected by a helpful sales associate at Saks department store while I'd occupied myself scoping "the competition" at the nearby Borders. When I say "competition," I don't mean men who are younger, buffer, and have more hair than me—I mean writers with books on the Featured Selections shelf. Bad boys and pink ladies. Dick and Chick Lit.

The new wardrobe was all part of Rachel's master plan that I should "reinvent" myself and thus resurrect my career. I failed to understand how multi ear piercings and a new 'do could persuade Steven "Satan" Krass, my new editor at Wheaton & Woodhouse, to reconsider his decision to dump me if my track record didn't speak for itself (eleven NYT bestsellers and over twenty awards). I couldn't imagine what argument black leather could make, but I was desperate. And scared.

From Boy Wonder to Has Been in one easy lesson. Well, maybe not easy, and it had taken sixteen years, but I was the victim of a kind of literary middle-aged spread—and I was barely forty.

"Steven feels that the sales on the last four books were... er...rather soft," Rachel had tried to explain. "The numbers aren't there."

"What numbers? *Miss Butterwith Closes the Case* is already in its third printing." I couldn't believe what I was hearing. They weren't renewing us? They weren't picking up my option?

"But that's way down from, say, the first six months of *Miss Butterwith Dispenses.*"

I felt numb. It had never even occurred to me that the day would come when Miss B. and I could no longer hoist ourselves over the transom.

"But *everyone's* sales are down, right? That's what I keep hearing. No one is reading, that's what everyone says. Everyone is watching DVDs and listening to CDs and playing computer games." Cold sweat popped out on my forehead. I felt nauseous. I don't take rejection well. Ask my ex.

"Not everyone's sales are down," Rachel said carefully. And the fact that she was being careful told me everything I needed to know. In New York publishing circles Rachel Ving is known as Ving the Merciless. "Look, Christopher, the market has changed. Miss Butterwith is—"

I couldn't bear to hear it. I had to interrupt. Portly and unfashionable though she might be, Miss Butterwith was my baby, the child of my heart. I cried, "Miss Butterwith is a classic, she's an institution. She's right there with Miss Silver and Hildegarde Withers." I swallowed on the last word, a kid-like gulp. I went on arguing, as though it were Rachel I had to convince.

"The critics have compared her to Miss Marple. I mean, Miss Butterwith and Mr. Pinkerton have solved more crimes than—" This wasn't just my livelihood, this was my—well, actually considering the fact that this was my livelihood was about all I could take in. I'd sold the first Miss Butterwith straight out of college. I'd been writing the series, three books a year, for sixteen years.

"Well, maybe we should think about spinning Mr. Pinkerton off," Rachel said, trying to be helpful.

"Rachel!"

She was still thinking out loud. "Yeah… You know, it's not a bad idea. Crime-solving cats are still popular. Look at the *Cat Who* books. Maybe he could get locked in a trunk of…of… I've *got* it. Weapons of mass destruction are being shipped to the States, and Mr. Pinkerton gets trapped in one of the crates."

My shattered silence must have said it all.

She said awkwardly, "Or maybe not. This isn't the end of the world. You're a very talented writer. You merely need another platform."

Platform? How about a window ledge?

"Simply because Wheaton & Woodhouse isn't going to pick up your contract—"

"You mean *Steven Krass* isn't going to pick up my contract," I broke in bitterly. "It's his decision, right? He's the Editorial Director, right?"

"It's business, Christopher. It's nothing personal."

"It ought to be personal. After all the money I've made for them. Do you know the offers I've had over the years?"

Well, yeah, Rachel knew. She was my agent. She also knew no one had tried to lure me away in recent memory, but instead of pointing out this painful fact, she came up with her brilliant scheme to have me ambush my former editor at Blue Heron Lodge where he was booked to bestow divine wisdom on acolytes all weekend long.

Rachel's idea of ambush was different from mine—less likely to land me in Tehachapi Correctional Institution. In my best consummate professional manner—whatever the hell that meant—I was going to propose a brand new and absolutely brilliant series. Now all I had to do was come up with the idea for one.

"This is the perfect opportunity to try something new," she urged.

"I don't want to try anything new."

"Well, you should. You're a thirty-something-year-old man writing about a seventy-year-old spinster and her cat. That *cannot* be healthy."

I was so flattered that Rachel thought I was still in my thirties that I didn't put up half the fight I should have.

I managed to locate one Reebok tangled in a knot of silken jockstrap (what had that kid in Saks been smoking?), found the other rudely nudging the crotch of a pair of Kenneth Cole trousers, and managed to exchange my footwear in a kind of squatting fumble, sort of like a Russian dancer after a few vodkas. As I balanced there, one hand planted in wet pine needles, one hand tugging on my boot, I caught a flash of color out of the corner of my eye.

I sank back—barely noticing that I was sitting on a pinecone—and stared. A small building sat in a clearing a few yards from me. It looked like a miniature Japanese teahouse. The shoji screen door hung drunkenly from its frame, and a bundle of rags spilled out onto the ground.

I felt the hair prickle on the back of my neck. Suddenly the woods seemed deadly silent. A single diamond drop of rain fell soundlessly from the branch in front of me. Nothing else moved.

Slowly, I got to my feet and limped past a bronze statue of the seated Buddha. As I drew near the teahouse with its broken door, the pile of rags came into sharp focus. I could pick out a glint of gold, splashes of purple, and rumpled khaki, and then I knew for sure that I was looking at clothes.

Clothes and hair.

A body.

I stopped a few feet away. It was a woman. A woman with blonde hair tumbled across her face. She appeared to be wearing plum-colored pajamas beneath a khaki trench coat. Her feet were bare. Small, bare, blue-white feet with red-painted nails and a gold toe ring.

I took another step forward and then stopped. She wasn't breathing. She wasn't moving. She wasn't the right color. You don't have to write crime novels to recognize a dead body when you see one.

A really good clue was the broken and bloody tree branch lying an inch from the tip of my boot.

CHAPTER TWO

I was out in the middle of nowhere with a corpse.

On the bright side, *I* was not the corpse.

For a second or two—or three—maybe four—I stood there showing none of the cool presence of mind demonstrated by Miss Butterwith in her forty-eight cases.

"Oh, *fuck*," I whispered. Usually I'm better at dialogue.

You would think that someone who made his living off death and danger would be better equipped to deal. Not the case, sad to say. After what felt like a very long time, but probably wasn't (one hopes) *that* long, I started looking around myself for...what? A convenient telephone booth? A cop? Miss Butterwith? I saw my suitcase lying open a few feet away. I saw the empty road beyond. The road seemed very empty, and the woods seemed dark and silent.

Of course it could have been a natural death. That broken branch could have come down in the wind and rain and conked the unknown woman.

And then bounced off her rubber head and landed two feet away?

Yeah, right. I was trying to convince myself of this at the same time I was working out that nobody, probably not even people desperate to escape a writing retreat, go for long strolls in PJs and bare feet in the middle of November.

So...chances were good that she was not the victim of a freak accident. So...this might actually be a crime scene I was standing on.

I took an apologetic step backward.

If it was a crime scene, it was not unreasonable to assume that there might be a criminal lurking somewhere. Somewhere nearby. I stared at the teahouse. A few feet to my left, a branch snapped. I jerked around. I couldn't tell if the wind was stirring the bushes or...

Movement in my peripheral vision. I turned back to the teahouse, and as I stared, it seemed to me that I glimpsed something black move behind the torn screen. Was someone standing inside the doorway, watching me? Or was that motion an effect of shadows and light? Lots of shadows and not much light. I strained to see more closely.

"Hello?" I called too loudly.

The rain pattered down softly on the leaves and roof. I glanced at the laughing Buddha. He looked less jolly—in fact, he seemed to be sweating bullets.

Writers are typically...observers. We're not action heroes. I mean, I don't even *write* about action heroes. I took another step backward, then another—and nearly tripped over a second tree branch. I caught my balance, turned, and sprinted the few feet to my suitcase, throwing myself down beside my bags, stuffing my things back inside, fumbling to lock it. Getting to my feet, I slung my carryall over my shoulder and made for the open road.

You know that thing about Death Be Not Proud? Well, Fear Be Not Proud either. And Fear Be Not Elegant. What Fear be is stumbling, bumbling flight, crashing through brush, slip-sliding on pine needles, sloshing through puddles that are always deeper than you expect.

I burst out onto the open road and paused, chest heaving as I tried to catch my breath.

No one seemed to be following me.

It—*she*—had to have come from the lodge, right? She couldn't have walked from town. She was wearing pajamas, so she had probably come out here in the middle of the night. *Why?* It was late afternoon; why hadn't anyone noticed she was missing? Why wasn't this place crawling with people looking for her?

It was just me and… Well, hopefully it was just me. I stared. Nothing moved in the dark impenetrability of the woods, yet I *felt* like I was being followed. I *felt* like I was being watched.

And standing out in the middle of an open road made it very easy to watch me. To pursue me, if it came down to it.

I jogged across the road and ducked into the trees on the other side. Standing in the shadows, I gazed out at the woods opposite.

Nothing happened.

It was so quiet I could hear my wristwatch ticking. How long was I going to wait? Till something happened? I didn't *want* anything to happen. Enough had happened already. Much better to hightail it out of there before the next thing happened. Especially if it was going to happen to me.

Picking up my bags again, I started race-walking toward the hill.

What else could go wrong? Did they have bears up here? I knew my California history, even if I did set all my own books in picturesque English villages with horrendous crime rates, and it seemed to me that this area had once been populated by grizzly bears and cowboys and other antisocial carnivores.

A covey of quail burst from the bush in front of me. I yelped. However, being short of breath, it came out more like a balloon losing air fast. The quail vanished into the wet silence, wings beating, making weird twittery sounds.

My thoughts kept circling back to the woman lying dead in the woods. How long had she been there? Not too long, from the looks of things. Even though we try to keep the forensic details to a tasteful minimum in cozy mysteries, I'd watched plenty of episodes of *Bones*. And not merely because of David Boreanaz.

At the crest of the hill I paused for another rest. Safe to say, I would not be winning the President's Challenge this year. My calf muscles were burning. I had a stitch in my side. My back was starting to twinge in that ominous way. Unbelievable to think I was struggling so hard to get someplace I hadn't wanted to go to begin with.

Below, I could see a rambling old-fashioned log-and-stone house and several outlying buildings and cabins. Lights twinkled in the many windows of the main house. A thread of pale smoke rose cheerily from separate chimneys. In the scattered cabins, the windows were mostly dark.

Beyond the lodge were the vineyards, rippling in the wind, with an eerie glint of red or blue or silver flickering here and there amidst the yellowing leaves—something metallic to discourage birds, I guessed.

The valley was encircled by a forbidding wall of mountains wreathed in storm clouds. Lovely. The kind of place the Donner Party might choose to vacation.

I dropped my bags then and there. Not that putting my back out wouldn't have been the perfect touch to this weekend. What the hell was I thinking buying all this stuff? Wasting money when I was technically unemployed? Even the mental picture of bears dancing around the woods in my brand-new Calvin Klein briefs couldn't convince me to haul my bags farther. New underwear. The sure sign of desperation. I hadn't bought new underwear since...

Yeah. Like the Road Not Traveled wasn't bad enough, I had to take a detour down Memory Lane.

Nope. Not going to happen. Gritting my teeth against the torture of heels rubbed raw—and memory rubbed rawer—I forged on.

And on.

At last the stone and wood homestead loomed before me like a painted backdrop on the set of *Bonanza*. Chimes made of rusted cowbells jangled on the breeze as I made it up the steps to the long porch. Pushing open the heavy front door, I nearly swooned with the combination of warmth and the homely scents of firewood and cooking.

I half collapsed on what appeared to be an abandoned— unless you counted the stuffed moose head mounted on the wall—front desk. There was a silver bell on the polished desk. I rang it.

Silence followed the cheerful ring.

"Hello?"

From down the hall I could hear voices and general merriment...like a party. Weren't these people supposed to be writing? How could anyone get any work done with that racket going on?

In a kind of sleepwalker's shuffle, I headed down a short hallway carpeted with faded Indian rugs. I caught a glimpse of myself in a long horizontal mirror and got a funhouse view of Quasimodo's kid brother. It was almost a relief to realize that it was me—I'd have been terrified to be alone with that creature.

A few yards farther down I found myself outside what appeared to be a meeting room. Huge picture windows looked out over a long deck and the vineyards. The mountains beyond could have been a painted backdrop. Open timber beams disappeared in the shadows of a soaring ceiling. An immense stone fireplace crackled cheerfully.

The room was packed with people, and everyone seemed to be talking at once—which, as I recalled, is pretty much how conferences go. A lot of the people were female and under thirty. Despite the chilly weather there were a lot of bare arms and bare legs. I'd seen fewer bare midriffs at a belly-dancing competition. That, of course, was the chick-lit contingent. They wrote mysteries called things like *A Whole Latte Death* and *Death Wore a Little Black Dress.* With their cartoon covers and glam author shots, they'd managed to turn murder and mayhem into something quite...frivolous.

An angelically beautiful guy with golden curls and a guitar sat in front of the fireplace. He wasn't playing—maybe it was a prop. I made a mental note to put in a request for "Michael, Row Your Boat Ashore."

I located Rachel almost immediately by the ring of spellbound people who appeared to be staring at their shoes. Rachel is five feet tall without heels and imposingly beautiful—like one of those tiny Mandarin empresses. Thumbelina meets *Vogue.* Despite the lack of inches, she's not easy to overlook. She was chatting with a knot of people, not one familiar to me. Rachel's crystal-clear Asian-English accent carried.

"Murder is *always* hot. *Always* topical. Auden said it best. 'The murder mystery is the dialectic of innocence and guilt.'"

Shoot me now.

To her far left was Steven Krass, who I recognized from his photos in *Mystery Scene*. Tall, blond, and handsome—the kind of recruit you seek when you're looking to people your Fatherland.

He was talking to a lithe and lean man dressed in black, sporting one of those dapper little mustache and beard combos like a young Spanish grandee.

Oh. Mah. Gah. As the natives say. J.X. Moriarity. How perfect. How...ironic. How perfectly ironic. The last time J.X. and I had crossed swords—and other body parts—was at the start of my career. By some ill luck, here he was in at the kill. For some reason the image clearest in my brain was the Full Living Color memory of his tanned and taut ass slipping out of my hotel bed and into a pair of Levi's.

Rachel turned and spotted me. "Oh," she said. It was more of a gasp really—like the kind of sound the Queen of England would make if someone slapped her on the back and called her Liz.

The people with her—she's always got a string of hopeful followers—turned to see what had alarmed their deity. It was like in a film where everyone zeros in on the newcomer and the soundtrack fades and action decelerates to slow mo—usually to be followed by a hail of bullets and the demise of everyone wearing white.

While Rachel did not actually pull an Uzi out of her Prada bag, she was not wearing her happy face as she detached herself from the others, pushing her way through to me. Grabbing me by the arm, she hissed in my ear, "Christopher, I told you to dress *up.*"

CHAPTER THREE

The implication being that this was how I usually looked?

I freed myself from her warden's clutch. Like the rival villain in a penny dreadful, I hissed back, "For your information, the bridge is out. I had to walk all the way from the main road."

"You walked?"

You'd have thought Rachel was a native Californian, given the horror in her voice.

"About five miles. I had a flat tire. That's the least of it." I took bitter satisfaction in delivering my bad news. "I found a body in the woods."

"You—" She couldn't even finish it. She stared at me. Light dawned in her almond-shaped eyes, then faded, as she read my grim expression. "Bloody *hell*. You're serious?"

Did she really think I was desperate enough to reinvent myself as the kind of nut who claims they've witnessed murders or been abducted by space aliens? Actually, I *was* that desperate, I just wasn't that imaginative.

"I'm serious. I stopped to change shoes by this Japanese teahouse in the woods, and there was a dead woman…lying there." As opposed to a dead woman doing what?

Rachel was staring at my encrusted trainers. In tones used by the medium at a séance she repeated, "The teahouse…in the woods?"

"Rachel, snap out of it. Maybe it was a temple. Or a gardening shed. How do I know? The point is the *dead* woman."

She swallowed hard. "Are you sure she was dead?"

"Affirmative. We need to tell someone." We were beginning to attract attention. Rachel's coterie crowded around asking what the problem was. Luckily, across the room, Steven Krass was still hanging on J.X. Moriarity's every word. Probably planning to give him my slot in Wheaton & Woodhouse's spring catalog. Not that I'm paranoid.

"Who's in charge here?" I asked.

"Edgar and Rita Croft," Rachel said.

An award-winning couple, I had no doubt. "Well, we'd better tell them. They'll have to call the authorities. Although, I don't know how anyone is getting in here, unless there's another road?"

"Bloody *hell*," said Rachel again. Turning, she led the way through the mob to a long buffet table where a tall, big-boned, impossibly raven-haired woman of about sixty was stuffing assorted muffins into plastic bags.

"Rita, something dreadful has happened."

Rita barely paused in the muffin retrieval. "Honey, they're trying to fix the cappuccino machine," she replied, bagging like she was in the express checkout line and shooting for employee of the month.

"This is Christopher Holmes, and—"

Rita paused, brown fingers sinking into a chocolate muffin. She stared at me with a kind of disbelieving recognition.

At last, I thought, and my spirits rose. A fan. She was the right demographic, though sadly the over-fifty demo isn't the one most publishing houses actively court these days.

"You're two days late, mister," she informed me crisply. "Get this straight. There's no refund on the cabin *or* the conference."

So much for fandom. I shot Rachel a look. She knew perfectly well I hadn't planned on really participating in this conference. I mean, I wasn't about to sit through workshops given by enthusiastic twentysomethings on Getting That First Novel Down on Paper or Finding Your Hero's Fatal Flaw (like you'd have to dig very deep to find a guy's fatal flaw). The very idea gave me cold chills. Or maybe that was my five-mile forced march in the rain.

"Sorry about the mix-up," I began, "but there's something you should—"

"There was no mix-up on this end," Rita retorted. "Your reservation was held in good faith."

"Okay, but—"

"This conference—retreat, whatever you want to call it— sold out over three months ago."

"Sure. I understand—"

"Cancellations have to be made two weeks in advance."

I blurted, "There's a dead body in your woods."

Rita stared at me with pale blue eyes while ripples of shock went around the pool of listeners.

"You might have broken that a bit more gently," Rachel muttered.

I ignored this, prompting Rita. "Blonde, late forties maybe, purple pajamas, gold toe ring?"

Rachel sucked in her breath. *"Peaches Sadler."*

More ripples on the pink pond—I was wondering how Rachel recognized the dead woman from a description of her PJs and toe ring.

Peaches Sadler. That had to be her real name. No marketing department would concoct "Peaches Sadler." But why was that name so familiar to me?

"Well," drawled Rita, seemingly unmoved. "That explains that."

That explains what? I wondered, but there wasn't opportunity to ask. Rita said something about finding Edgar and disappeared through a side door off the meeting room. Meanwhile, the news of Peaches' demise was being passed from person to person in a grown-up version of Telephone—and probably about as accurately.

"I'm getting old. I had to leave my luggage by the road." I automatically reached for one of the chocolate muffins in the bag left lying there. Despite a decent lunch at the Encounter Restaurant at LAX, I was starving. Running for my life does that to me. "So who's Peaches Sadler?"

Rachel's eyes did this uncharacteristic slide away from mine. "Peaches Sadler is the author of *Some Like It Haute*. The bestselling comic crime novel of last year. You know, literary, but with that sexy chick-lit sensibility. She's huge. She…was."

I was listening to Rachel's tone rather than her words as I crammed the muffin in my mouth, the chocolaty sweetness melting on my tongue. "Hold on a sec," I said thickly, and dusted the crumbs from my chin. "Isn't she the broad who wrote that essay in the *New York Times*? 'Who Killed Miss Marple?' was the title, and she basically blamed the decline of the classic mystery on hacks like me. 'Sherlock Holmes's *other* brother and his ilk,' that's what she wrote."

Rachel gnawed her carmine-stained lips—something I'd never seen her do before. "I don't think she was singling *you* out so much as generalizing about the—"

"The hell she wasn't. That bitch dissected—savaged—three of my most popular titles. She called Miss Butterwith a nosy old bat with ugly shoes and no sense of humor. She said she was like Frankenstein's Bride, a grotesque *pasticcio* of her older and more clever sisters."

I hadn't even known what "*pasticcio*" was before reading that essay—every word of which was branded into my memory.

Rachel looked more uneasy than ever. "Do keep in mind that Peaches wrote that in answer to another essay very critical of the new direction that mystery fiction has taken—" She glanced past my shoulder and pasted on a twitchy white smile. "Hullo, J.X."

Instantly my body went so rigid that my head shook—and for the life of me I couldn't have explained why. I thought of the man in purely professional terms—and that's about *all* he was wearing when I thought of him. I glanced around, trying not to crack my fused spine. J.X. Moriarity offered that sardonic grin that was so effective on his book jackets. A tiny gold stud glinted in his ear.

"Kit Holmes," said the only person in the world who called me Kit instead of Christopher. "As I live and breathe."

"*Such* a bad habit," I murmured.

"I thought I recognized you."

Really? He remembered me looking like Swamp Thing? How flattering.

"We meet again," I said as casually as though I'd stumbled over him on Park Avenue—or maybe under a bush in Central Park. "How've you been?" Not that I had to ask. He looked great, and you had only to open *Publisher's Weekly* to see his latest thriller climbing the charts like Jack the Giant Killer scaling the beanstalk. Not that I begrudge anyone his success. Much.

"Good. Great." He offered his hand, which seemed formal given the vividness of my own memories. I switched the muffin to shake—hoping that I was not smearing his palm with chocolate. He raised his eyebrows. "Cold hands, cold heart," he said.

"Ha," says I.

He looked me up and down. "You're soaked through."

"You really *did* use to be a police detective."

"Have you heard about Peaches?" Rachel whispered, forestalling further civilities.

He still had my hand, which is why I felt him stiffen. "What about her?" He sounded...frosty. Or maybe I was projecting. I'd have sold my soul for a hot shower and a change of clothes about then.

The side door swung open, and Rita returned with a tall, square-jawed man with a gorgeous shock of silvery hair like a well-aged Clark Gable. He wore cowboy boots and an olive shooting jacket.

"You're the young fella who found Ms. Sadler?" He had an attractive raspy voice, very different from J.X.'s husky tenor.

Speaking of which, J.X. was stone silent.

I nodded. "She was lying by that Japanese temple in the woods."

"The shrine? And you're sure she was..."

"I'm sure."

"This is a real tragedy." He shook his head regretfully. "A real shame."

"It's bad news for the conference, that's for sure," Rita said. "And it's bad news for us. What would she have been doing out there in this weather?" She sounded indignant. "She was asking for trouble!"

Edgar said to me, "Young fella, would you mind showing us where she is?"

I did mind, actually. I was dirty, wet, exhausted, and I prefer my dead bodies between the pages of a mystery novel. "*Me?* She's right there at the shrine. You know where the shrine is, right?"

His silvery eyebrows rose. "Sure, but—"

"I mean, you've called the sheriffs, surely? They're on their way?"

"The phone lines are down," J.X. said curtly. "They've been down since noon."

I glanced his way. His chiseled features looked sharper than they had a few moments before.

"Well, what about cell phones?" As a self-proclaimed recluse, I didn't bother with one, but I couldn't believe the rest of these minions of technology weren't packing.

"Have you noticed the mountains around us? Reception is impossible." Rachel too wore a weird expression. Maybe it was the dawning realization that we were trapped here. Not exactly heartwarming news for me, either.

"Internet access?"

"The lodge doesn't offer internet access," Rachel informed me. "Writers don't get anything done with internet access."

"A two-way radio? Walkie-Talkies?" I turned to Edgar Croft.

He shook his head regretfully. "Somewhere around here we must still have an old radio set. We'll have to try to dig it out later."

"Carrier pigeon?" I have a tendency to babble when I'm nervous. "Blanket and campfire?"

J.X. made a snorting sound.

Yep, the inference was that we were here for the duration. We could not phone out, and apparently we could not drive out. Which meant the police could not drive in—they could not even land a helicopter until the storm passed.

"Meantime…" Edgar said slowly. He didn't finish the sentence. He didn't have to.

J.X. seemed to shake off his preoccupation. "Right," he said briskly. "We're losing daylight."

They both gazed at me expectantly. "But…you don't need *me*," I protested. "You know where the shrine is. And I've got to get out of these wet clothes. Really. I'm prone to ch—"

"We can wait," J.X. said. "It will save us time in the long run."

Oh, he was loving this. And what was with the "we" stuff? Was he planning to join the expedition? Once a cop always a cop?

"No, it won't. She's right there. You can't miss her." First body to the right.

He frowned at this non-civic mindedness, but what did I care what he thought? He was just a guy I had once—er—well, he was just a guy.

"I'm sure we can borrow some dry clothes for you, Christopher," Rachel said, and I gave her an ungrateful look.

"Sure," Edgar returned easily. "I'll bring up some jeans and a flannel shirt."

"We'll meet you in the front lobby," J.X. said. "Say ten minutes?"

If I was going to *say* anything, it would not be "ten minutes." But I refrained, letting Rachel drag me away to her room. There was no sign of Satan Krass as we made our way through the crowd. He was probably off booby-trapping careers and destroying other unsuspecting people's lives. The rest of the room had fallen into disbelieving and shocked murmurs. Bad news travels fast.

The hallway outside the dining room was deserted—as was the front desk. We climbed a steep rustic stairway to the second level. More Indian rugs and Indian baskets by way of decoration. Wrought-iron light fixtures that suggested cacti and tree branches hung from the sloped ceiling and cast a mellow glow over Charlie Russell prints and black-and-white photos of the winery back in the fifties. Rachel led the way down a long hallway. The murmur of voices from behind closed doors reminded me of bees in a hive.

I tried to avoid the mirrors in Rachel's room, but it was like trying not to look at a traffic accident. All trace of the suave literary lion I'd been impersonating before I arrived at Hell's Half Acre was gone—killed on safari. What remained was a forty-year-old man, average height, average weight, brown eyes, and dishwater blond hair cut in a very expensive haircut that, sopping wet, looked like every other haircut. The head-to-toe mud-coating was the most interesting thing about me.

Somewhere on my wilderness trek I'd lost one of the two tiny earrings gracing my right ear. I mean, wearing one earring was enough out of character. *Two?* And the damned things cost a fortune because I was allergic to any metal but platinum. I dropped the remaining stud on the glass shelf and opened the door to the shower.

I took a quick and scalding shower, toweled off and dressed in the oversize jeans and plaid flannel shirt Edgar Croft had dropped off for me. Edgar was about five inches taller than me. I looked like a little kid playing cowboy dress-up. I opened my mouth to bitch to Rachel, then realized she hadn't said a word since we'd come upstairs.

"Hey, are you okay?" I asked, poking my head out of the bathroom. She stood smoking at the open window, blowing a thin blue stream into the rain-swept air.

She didn't turn. "Naturally."

I'd have to take her word for it. My ten minutes had been up fifteen minutes earlier. I returned to the steamy bathroom, blow-dried my hair without regard to the sleek and spiky style I'd left home with. Don King suited my mood about now, and anyway I was warm and I was clean. That was all that mattered to me.

Rachel turned to survey me when I had finished my repair work. "Maybe you should borrow my bronzer," she said, breaking the uncharacteristic silence.

"Rachel, d'you mind? I'm gay, not European." Like bronzer was going to make a difference? Maybe a facial. Maybe a facelift. "I think Peaches will appreciate my interesting pallor."

She shook her head like it was hopeless. I tended to agree with her. In fact, I had always believed my mission was hopeless—even before I had stumbled over the body in the woods. I hadn't understood half of what she'd talked about that black afternoon on the phone. All that stuff about Candace Bushnell and *Sex and the City* and shoes—*shoes?*—it was like she was speaking a foreign language. Very soon I was going to have to admit to her that I still hadn't come up with the idea for my brand new and absolutely brilliant series. Come to think of it, maybe this gruesome delay wasn't such a bad thing.

I took the giant quilted plaid jacket Edgar had supplied in exchange for my soaked Burberry, and, looking ready-for-action in what probably looked like my dad's bathrobe, went downstairs to meet J.X. and Edgar.

I found them in the lobby, standing by the heavy front door, engaged in undervoiced conversation. Edgar looked like the Marlboro Man, and J.X. looked like he had stepped out of the pages of *GQ*. It's hard to like a man who's younger and more successful than you are. His being better groomed endeared him even less.

Rita greeted me from behind the front desk. "You'll be staying in one of the cabins. Number nine." She pushed a key across the counter.

Number nine, number nine... The ominous refrain from the Beatles' *White Album* ran through my mind.

"Rita, that can wait," Edgar said. "We've got to get a move on."

"Doesn't sound like Ms. Sadler's going anywhere to me," Rita said laconically. A young woman with thick glasses and hair that somehow reminded me of Velma in *Scooby-Doo* also stood behind the desk. She gasped at Rita's words.

I could see that Rita was one of these blunt call-a-spade-a-spade types, but she had a point. "The thing is," I said, taking the pen she handed me and automatically signing the paperwork she pushed my way, "aren't the police going to be unhappy about our tramping all over their crime scene?"

All four of them—five, if you counted poor Bullwinkle looming over the desk—stared.

"*Crime scene.*" They said it in unison. You'd have thought they'd been rehearsing while I was in the shower.

"Uh," I faltered. "I thought I mentioned that."

CHAPTER FOUR

"Uh, no," J.X. said after a pause. "You didn't."

I was liking him less and less.

I stared at the ring of faces. The kid in the horn-rims looked ready to swoon. Between J.X. and the stuffed moose, it was hard to tell who looked more put out. "Well," I said. "It was just a thought."

"It must have occurred to you for some reason."

I had a sudden vision of what he must have been like when he was a cop—curt and sarcastic and no-nonsense. Nothing like my own delightful Inspector Appleby, who so ably assisted Miss Butterwith on all her cases.

"It looked to me like she was hit over the head with a tree branch."

Rita made a sound like seals do when they see sardines flying their way. Her husband gave her a warning look.

"A branch could have broken in the wind and hit her," J.X. objected. "That was a hell of a storm last night."

"True," I said. I mean, why should I argue? I hoped it was an accident. Murder would complicate an already complicated situation, as I could see from the Morse code looks passing between him and Edgar.

"Why would *anyone* want to hurt *Peaches*?" That high wobbly voice belonged to the kid with the Velma hairdo—and she seemed to be talking to me.

I opened my mouth to assure her that I hadn't the foggiest—that despite the knife Peaches had dug between my shoulder blades, I wished her nothing but long life and prosperity (well, long life anyway). But J.X. cut me off with a crisp, "We can discuss it on the way."

It appeared we were under martial law. However, since nobody else seemed willing to challenge J.X.'s assumption of authority, I figured protest would be a waste of time. The sooner we got this over with, the sooner I could eat some supper and get into bed—preferably with the covers over my head and a chair jammed beneath my room doorknob.

The rain had resumed as we filed out the back entrance, and Edgar handed me a battered felt hat from the rack next to the door. It was the kind of hat homely fat squaws wear in politically incorrect cartoons. I pulled it on and followed them outside.

We scuttled across the rain-slick wooden deck and down a rickety set of steps. I reached for the wet railing. Not that a broken leg wouldn't have been a piquant touch to an already *novel* vacation. Or should this descent into hell really be called a vacation? No way would it be classified as such on my tax return.

We reached the lower level safely and started down a slippery walkway which snaked through a small courtyard with dripping patio chairs and tables stripped of their umbrellas. The overhead lights cast blurred reflections in the cement as we hurried past.

We came to a long arbor wreathed tightly in woody vines. It was as dark as a tunnel. The sharp, dry smell of summer reached my nostrils. The withered vines deadened the sound of the rain. Ahead of us, I could hear the steady clomp of Edgar's boots, though I could barely pick out his bulk moving through the dim light.

"Watch your step," J.X. threw over his shoulder as the cement path abruptly gave way to a much rougher wooden walkway. I realized this must be one of the original structures on the property, and put out a hand to orient myself. My fingers brushed J.X.'s jacket.

His voice drifted back to me. "Afraid of the dark?"

"Only the things that go bump."

I meant that literally, as in I didn't want to trip or bang into anything, but I heard his laugh and realized that he took that quite a different way. Which shows how little he knew me; I hadn't flirted with anyone since... Frankly, I couldn't remember the last time I'd flirted with anyone.

Exiting the arbor, we seemed to have traveled back in time. The walkway had given way to hard-packed earth. There were no reassuringly modern overhead lights here, and the lights glinting through the tall hedge of dwarf yew seemed a long way away. We passed a long, low line of chopped firewood. An axe perched in a stump, glistening in the wet. Ahead was a tall brown wooden building, probably the former carriage house.

We dived in a side door, and Edgar turned on the wall switch. Two mini buses, a Land Rover, and a giant pickup with a double cab gleamed in the waxen light.

"Better take the truck," said Edgar. "Don't want to take a chance on getting stuck in the mud."

I murmured agreement. I must have sounded pretty vehement, however, because J.X. glanced at me. His thin mouth twitched with amusement—probably the look the old

Conquistadors wore when they were torturing helpless Indians. "What do you have in the way of a tarp or canvas covering?" he asked Edgar.

Edgar moved off toward one of the well-organized shelving units, and J.X. followed. I tuned out their grim debate on what to bring. Pick axes? Shovels? Spray paint? Were they planning on putting in a new swimming pool while we were out? No need to bother. The back forty was now a lake.

Finally they loaded their toys into the back of the pickup, and J.X. gave me a hand into the cramped confines of the double cab. Maybe he thought I had time-warped into my dotage. I took his hand, felt the hard calloused strength of it as his muscles flexed.

Climbing into one of those giant trucks is never the most graceful maneuver, and my ascent was made less graceful by the fact that my foot caught in the giant cuff of my left jeans leg and I nearly pitched headfirst into the narrow confines of the backseat.

"Easy there, young fella," Edgar advised, watching me right myself with a hostile look at J.X. He started the engine as J.X. swung up with ease and slammed the door shut after him. The cab seemed very crowded; the scent of leather and after-shave and cinnamon was overwhelming. Granted, the cinnamon was me—or rather, Rachel's scented bath gel.

Edgar hit the remote, and the now-mechanized carriage house doors swung up. We had a stark panoramic view of flooded landscape and the black bulk of the hills beyond.

"Lonely out here, isn't it?"

"Sometimes," Edgar agreed, putting the truck in gear.

"Explain to me exactly why you think Peaches was murdered," J.X. requested as we bumped and bounced down the soggy road.

"I said it was a possibility. I didn't say I knew it for sure."

"What you said was, aren't the police going to have a problem with us traipsing over their crime scene? Sounds to me like you were pretty sure."

Did he have phonographic recall or something equally annoying? Imagine the horror of being with a man who remembered precisely everything you ever said. And what kind of shelf life did his recollections have?

"It's kind of a blur now," I said vaguely. "But, okay, the one really odd thing was that Peaches was out there in her pajamas and bare feet. Doesn't that seem unlikely in this weather?"

"Go on."

The truck wheels slipped and spun as we splashed through a pothole the size of a small lake. I held my breath until we had regained firm ground, then replied, "And I already told you about the broken and bloody tree branch a couple of feet from her body."

"Sounds like an accident to me," Edgar commented, his attention on the muddy road.

"Yeah, I'm not following." J.X. directed that my way.

"Look, it was only an impression. I'm probably wrong."

"Probably."

I was leaning forward, so we were practically cheek to cheek. Close enough to whisper sweet nothings into his ear. *Nothing* being about all I had to say to him.

Glancing up, I caught Edgar's gaze in the rearview mirror.

"Okay, except what was she doing out there in her jammies in that weather?"

"Who the hell knows." J.X. faced front again. "She was eccentric. To say the least."

"She was a high-spirited gal," Edgar agreed. He added after a moment, "What made you go into the woods there?"

"Bad luck," I said. "I was trying to find a dry place to change shoes."

As we crested the hill my suitcases appeared in the truck's headlights. Edgar slithered to a stop, and J.X. got out. He tossed my suitcases in the flatbed and climbed back in the cab.

We continued on our way in grim silence. It was only a few minutes' drive, but all the same it was dark by the time we reached the shrine.

"I think it's along here," Edgar said, pulling up on the side of the road. "This look about right to you?"

"I guess. It all kind of looks alike this time of night."

J.X. opened his door. Edgar turned off the engine. "You can stay here if it'll be easier."

"Not that a little practical experience wouldn't do your books a world of good," J.X. tossed back.

It would have been definitely easier—and preferable—to stay in the truck, but after that crack I didn't have a choice. I climbed down and squelched after them into the wet and silent woods. The smoke from our breath hung in the air, the shadows were deep as night.

It didn't take long to find the temple.

Frankly, I half expected that the body would be gone, like the corpse in *Miss Butterwith and the Dear Departed*. But there she lay, her hair plastered and dark against her gray-white skin, her clothes colorless in the gloom. I could see by the stiffness of her limbs that rigor mortis was now advanced.

"Sure you wouldn't rather wait in the truck?" Edgar asked, switching on one of those industrial-sized flashlights. Peaches' toe ring glinted in the beam.

Oddly enough, I no longer wanted to wait alone in the truck. I stood to the side, sheltered beneath the tree branches, and watched them.

J.X. circled the body and took picture after picture from different angles with a small digital camera.

"I wish the light was better," he muttered. He snapped, and the flash briefly illuminated Peaches' face. Not pretty.

"There's the branch." I pointed.

J.X. took a couple of photos of the bloody branch, and then he and Edgar measured the distance from the body to the branch.

"About two feet," Edgar concurred. He glanced at me. "You've got sharp eyes."

I shrugged.

To J.X. he said, "She could have staggered a foot or two after she was hit, I guess."

"Maybe." To his credit J.X. sounded more polite than convinced.

"You didn't see anything...funny...when you found her?"

Funny? Well, no. I shook my head. Edgar looked like I had confirmed his own thoughts on the subject.

"What about footprints?" I asked J.X.

"Can't tell a damn thing in this light. Pine needles would cushion them, I guess."

Between the steady rain and the pine needles, I guessed that there probably wasn't much chance of tracking Peaches' footsteps—or the footsteps of anyone following her.

"There's no way she walked out here," I said. "And she obviously didn't drive herself."

Neither man answered. I knew what they were thinking—that the day's rain would have eradicated any tire tracks.

"We should probably stake a tarp over her," J.X. said at last. "I don't want the crime scene compromised any more than it has been."

He didn't look my way, but I still felt this was a criticism.

"The thing is," Edgar said slowly, "the critters are liable to..."

He didn't finish it. He didn't have to. Maybe there weren't bears in these woods, but there were certainly coyotes, foxes, ravens—even ants and bugs would contaminate the crime scene.

No one spoke. The rain pattered down softly around us.

"You think they'll be out tonight?" J.X. inquired. "In this weather?"

Edgar gave him a look that in a salsa commercial would convey a certain *New York City!* sentiment. It occurred to me that if we weren't leaving Peaches, she would be a travel companion on the way back to the lodge.

J.X. wordlessly considered what Edgar refrained from saying. Then he knelt, pulled the can of spray paint out of the bag they had brought. He scooted around the dead woman, carefully brushing the pine needles and leaves away from around her body. Rising, he slowly, painstakingly sprayed a thin line of navy blue paint around Peaches' sprawled form.

"Seems a mite disrespectful," Edgar muttered. I couldn't seem to speak around the obstruction in my throat.

J.X. said nothing. When he had finished roughly outlining the body and the possible murder weapon, he and Edgar spread the tarp out beside Peaches.

He looked at me, and I saw what he expected. I said—and it was God's truth, but it sounded horrifyingly lame, "I've got a bad back."

His expression told me that this was exactly what he had thought I would say, and I opened my mouth to refute it—but I'd have sounded lamer than I already did. In silence I watched them lift her up, depositing her body on the canvas and folding the flaps over her like they were wrapping a sandwich.

They picked her up and carried her to the truck. I moved out of the way, though I was not in the way.

Circumnavigating the crime scene, I walked over to the Japanese building and peered inside. It smelled of damp wood and something animal. I studied the floor and the torn screen. No convenient cigarette butts or a scrap of material or a matchbook. Real life is so unsatisfactory compared to fiction.

I peered more closely. There seemed to be two shadowy shapes in the darkness.

I jumped at a whisper of sound behind me.

J.X. knelt beside where Peaches had lain. As I watched, he slipped something in his pocket. Then, with gloved hands, he quickly shoveled the pine needles over the spray-painted outline of the body to preserve the paint from further rain.

"I think her suitcases are in here."

His head snapped up, and he rose, coming to join me. He stared inside the small structure.

"Edgar," he called.

"Do you think he'll return to the scene of the crime?" I asked.

He glanced at me but didn't respond as Edgar rejoined us.

"Her suitcases are inside there."

Edgar didn't seem to hear. He handed J.X. an empty trash bag. "You want to put your murder weapon in that?"

By his tone of voice it was clear to me that Edgar still clung to the belief that Peaches had gone for a midnight stroll and been unfortunately conked by a fallen branch. I couldn't blame him. Murder would not be good for business.

J.X. said, "Someone wanted us to think she left voluntarily."

"Maybe she did," Edgar said stubbornly. "Maybe she stashed those suitcases in there herself."

J.X. didn't bother to argue. He picked up the branch with his gloved hand and began to wrap it in the black plastic.

Then he hesitated—just for an instant.

I looked from the branch to his face and then back to the branch, which he finished wrapping in the black plastic.

"Something wrong?" Edgar asked.

J.X. shook his head.

But there was something wrong, and I knew what it was thanks to Miss Butterwith, the retired botanist with an insatiable love of gardening. All those nights spent reading seed catalogs and planting journals were paying off. The branch that hit Peaches over the head had not come from any low-hanging pine tree. For one thing it had been partially sawed off on one end. For another, it wasn't pine. It was black oak. And there wasn't an oak tree anywhere around us.

CHAPTER FIVE

Murder is a lot more fun in books.

The burst of adrenaline that had carried me through our ghastly trip seeped away, leaving me chilled and sick. I hugged my arms around me for warmth, sliding back in my rear seat. The cold glass of the cab window felt good against my aching head.

My suitcases were knocking against the back of the cab. Turning, I glimpsed the mound of tarp sliding gently along the truck bed. I quickly faced forward, staring out the windshield. After a minute or two I closed my eyes and rested my head against the chill of the glass behind me.

"We're liable to have a panic on our hands once word of this gets out." Edgar's voice was as loud as Surround Sound. I jerked back into wakefulness. "Some of those gals are a mite high-strung."

I had an instant visual of the pink ladies in pastel panic—it *was* frightening. We might be trampled beneath all those stiletto heels making for the open road.

"They're not going anywhere," J.X. said indifferently. "Not till the road's open again." He glanced back at me. "Did you faint, or were you sleeping?"

"Just resting my eyes."

"Uh-huh."

"It's been a long day," Edgar sighed.

I must have dozed off again because the next thing I heard was J.X.'s quiet but heartfelt, "*Jesus.*"

I opened my eyes to find his hand planted in my chest, bracing me—which sort of played into the weird dream I'd been having, and then I realized the truck was fishtailing on the slimy hillside while Edgar struggled to regain control. J.X. and I sat in rigid silence as the headlights swung back and forth, catching glittering eyes beneath a bush, the lights of the lodge, the bulk of distant mountains.

Edgar yanked the wheel. We slid sideways a few feet and lodged in a deep rut. He swore under his breath and gunned the engine.

"You've *got* to be kidding," I said.

"Steady." J.X. sounded for all the world like Inspector Appleby in a tough spot. As an afterthought he removed his arm from my chest. I kind of missed the warmth.

Edgar gunned the engine again, and the pickup gained some traction. Mud flew. We jolted and bumped our way back onto what was left of the road. Out of the corner of my eye, I saw J.X. relax. He glanced my way. We shared a grimace of relief.

"Nice driving," he told Edgar.

Edgar grunted.

A few minutes later we reached the outlying buildings of the lodge. The small cabins reminded me of the house tokens in a Monopoly game. Edgar cruised slowly, headlights picking out the black windows.

"Are the cabins all in use?" J.X. asked. "We need a secure location to store her."

Edgar didn't seem to know what to say to that.

Mr. Diplomacy added, "I'd suggest we dump her in the deep freezer, but I don't know how the ladies might react to no frozen yogurt."

"*Jeez*," I said. "How about a little sensitivity here?"

"Hey," he said. "It's not all tea and crumpets."

"It's not all serial killers and rogue cops either, although I admit they seem to sell your books."

Edgar interjected, "I guess you folks have known each other awhile."

"We've exchanged a few barbs online," I said. No point going into what we'd exchanged off-line.

J.X. opened his mouth.

Don't say it, I thought. Or the next murder you investigate will be your own.

He closed his mouth.

Edgar said slowly and thoughtfully, "There's the icehouse. Hasn't been used in years. We could put her there."

"The icehouse?" That was J.X.

I said, "Icehouses were used to store ice all year long back in the days before refrigeration."

Edgar was nodding. "Back in the 1800s they built a cellar into the hillside behind the stables. The pond freezes in winter, and they used to cut the ice in blocks and store them there. There's no ice now, but it's still plenty cold."

"Can it be secured?"

"It's kept locked. We don't want any of the guests getting injured, fooling around in there."

J.X. nodded. "The icehouse it is."

I opened my mouth, but before I could form a protest he added, "We can drop Kit at the main house first."

"We could do that," agreed Edgar.

We drove back past the carriage house and the long vine-covered arbor to the walkway that led back to the lodge. J.X. got out, and I climbed stiffly down after him. Sleet blew in my face as I watched him lift my suitcases out of the back of the truck.

I took the suitcases from him and wondered why I had packed them with bricks.

"Go back the way we came." He pointed at the walkway. I nodded.

"And don't say anything about a possible homicide to any of the others."

I nodded again.

As I hurried down the path I heard the truck door slam and the engine die away. If it had seemed deserted when we came through a couple of hours earlier, it was like a ghost town now despite the smell of woodsmoke lingering in the air. The silhouette of yew branches wavered in the dull yellow pool of the overhead lights, the patio tables and chairs formed a crisscross of bars and boxes like a shadow crossword.

The lodge loomed before me; the rain pouring off the eaves was deafening. I paused, panting at the foot of the stairs leading to the deck, and stared up at the tall black building.

Was there a killer in the house?

Maybe the danger was past. Rigor mortis can set in within a few minutes after death and reach maximum stiffness twelve to twenty-four hours later. Even without the evidence of her pajamas, it was clear to me that Peaches had died during the night. At that point the bridge had still been usable—as were perhaps some of the other roads out of the valley. Peaches' killer could have escaped to the outside world then. If I had committed murder, I wouldn't hang with the girls talking publishing contracts.

The simplest thing would be to ask around and find out who, if anyone, had left during the night or earlier that day—an unexpected departure would be especially interesting. To the police, that is. Not to me, because my only interest was getting out of Hell's Half Acre as fast as possible. It was one thing to write about an amateur sleuth. I had no desire to become one.

I put one foot on the steps, and a new thought occurred. Maybe a passing madman had stolen into the lodge and abducted Peaches Sadler from her wee trundle bed, murdered her in the woods, and then continued on his merry way. I liked that idea. A lot. If only I could convince my inner Miss Butterwith.

I clambered up the stairs, crossed the slippery deck, and grabbed the handle of the lodge's back entrance with my free hand.

The door was locked.

For a moment I stood there shaking with cold and weariness. I dropped my suitcases, took the door handle with both hands, and tried to wrench it open.

It didn't budge.

I banged on the wet wood.

Nothing.

Where *was* everyone?

I looked down the walkway shining and black in the rain. The night was alive with weird shapes and crouching silence. There was a buzzing sound above me. I looked up. Rain glinted in the artificial light like rice. One of the overhead lights flickered. Went out.

I pounded on the door. Yelled.

Nothing.

I *couldn't* go back that way. Walk down that lonely path into the darkness where no one could hear me yelling for help?

I brushed the wet from my face. I hoped it was rain. Maybe I wasn't the most macho guy on the planet, but I was too old to stand here bawling in the rain.

Okay, I'd already walked a few miles. A couple more yards wouldn't kill me—unless something waiting in the shadows did.

Stop it.

I picked my suitcases up and started back the way I had come.

Scuttling along the slippery walkway, I rounded the corner and walked straight into a man carrying an axe.

CHAPTER SIX

I had a quick impression of a tall, dark figure and a cowl without a face—exactly like the ghost of the murdered monk from *Miss Butterwith and the Holy Terror*. I sucked in my breath to vent all my fear—and a lot of my frustration.

Then my eyes adjusted to the light, and I realized I was staring at a man in a hooded jacket. He was still holding an axe—but he was also holding a wood carrier.

"Shiiiiiiiiiiit," he said in shocked and startled tones. "You scared the *shit* out of me."

"The back door is locked," I informed him breathlessly.

"Well, yeah, it's locked. There's a maniac on the premises." His tone indicated he thought he'd located the above-mentioned maniac. And I agreed with him because I now knew for sure that I had been totally insane to ever agree to this scheme of Rachel's.

"How do I get in?"

"What are you doing out here? Did you just get here?"

"Yes—that is, *no*."

"No," he confirmed in the tone of Sherlock Holmes when he's about to explain something amazing about pipe tobacco to Dr. Watson, "because the bridge is out. There's *no way* you could have just arrived from the main road."

"Elementary, buddy," I said. "I was here earlier. I've been out with Edgar and J.X."

He looked startled. I mean, I couldn't really see his face in the dismal light, but his body language indicated surprise. "So you're the one," he said. "You're the one who found…*her.*"

I thought that "her" was revealing. It reminded me of J.X.'s curt, *She was eccentric. To say the least.* Peaches seemed to have had an unsettling effect on the menfolk.

"Yes. I found her." I couldn't think of anything to add to that. My brain didn't seem to be working properly. Too much fresh air.

"Was she—"

"Dead?"

He shook his head. "Murdered," he said huskily.

So much for J.X.'s hope to keep a lid on it.

"I don't know," I lied.

"What happened to her?"

"I don't know."

"You must know something."

A lot of things. And none of them pertinent. "I knew where to find her," I said. "Were you close to her?"

He was silent, considering.

"No one was close to her," he said.

I wondered if that were true. I recalled Miss Butterwith once pronouncing that murder always indicated a certain degree of intimacy. But people in Miss Butterwith's world were never killed by maniacs or serial killers, and I had my heart set on Peaches being offed by a passing madman.

"I'm Christopher Holmes," I said, and shifted suitcases to offer a hand.

"George Lacey." He chopped the axe into a broad tree stump with casual, unerring aim, and shook my hand. "Where did you find her?"

"I had to walk from the main road after the bridge washed out. I stopped in the woods near a tiny Japanese shrine—and there she was."

"Wow."

"My words exactly." I'm not sure where the thought came from, but I heard myself ask, "How come no one noticed she was missing?"

He gave a funny laugh. "Maybe it was a relief to most of them when she was a no-show."

"What do you mean?"

"She wasn't exactly *Ms.* Popularity, you know what I mean?" He took my big suitcase with his free hand—jeez, random acts of kindness practiced right before my very eyes. "Come on, we can get back in this way." He proceeded in the direction opposite of the way I'd come. I gathered my wits and started after him.

"Christopher Holmes, huh? Your name's familiar. I think I've read your books." He glanced over at me. "You write about that Welsh policeman in the mountain village, don't you?"

"Er—no. I write the Miss Butterwith series."

"Oh." He sounded doubtful. "The syrup-bottle lady?"

"That's Mrs. Butter*worth*. No relation."

"Oh."

"Are you a writer?"

He made the sound that Miss Butterwith would have referred to as a raspberry. "Me? Nah. I'm here with Mindy."

"Ah-ha," I said. Mindy, Mandy, Buffy, Trixie. They were all interchangeable. Bright young things with enthusiasm and ambition and occasionally talent, eager to discuss topics like Should You Trust Your Computer's Word Count? Or What Color Did You Paint Your Home Office?

"You probably know her," George added.

"I doubt it."

George and I trekked through the vine-covered arbor and cut back between a vegetable patch and another outlying building, probably a smokehouse from back in the days when smoked meats were still accepted in polite society.

"How many people are trapped here?" I asked.

"You mean guests?"

"What a quaint way to put it. No, I mean literally. Everybody. We're cut off from the outside, you know."

"Oh, yeah. Right. There are fifty conference attendees. I'm not sure if that's counting you or not. And then the lodge staff. It's off-season, so they don't have a big crew."

"Did anyone leave during the night?" Look at me, making like the long lost Hardy Boy. Frank, Joe, and now Dick.

"I don't know." He didn't sound particularly interested, and why should he be?

Why should *I* be?

We reached the long front porch where the cowbell chimes clanged on the breeze, and pushed our way through the heavy doors. The front desk was deserted again.

"Hey," said George, pushing back the hood of his jacket. "Where is everybody? Someone's supposed to be watching the front entrance."

I now recognized George as the angelically beautiful guy with the guitar, whom I'd spotted earlier. Music and wood-chopping. What more could you ask of a man? Besides fidelity, I mean.

"It sounds like they're having a meeting," I said, listening to the sounds from down the hallway. "Or a lynching."

"Those babes can talk," George agreed. He set my suitcase down and pulled the heavy bar across the front door.

"I guess you aren't expecting any more late arrivals," I said, and no pun intended as I thought of poor old Peaches even now checking into the icehouse.

"I guess," George replied. "Well, let's see what's cooking..."

Speaking of cooking, I was starting to get that low-blood-sugar feeling. Not sure if death and disaster were supposed to actually stimulate one's appetite, but I was close to hallucinating at the thought of stale saltines or a lonely chocolate mint that might even now be waiting in my cabin. I wasn't sure I had the strength to follow George as he started down the long hallway. I was debating how to wisely use my last milliseconds of energy when I heard my name whispered in a very sinister fashion.

"*Christopher*," the voice hissed again as I looked wildly around the lobby. "Here. Up *here*."

I looked up. Two stories above me, Rachel leaned at a death-defying angle over the staircase railing. She beckoned sharply to me.

I gestured to George's retreating back. Rachel made waving motions like I was out of bounds. I obediently peeled off, dropping my bags at the front desk and hiking up the staircase to where she stood gnawing her long acrylic nails.

"*Well?*" she demanded as I reached the top step. She sounded as breathless as I felt.

"Well what?"

She was haggard. Hollow-eyed. That's what comes of these writing conferences. "Was she...?"

"Dead? Yes. Of course."

"Murdered."

"That too." Guiltily I remembered J.X.'s orders. "I mean, I think so." I dredged up one of Miss Butterwith's favorite phrases. "We can't be sure until we see the coroner's report."

Did they have coroners up north? Or were they MEs?

"Why would you be looking at the coroner's report? Are you working with J.X. on this?"

"It's a figure of speech. No, I have nothing to do with any of this." Positive affirmation: if I kept saying it, maybe it would be true.

Rachel whispered, "How was she...killed?"

"A tree branch crushed her skull."

She closed her eyes for an instant. "But that could have been an accident."

"Absolutely," I said. "Maybe it was."

Rachel's lashes lifted. She stared at me, perplexed. "What does J.X. say?"

"Very little and most of it's pretty damn rude."

She chewed her lip.

"What's going on?" I asked.

She stared at me, wide-eyed and wordless. She's not the wide-eyed, wordless type.

"You're acting very weirdly," I said. "In case you hadn't noticed."

"It's...shocking."

True. I studied her doubtfully. "How did you know it was her?" I asked suddenly.

Her gaze zeroed in on mine. "Sorry?"

"When I described what Peaches was wearing, you seemed to recognize her from the description." The description of her pajamas and toe ring.

She shook her head. "No. It was simply that no one had seen her all day. We'd all been wondering where she was."

Maybe that was true. It sort of meshed with what George had said. Besides, if Rachel wanted to lie about it, that was her business.

Why, then, did my mouth flap open and the words, "When did you last see her?" slip out?

"What?" She seemed confused. "I…yesterday. No. Last night. In the bar. She was with J.X. and Steven Krass. Why are you asking me all these questions?"

"A writer's curiosity. Forget it." I turned to go downstairs. "I'm heading to my cabin, and then I'm going to bed," I informed her. "Is there any kind of room service around here?"

"No." She shook off her preoccupation. "Anyway, you can't go to bed. Your meeting with Steven Krass has been moved up to tonight. We're going to have drinks in the lounge."

"You expect me to have drinks and pitch a new series *tonight*?"

"Christopher, he's booked practically every minute of this retreat. We have to squeeze in where we can. I mean, that's why you're here, right?"

I met her strained gaze. "Uh…right."

"So go lie down for an hour or two and then make yourself presentable. You have to make this opportunity count."

Oh, God. Here it was. The moment of truth.

"The thing is, Rachel," I said. There was no easy way to put it. "I don't have an idea for a new series."

She lost that wild-eyed look and focused on me.

"*What?* What have you been working on for the past weeks?" She sounded almost like her normal obsessive work-aholic self.

"All kinds of things, but none of them gelled. I just… can't…" I took a deep breath and said good-bye to my career, "… write something with a twentysomething female protagonist. I don't get that thing about the shoes." I delivered the death blow. "I can't write chick lit."

There, it was out.

"Chick lit? Don't waste time on chick lit. Chick lit is over. Dead."

Wow. Coincidence. Peaches *and* chick lit in the same week.

"But I thought you said—"

"That was before. All the data indicates the latest industry trend is veering toward thrillers. Techno thrillers in particular. Erotica is hot. Paranormal is hot. Sexy demons in techno thrillers are *very* hot." She waved her hand as though she had burned her fingers on the latest demon-techno-thriller romance.

"But…"

"No worries." Her acrylic talons sank into my arm although her voice was even. "We'll get together for an early dinner and brainstorm. We can come up with something utterly brill before your meeting with Sata—Steven. Don't panic."

"I'm too tired to panic," I said. "I'm too tired to care one way or the other."

"That's not the right attitude, Christopher. This is your career we're talking about. You have to be willing to do whatever it takes to survive. This is your *life*."

I met her fierce gaze. The sad thing was, she was right. My career *was* my life. And up until now it had been a supremely rewarding one. It had been my pleasure and my passion. It had provided a very comfortable lifestyle, and it had nearly made up for one spectacularly awful relationship—and everything else I might have missed.

"All right," I said. "I'll take a shower and a quick nap and meet you back here for dinner at..." I checked my watch, "... six."

"Remember what we talked about, Christopher," Rachel warned. "It's also about The Look. It's about the whole package. Platform *and* presentation."

"And all these years I thought it was about the writing," I said bitterly.

CHAPTER SEVEN

"They were all jealous of her," Velma told me as we slogged our way through the obstacle course of puddles and mud holes to the guest cabins located a pasture length from the main house.

"Really?" I said with polite disbelief. Granted, Peaches had not been at her best during our brief acquaintanceship. "Why do you think so?" Not that I cared. I was making conversation strictly to keep myself from falling asleep on my feet.

"I *know* so," said Velma.

My back ached. Everything ached. I had never been so tired in all my life. Maybe I was dreaming. Maybe even now I lay in a soft warm bed and merely dreamed that the rain was blowing in my face and I was stumbling through weeds and mud to a little sod shanty on the plains.

"Even Mom…I can't believe she said those things…"

I tuned back in. Velma, who was actually named Debbie and turned out to be Edgar and Rita's daughter, had been designated to guide me to my cabin. Either the kid was the only expendable member of a reduced staff or her parents still clung to the belief that Peaches had died an accidental death.

"People say things when they're in shock," I said. "Don't take it seriously."

"Mom's not like that. She's like…a…a…pioneer person. Nothing shocks her."

"Well, maybe Peaches wasn't a very pleasant guest. I don't know." And I cared even less. But I heard Debbie catch her breath like she was close to tears, and I said gruffly, "I'm sure your mom is dealing with it the best she can. She's probably worried about how this will affect business. I know that sounds kind of callous, but—"

"Last night?"

"Huh?" I said, stopping in my tracks. Debbie stopped, too, turning to face me.

"Was she worried about her business last night? Because last night she said..." She shook her head. "It doesn't matter." She swung away, sloshing right through the nearest puddle.

"You mean your mother and Peaches argued last night?"

"It doesn't matter."

"Uh...probably not. What did they say?"

"It doesn't matter."

We were now at my cabin, which Debbie unlocked. She pushed the door wide, felt inside, and turned on a light switch.

"The phones aren't working now," she informed me. "There are candles and matches in the bureau drawer, in case the power goes out."

"Is that likely?" I looked around uneasily.

The cabin consisted of one room with a charming print of Indians killing buffalos—or, in one instance, buffalos killing Indians—over the full-size bed. There was a table and a lamp and a metal fireplace and a door leading off to a tiny bathroom with a scary shower curtain straight out of *Psycho*. No television and no internet access—and seemingly no phone. It was like prison for writers. Even killers get TV.

"It happens. We start serving dinner at seven in the main dining room."

I thanked her. She wasn't meeting my eyes, perhaps regretting her earlier need to confide. Without further ado, she slipped out, closing the door behind her.

I wondered if it was worth my while to unpack. The rain couldn't last forever, and the minute it let up, I was out of here. Murder investigation or no murder investigation.

In the end I arranged my toiletries around the bathroom cubbyhole, hung the evening's apparel on the back of the door, with the shower taps blasting out hot water in the hopes the steam would shake out the wrinkles. If only it were as easy to shake out my own wrinkles, I thought, gloomily studying my face in the Halloween glow of the bathroom overhead.

I happened to know from a *Publisher's Weekly* article that I was only five years older than J.X., but tonight I looked at least a decade or so. Granted, today had not been the stuff of beauty treatments. Seeing him so unexpectedly had brought back the past in a vivid and disconcerting rush. I didn't want to think about the man I had been back then when my career was taking off. I found the memory distracting. Maybe even depressing, although I wasn't sure why. The best thing was not to think about it.

I flopped down on the calico bedspread and passed out.

Half a second later, it seemed, the alarm on my wristwatch went off. I rose and stumbled into the bath to splash some cold water—very cold water—on my face. I shaved and tried to get my hair to behave in a way that might fool someone into thinking I wanted it to look like that. Studying the bewildering array of grooming products foisted on me by the cosmetic counter consort: scrubs, cleanser, moisturizer, sunscreen (no worries there), and mask (not much of a disguise if you asked me), I wondered what the hell happened to soap, toothpaste, and aftershave? One thing I've noticed about getting older, it takes twice as much work to get half the results one formerly achieved by falling out of bed. Not that I didn't enjoy the architectural challenge of pitting hair and gel against the elements, but there was really no contest. All this effort wasn't going to last three minutes in the wet and windy trek back to the main building.

I dragged on the Kenneth Cole trousers and shrugged into the coordinating classic stripe shirt the sales associate had selected for me. After consideration I decided a tie would look desperate. Pulling my still damp Burberry back on, I shoved my Bruno Magli loafers in my raincoat pockets and stepped into my muddy boots once more.

The nap had slightly refreshed me, but it was nervous energy that propelled me across the wet and lonely stretch back to the lodge. Behind me most of the other cabins were still dark, the majority of guests choosing to hang out at the main house rather than face their lonely cells. I wondered where the ice-house now containing Peaches was located.

Reaching the main house safely, I finger-combed my wet hair, changed my muddy boots for my loafers, and went to find Rachel in the main dining room.

Down the hallway I nearly ran into "Satan" Krass and his entourage. Even if I hadn't known him from his photos, I'd have picked him out of the crowd as the man to be reckoned with. I had to admit he had presence. Though he wasn't as tall as I'd previously thought—in fact, he was shorter than me—he was broad-shouldered and powerfully built beneath an Aran-knit sweater and charcoal trousers. Like a fashion magazine's version of what people wore in ski lodges.

He was surrounded by a fluttering flock of mostly young and mostly pretty women. I wondered if he was married and what Mrs. Satan thought of the harem.

The comely George was also present. He noticed me scrunched to the side as the chickadees crowded past into the bar, and nodded a friendly greeting. I nodded back and happened to catch Steven Krass's chill gaze. He showed zero recognition as he swept by. I tried not to take that as a bad omen.

Peaches' death didn't appear to be hurting anyone's appetite. The dining room was crowded. Rachel sat at a table near the picture windows, clicking away on her laptop. As I pulled out a chair she looked up and nodded approvingly. "Much improved. Very professional. Gray suits you."

"No, it doesn't." I touched the white collar of my shirt, resisting the urge to tug at it. "Gray doesn't suit anyone."

She shook her head as though age could not possibly be a real concern for anyone in these days of plastic surgery and implants. "Let's order; then we can focus."

The all-purpose Debbie arrived to take our drink order—which was a huge relief. I had feared this was one of those dry—literally—meeting of minds.

I ordered gin and tonic. Rachel ordered the house merlot, which Debbie earnestly explained was not the house merlot after all. It turned out that Blue Heron grapes were harvested and bottled by a neighboring winery.

"Isn't that interesting," Rachel commented. It was clearly rhetorical; but encouraged, Debbie burbled on about metal gondola trucks and crushers and fermentation. My attention wandered. I studied Rachel. She looked better than she had earlier. She must have taken time for a nap as well. She appeared fresh and carefully made up as she always did. It occurred to me that although I'd known her for nearly a decade, I really knew very little about her. She had been born in British Hong Kong, wasn't married, didn't have children, and was allergic to dairy. That was the entire extent of my knowledge. Well, and she was a good agent. Yet I felt I knew her well enough to be sure that her reaction to Peaches' death was not that of a casual acquaintance.

When I tuned back in, Debbie had departed with our drink order, and Rachel was frowning into her laptop screen like a gypsy fortune-teller gazing into her crystal ball.

She muttered, "We're seeing some success with these mystery hybrids. The chick-lit heroine is a close relation to the contemporary amateur sleuth, you know."

"Their shoes are too tight, their credit cards are maxed out, and all the men they know are jerks," I replied. "Why wouldn't they turn to murder?"

"Still…" She got that faraway look in her eyes. "We might be better off taking a completely fresh direction."

I nodded encouragingly.

Speaking of completely fresh directions, Debbie returned then with our drinks. I gratefully slammed half of my G&T. Rachel took a ladylike sip of wine as Debbie recited our dining options. Rachel went for the herbed chicken fillet, and I opted for veal medallions. Debbie retreated once more, and Rachel resumed clicking and scowling.

"Sexy demons, I believe you said."

She wrinkled her nose. "Mmmm. Of course once something is openly recognized as hot, it's already starting to chill. Let's dig deeper."

"Sure. Let's mine for coal." I ran my hands through my hair, which brought a frown to those tiny features so reminiscent of Japanese hina dolls.

"Christopher, petal, hair sticking on end is truly *not* a good look."

"But very appropriate for this place."

She ignored this. "Right. Let's think back to the late eighties. Vampires, werewolves, sexy historicals—these were all huge then, and we're seeing their resurgence now, so my instinct is we're starting to cycle around once more. If we can anticipate what will recrudesce..." She typed away. "What else was selling well in the late eighties?"

I tore my thoughts away from her use of the word "recrudesce." I mean, who talks like that in real life? "Spinster sleuths were very popular in the late eighties," I said. "Maybe Miss Butterwith is due for a revival."

"Oh, Christopher," she muttered, not even bothering to answer that.

"Regency novels," I said gloomily.

She flicked me a thoughtful look.

"The Regency is tricky right now. A number of houses have cut the Regency from their roster, but it's been in decline for so long it might be due to—"

"Recrudesce?" I suggested.

She was nodding thoughtfully to herself. "It's not a bad notion. Time travel is still strong. But think Regency spec fiction. Space captains, vampires, werewolves, ghosts, and witches have all been done. What's new?"

"Centaurs."

"Christopher, do *try* to concentrate."

"Centaurs are sexy," I argued. "Or maybe satyrs." Not that I personally have a thing for cloven hooves—or I'd have stayed with David—it was more to make a point.

Raucous laughter from the bar next door. The knots in my stomach pulled tighter still.

I drained my glass and leaned across the table toward her. "This is hopeless. Can't we postpone even a few hours?"

"We were lucky to get this meeting." I could tell Rachel instantly regretted the words.

I sat back as though she'd slapped me. "What does *that* mean?"

"Nothing. Steven Krass is a very busy man, that's all."

"He didn't want to meet with me, did he?"

"Of course he wanted to meet with you." You'd think for a high-powered agent, Rachel would be a better liar. "It's only that he's *extremely* busy."

"This isn't going to work," I said. "His mind's already made up. He isn't going to be interested in anything I have to offer. I'm going to humiliate myself. More."

Rachel's hands fell away from the keyboard. "What are you talking about? That's not true. Of course he's interested. He agreed to meet with us, didn't he? No one bribed him. No one threatened him."

Why was she looking at me like that? Was she wondering if *I* had bribed or threatened him?

I glanced away from her tense face and caught sight of J.X. weaving his way through the crowded tables. He seemed to be making straight for us. I couldn't help noticing—and being unreasonably irritated by—the interest he stirred as he made his way across the sea of herbed chicken and veal medallions and veggie plates, but then attractive single guys are always at a premium at writing conferences.

He pulled out one of the extra chairs and sat down, barely returning Rachel's startled greeting before leaning across to me. "I thought I asked you to keep a lid on any possible homicide investigation," he said shortly.

"Speaking of lids," I returned equally terse, "you've flipped yours. I haven't said a word to anyone."

"Really? Then how is it everyone in the damn place seems to know Peaches was murdered?"

Rachel's breath caught.

I said, "Newsflash. Everybody in the damn place was speculating that before we ever left to go find her."

"That's true, J.X.," Rachel said. As mad as I was, her flat tone caught my attention. She repeated slowly, "It's true. So… it *is* true, then?"

He glanced at her briefly, as though he'd forgotten she was sitting there. "We won't know for sure till we get the autopsy results."

"We?"

"Edgar set up a makeshift radio, and I managed to talk briefly to the sheriff's department. They've asked me to…hold the fort till they can get through. Hopefully sometime tomorrow evening."

"Hold the fort. What a piquant term." Rachel's tone was light, but her expression was distracted. The bleak look was back in her eyes.

"It reminds me of that movie, *Beau Geste*," I said. "You know, the one where the Foreign Legion mans the fort with dead bodies to fool the Arabs. You don't foresee that happening here, do you?"

If possible, J.X. looked even more unamused.

"I credited you with more sense," he said. "Do me a favor and don't speculate on this in public anymore. It could be… dangerous."

I couldn't help noticing that Rachel's hand shook as she put her wineglass down. She asked, "What do you mean?"

I said to her, "He means it's safer for all of us if the murderer believes that he or she is getting away with it—at least until the police arrive and can give the rest of us some protection."

J.X. stared at me for a long moment. His long-lashed brown eyes were rather pretty for a man—the expression in them was anything but pretty.

I nodded toward him, adding, "Unless *he's* the murderer. In which case, it's to *his* advantage that we don't—"

"You're a laugh a minute, Kit." J.X. rose. "Don't say you weren't warned."

And with that he was gone. I picked up my empty glass, shook the ice in it, doing my best not to watch him threading his way through the tables. "Maybe that *was* a threat," I joked.

Rachel gave a strained laugh. "After all, I suppose he does have a line on this. He used to work for…SFPD, wasn't it? Some law enforcement agency."

"The Gestapo?"

Debbie appeared at my elbow with a tray of fresh drinks. I took mine gratefully.

Rachel sipped her wine like she badly needed it, then said, sounding more like herself, "What is it between you two? I'd no idea you even knew each other. Let alone that there was bad blood."

"Ancient history," I said. "We had a five-minute thing way back when."

Not that I wasn't delighted to help take her mind off her troubles, but her astonishment seemed out of proportion. "When?"

"Years ago. Before David and I were…committed." About a week before we were committed. And committed was pretty much the right word—as in, I should have been for even thinking of it, considering what I'd already known then about David. "Maybe J.X. is still carrying a torch," I added lightly, my ego still smarting.

She giggled. She is not a woman given to giggling.

"Or maybe he just wants to burn me at the stake."

She burst out laughing.

"Hey, it's not *that* funny."

"It is actually," Rachel retorted. "My God, Christopher, didn't you know that he's *straight*?"

CHAPTER EIGHT

A lesser man would have sprayed gin and tonic across the table. I managed to choke mine down and demand, "Since *when*?"

Rachel raised her elegant eyebrows. "Since...forever, I suppose. It's not a secret. He's married."

"He's not wearing a ring." I blushed as soon as the words were out, but yes, I *had* noticed. But that's because I'm a mystery writer and we...notice things.

"Not everyone wears wedding rings. He's straight. He's married." Rachel delivered it like an official pronouncement. Like she was one of the fairies gifting Sleeping Beauty's christening: Beauty. Intelligence. Heterosexual.

"That's *impossible*."

She shook her head, like it was all she could do not to break out into guffaws.

"I'm telling you, I would know," I said a tad heatedly. "I spent four days and three nights with him. He was not *faking*."

"Maybe he was experimenting," she said. "Maybe it was just a phase."

"No."

"I'm only telling you what everyone knows." Her eyes were curious. "Does it bother you so much?"

Yes. It did. And I wasn't sure why—unless it was the idea that three nights with me had turned him straight?

Rachel's fingers absently caressed the keys of her laptop. "Christopher, you're a mystery writer. Look at the evidence. He's gorgeous, rich, talented, over thirty. Why wouldn't he be married?"

"I'm thinking it's because he's a pain in the ass—don't say it—perfectionist."

"He's married, and they have a baby."

I swallowed hard. "Okay. I grant you that he's probably in a relationship with someone, but I don't believe he's straight. How would you know this? I've read interviews with him, and he's never said a word about his sexuality. Nothing. Ever."

"I read *People* magazine. I remember the article."

"When was this?"

"Five years ago."

"Maybe he's divorced."

"Maybe he is." Rachel was losing interest fast. "Why don't you ask him?"

Yeah. Right. I said, "He lives in San Francisco. He writes a series about a gay San Francisco homicide cop."

She shook her head. "Dirk Van de Meer is totally heterosexual. His partner Gabe is gay."

"That's obviously a commercial compromise—gay lit is in a slump."

She sighed. "Christopher, you really need to pay attention to what's happening in the market. Erotica is—"

"Everything is not always about books and publishing."

Rachel's face mirrored astonishment. "What an odd thing for *you* to say."

It was.

I said, "This is all totally hearsay. Circumstantial."

"Well, we're not actually trying him in court." Rachel's restored good humor was irritating me beyond belief. "But I can see why you were confused. He is *very* well-groomed."

"*There*," I said triumphantly. Even impeccably turned-out Inspector Appleby didn't dress "gay vague."

"And he does wear an earring," Rachel admitted, glancing at her wristwatch, "so he doesn't mind wearing *some* jewelry."

I could see she was only saying this to make me feel better. I said shortly, "Or maybe he's in a rock band or has been ship-wrecked a couple of times. It's not like I really give a damn one way or the other."

She closed her laptop and rose. "Exactly. You don't even like each other."

"That's right." I pushed my chair back.

There was really nothing more to say, and anyway, as the Lady of Shalott would have said, my curse was come upon me. I watched Rachel shove her laptop into the carrying case and followed her, my heart pounding in a sick mix of nerves and dread, into the bar where Steven Krass was holding court at three crowded tables that had been dragged together. He was regaling the assembly with a story that had the ladies all screaming with laughter.

I felt like screaming too, but I didn't suppose it would help. Rachel seemed determined to throw me off this cliff.

I glanced around the room. It was a comfortable-looking hole in the wall with cozy leather booths—mostly filled with young women staring enviously at the center tables taken up by the Wheaton & Woodhouse retinue. There were Western-themed prints on the wood-paneled walls and an impressive array of bottles behind the massive bar. Every seat was taken. I picked out J.X. leaning on the bar, one boot propped on the foot rail like he was posing for a magazine layout.

Our eyes met. His gaze was level and not particularly friendly. Thinking of my recent conversation with Rachel, I glanced guiltily away.

Steven Krass beckoned to us. Maybe he'd suddenly remembered where he knew me from or maybe he was simply feeling sociable.

"Chris. Isn't this delightful? Grab a chair. Join us."

Chris. No one calls me Chris. My parents didn't call me Chris. David didn't call me Chris. Rachel and I exchanged looks. A couple of chairs scooted out. I squeezed into one, and she snagged the other. I found myself sitting across from Krass. Rachel was a couple of seats down.

"Delightful," Krass repeated solemnly.

His handsome face was flushed, his eyes rimmed with red as though he had been drinking all day—or crying himself to sleep over the nasty things he did to people.

I offered my hand across the table littered with soggy napkins and empties and smudged glasses. "It's a pleasure," I lied.

His hand was soft, but his grip was hard. One of those assholes who has to try and crush your fingers to make up for having a short dick.

"Chris, you look like you could use a drink," he remarked. "In fact, you look like you could use a lot of drinks." He smiled—a personable, practiced smile. He tapped a teaspoon against an empty Tecate bottle as though signaling for a speech. "Drinks," he commanded. "Drinks for Chris Holmes and... sorry, dear, what was your name?"

"Rachel." Rachel had to raise her voice to be heard. At Krass's look of non-comprehension, she clarified curtly, "Ving. Rachel Ving."

"Right, right. Rachel...like the cook." Krass beckoned to the sole and harassed-looking waitress.

Thirty-minute meals—and drinks with Satan. I really had descended into Hell. Maybe we could spend the evening discussing recipes or reading *War and Peace* aloud or just driving spikes into my head.

Did Krass even recall that we had an appointment? Or was I supposed to make my pitch surrounded by the tipsy courtiers and bar patrons?

The waitress wriggled through the crowd, and Krass remarked, "New meaning to the words waitstaff." He paused for the laughs from those around him, before adding, "Look, dear, can we get some more help out here?"

"Christopher Holmes," cooed a voice to my left. I glanced over. An apple-cheeked elderly woman with pink spectacles and lovely gray hair was beaming at me.

"Good God," I said. "Mindy Newburgh."

She chuckled at my amazement. I noticed the beauteous George sitting to the other side of her—a faraway look in his eyes.

"So you're George's Mindy. I don't know why I didn't make that connection earlier." Probably because Mindy was old enough to be George's grandma. Maybe she *was* George's grandma, although in that case, I'd have preferred him to stop stroking the back of her neck.

Mindy gave that comfortable chuckle again. "I couldn't believe it when Georgie told me you were here, knowing the way it went down with Wheaton & Woodhouse. No hard feelings?"

Above the pink rhinestone specs her eyes were shrewd.

"I try not to burn bridges." As though my finger wasn't trembling on the trigger of a flamethrower at that very moment. "You're still with them? You do the Rock Montana political thrillers, right?"

Mindy knocked back what appeared to be the last in a long line of Bloody Marys (if a forest of limp celery was anything to go by). "Well, kiddo, I saw the writing on the wall a year and a half ago, and I put Rock Montana out to pasture. I spun off a minor character—the divorced Jewish female CIA assassin from one of the early novels—and started a new series. It's actually worked very well. It has that sexy chick-lit sensibility."

"Are you *serious*? I mean, smart thinking," I said hastily.

"It was. Of course I've been in this business a long time. I brought my Romance fan base with me when I moved into political thrillers."

How? In her knitting bag? "That was lucky," I said. Romance had never been a problem for Miss Butterwith. Her one true love died heroically and chastely in World War I.

Mindy bridled. "It was *not* luck. Luck has nothing to do with success in this business."

That was what I used to think—back when I was successful.

We placed our drink orders. "Are we going to order any food?" Steven called to the table. He got a number of loud assents.

"We can't serve food in here," the waitress said.

He gave her an irritated look. "It seems you can't serve drinks, either. I'd like to speak to the manager. You've been rude and borderline incompetent this entire evening."

She looked like he'd slapped her.

"Go away," Krass said. He waved a hand like he was fending off a fly. "Get me the manager. Now."

She opened her mouth, then thought better of it and retreated to the bar. I could see her making her protests to the bartender.

"Did you know Peaches?" Krass asked, turning suddenly to me.

"No," I admitted.

"She was...amazing. An amazing woman. And a hell of a talent."

She had struck me as an arrogant bitch, but I'm sensitive about unprovoked attacks from people I don't know—or even people I do know. I said, "I guess you knew her pretty well."

"I knew her very well." He raised his glass and said loudly, "To Peaches."

Everyone down the length of the table grabbed their glasses, empty or full, and obediently echoed, "To Peaches."

Krass drained his glass and focused blearily on my face. "I understand you went with J.X. to reclaim the...the body. What happened? Why is he being so mysterious?"

"Is he? I don't know. I only showed them where to drive."

"Yeah, he's being mysterious. He's being an asshole is what he's being." He turned around and flipped off J.X.

J.X.'s back was to us, but I could see his face in the long mirror behind the bar. I caught his gaze and knew he had not missed Krass's gesture.

"Oh dear," murmured Mindy, sounding amused. "Those two have a love-hate relationship."

What did *that* mean? Surely J.X. and Krass weren't...the mind boggled.

I leaned forward, trying to attract Rachel's attention. She seemed to be avoiding my eyes. Obviously I was not going to be making any pitch tonight. Either Krass didn't remember or he was cancelling our appointment in his own inimitable fashion.

The weary-looking waitress brought our drinks.

"Here's to friends," Krass said, taking his glass. "Friends and lovers." He sipped and added, "Old friends and young lovers."

Okay...so did that mean that Krass and Peaches had been an item? Or was this sort of a generic toast? He couldn't be having relationships with Peaches *and* J.X., right?

His expression changed. He snarled at the waitress busily distributing drinks. "Where's the manager?"

"On his way," she said tersely.

"On his way *out* when I get finished with him."

"Yeah, whatever," she muttered.

"Piece of work," Krass said, shaking his head as though it were sort of funny, like what could you expect here in the wastelands? His eyes met mine over the rim of his glass.

"So, Chris, I hear you're working on a new book."

"Oh," I hedged. "This probably isn't the time." I felt Rachel's elbow in my ribs—which was pretty amazing since she wasn't sitting next to me. I blabbed, "It's about a female private eye in the Regency era."

Krass winced. "Historical P.I. novels are death at the bookstore." He turned as Edgar Croft appeared at his shoulder. Edgar leaned down and spoke low-voiced into his ear.

Anger crossed Krass's flushed features.

"You've one hell of a nerve, *pardner*, considering the fact you've got us trapped here like ducks in a shooting gallery."

Edgar's face tightened. He bent still lower.

Not low enough. Krass snarled, "I've got news for you, cowboy, this will be the last writers' conference you *folks* hold, if I have anything to say about it—and I will have plenty to say about it."

It didn't sound like much of a threat to me, but Edgar's expression was grim as he straightened up. Whatever he might have answered was forestalled as J.X. wandered up to the table.

"Come on, Steven," he said easily. "Everyone's doing the best they can under the circumstances."

Krass's smile reminded me of a great white shark charging at the bars of an underwater cage. "J.X., sport. Pull up a chair. Chris was telling us about this evening. About bringing Peaches...home."

J.X. gave me a long, level look.

I opened my mouth and then gave up.

"No need to look at him like that," Krass said. "The best thing would be if we all pooled our knowledge, right? Isn't that what all the law enforcement agencies do? Pool their knowledge?"

J.X. said dryly, "What law enforcement agency is this supposed to be? The Torchwood Institute?"

Krass laughed. "Very funny." He said to me, "He's very funny, isn't he?"

"I thought I'd die laughing earlier," I said, and reached for my glass.

Krass drawled, "Funny ha ha or funny queer?"

Stillness seemed to vibrate from J.X. I couldn't look at him.

"Yeah," Krass said. "I think we ought to pool our knowledge. Like the last pages of one of Chris's novels. You might be surprised at what you learn, J.X. One of us might easily have seen something last night."

Everyone was still talking at once, yet I had the oddest feeling that someone was listening very closely to this conversation. I glanced around. No one seemed to be paying particular attention.

"If you do know something about Peaches' death, your best move is to speak up now," J.X. said.

Krass laughed. "Are you sure about that?"

Something flickered in J.X.'s eyes.

Krass turned his back on him. "Anyway, Chris, continue telling us about this marvelous new idea of yours."

A minute earlier the sound level matched Shea Stadium during a Beatles concert; now you could practically hear crickets chirping. I moved back to allow Rita Croft room to gather up the dirty glasses.

"Uh…it's about a private eye in an alternate universe very similar to the Regency Period but magical."

"So it's fantasy?"

"But with that sexy chick-lit sensibility," Rachel put in.

"Half mystery, half fantasy, half romantic comedy," I said.

"That's three halves," J.X. noted, for the record. I ignored him. With those math skills why the hell had he wasted himself on popular literature? He could have been giving Stephen Hawking a run for his money.

"Tell him about the demons," Rachel urged over the clink of glassware and bottles.

But Satan Krass wasn't having any part of my Regency demons.

"To tell you the truth, Chris, we already bought a manuscript very similar to this a few weeks ago."

"Christopher has several projects," Rachel started, but again Krass cut her off with a look.

"I'll be frank, Chris," he said. "I pride myself on being honest with my writers. You write with a lot of warmth and… understanding. Understanding of *what* I have no idea." He laughed heartily. "Kidding, Chris. Your books are wonderful. Really. Very pleasant. But you're simply not in sync with what's happening in publishing right now. We're looking for edgy, new voices. We're looking for fresh, for fat."

"For *what*?" Because if he said what I thought he said, I figured I was still in the running—not too much running, obviously.

"Phat. P.H.A.T. You don't know what that word means, do you, Chris? And that's the problem in a nutshell."

"Sexy, first-rate, excellent," supplied Mindy out of the side of her mouth.

"God knows, I love your stuff, but you don't fit the new direction of Wheaton & Woodhouse. Try one of the smaller houses; try one of the indies. They're not under the same pressure to perform."

I could feel myself turning red, then white, as anger and embarrassment hit the litmus paper of my nervous system. In a minute he was going to advise me to self-publish. Rachel's chair scraped as she got to her feet. I was already standing. Everyone at the table seemed to be looking at me. Even J.X.'s dark gaze was sympathetic—that was probably the worst thing of all. He was sorry for me.

"Now, now," Krass said, full of sudden good humor. "No need to hurry off. Tonight we have to put aside our differences.

Tonight we say good-bye to one of the greats in our industry. Tonight we bid farewell to an old and valued friend...Peaches Sadler. Stay and have that drink."

"That might not be a good idea," I said, almost managing a smile. "I might be tempted to slip poison into yours."

He raised his glass in a mock salute.

CHAPTER NINE

"Well, that's that," I said as Rachel and I reached the hall outside the bar. I felt like I was in shock. Sort of cold and distant. "I guess I can still have a full and rewarding career writing *Diagnosis Murder* spin-off novels."

Rachel stared at me as though she'd seen an apparition. Maybe we were looking at the same thing—the bloody wreckage of my career.

I couldn't resist one last glance back into the bar. Krass, slightly swaying, was on his feet, making a toast to Peaches. From the sound of clinking glasses you'd have thought the bride and groom were about to kiss.

"The man's a pig," Rachel spat out.

It took all my willpower not to say, *I told you so.* Her face was dusky with fury. At least, I thought it was fury. Her next words gave me pause.

"Do you suppose he meant it—about knowing something about Peaches' death?"

I tried to process this. No go. The little gray cells seemed to be burning out at an alarming rate.

She said impatiently, "Krass's remark about seeing something last night? Do you think it's true?"

"How would I know? Rachel..." Was there a tactful way to put this? Did I really want to know? Could I take one more piece

of bad news tonight without coming apart at the seams? "Uh…
you didn't…have anything to do…anything against Peaches,
right?"

Her elegant features hardened into old ivory. "What are
you suggesting?"

"It's not really a suggestion." More like craven beseeching
for reassurance. Naturally I didn't say *that*, and she wasn't listening anyway, her gaze riveted once more on Krass. It was like
he had brought his own laugh track with him. Shrill hilarity
echoed off the hardwood floors and open beams.

It's over, I thought. My career is over. Done. Dead. He
killed it. Without a second thought.

From a distance I heard Rachel's bitter voice. "All that sor-
ry-dear-what-was-your-name *bullshit.* Do you know how many
times he's pulled that? I represent three—two—of his bestselling writers. I *spoke* to him this morning. Pig. Chauvinist
pig."

Krass struck me as an equal-opportunity swine, but perhaps she knew him better. Somehow it didn't seem important.
Standing numb amidst the carnage of my career, I was having
trouble focusing on her words, let alone forming a polite
response.

She fumed, "What a pity no one thought to cosh *him* over
the head."

"You go, girl," called a voice behind us.

We turned. A small Hispanic woman with cropped black
hair was seated at one of the conversational groupings of chairs
and small tables. She looked a few years younger than me, which
was how everyone looked these days. She wore red Audrey
Hepburn capris that matched the scarlet slash of her laughing
mouth.

Rachel swept toward the empty chairs like the last empress washing her hands of the Forbidden City once and for all. I followed on wobbly legs, collapsing onto the nearest seat. If Krass thought I'd looked like I needed a lot of drinks before, he should see me now.

"Espie Real." The woman reached across the table, and we shook hands. "I'm another of Rachel's clients." To Rachel, she said, "You look like shit."

Rachel glanced at her, unspeaking.

Espie said to me, "I guess it didn't go well?"

"That would be putting a positive spin on it." She had to be about the only person at the conference who hadn't been an eyewitness to my humiliation, and even she, it seemed, knew why I was visiting this particular ring of Hell. Maybe it was actually listed on the schedule of events—right there between Morning Mixer and Brainstorming for Beginners.

"Join the crowd. We're all on the endangered species list these days."

"The cop bought you two a drink." Rita materialized at our table and set glasses down in front of Rachel and me. I guess there was something to be said for sensitive men. I reached for mine like I was trying out for a role in *Lost Weekend*.

"You need another one?" Rita asked Espie.

"Yep." Espie drained her glass. I noticed she had a tiny teardrop tattooed beneath her left eye. Wasn't that a prison tattoo?

Espie caught me staring at her and winked. I felt myself redden. She grinned.

"You folks are missing the wake," Rita informed us.

"It's enough to know the bitch is dead," Espie remarked. "I don't need balloons and streamers. Maybe if there was cake..." She shrugged.

Rita gave that harsh bark of a laugh and walked away with the tray of dirty glasses.

I came up for air. "I take it you weren't a fan of Peaches Sadler?"

Espie's tone was cool. "You take it wrong. We had a mutual admiration society going. She was a big fan of my work, and I was a *big* fan of hers."

I didn't follow the intended insult. Did she mean, *I was a big fan of her work, and so was she?*

Rachel said sharply, "Espie."

"Oh, please." But she fell silent.

I glanced at Rachel, did a double take. Her wineglass was empty. Focus on someone else's problems for a change, I instructed myself. You need the practice. From now on you'll have to live in a world you didn't make up. Horrible thought.

"I never met her," I said, "but she sounds like the kind of person you either loved or hated." Mostly hated.

"She could be very charming," Rachel said flatly. She rubbed her temples.

Espie hooted with laughter. "She charm the pants off you last night, *querida*? Maybe not literally. Not this time, anyway."

I choked on my drink.

Rachel looked at me sideways. "It's not what you think."

"Probably not, since I haven't had a coherent thought in hours."

"We…go back. The three of us."

"The Three Mesquiteers," Espie put in. "That's us."

"I used to represent her," Rachel explained.

"You're kidding."

"I never kid," said Rachel, which was the truth.

Not that Rachel wasn't a great agent, but Peaches Sadler had dwelt in the rarified stratosphere of authors who get the thumbs-up from Oprah and options for cable TV miniseries. "So what happened?"

"Nothing." She ignored Espie's sardonic laughter. "She moved to another agency. It happens."

"Easy come, easy go," Espie said. "I guess you two were renegotiating last night. At the top of your lungs."

Rachel glared at her. "Yes, we argued. What of it?"

Espie opened her mouth but bit off whatever she was going to say as Rita arrived with her drink—and Mindy Newburgh in tow.

Mindy pulled out the last empty chair without being invited. "You three are missing the canonization of Saint Peaches." She was slurring the teeniest bit as she gave her drink request to Rita. Rita said something under her breath and returned to the bar. I wondered where Gorgeous George was.

"Krass seems to have been genuinely fond of her," I remarked.

"Why not? They were two of a kind." Espie smiled at me.

"Oh, I think he truly loved her," Mindy muttered. She rooted around in her purse until she found a pack of peppermint Life Savers, which she offered around.

"You used to write romance novels, what do you know?" Espie reached for a Life Saver.

Mindy offered me a Life Saver. I took it and crunched morosely. "What do you write?" I asked Espie. I didn't care, really, but if I didn't keep talking I was liable to start crying.

"The Marcie Marquez series. She's a part-time flamenco dancer and bounty hunter," Espie informed me. "I've got something else going, though. Something big."

"Chica lit is hot right now," Rachel recited, without pausing in massaging her temples. "The Hispanic market is about to crack wide open." Along with poor Rachel's head, it appeared.

"Marginalization is always a danger," Mindy remarked knowledgeably. Her glassy eyes studied me behind the glittering rhinestone specs. "I must say, Christopher..." And then she seemed to lose track of what she must say.

Rachel stopped rubbing her temples. "Look, Christopher, try not to worry. Your idea was wonderful. Truly. I'm proud of you. I know we can sell this next book somewhere."

She couldn't be serious. Never in a million years was I going to write a book about a Regency P.I. and her demon lover. "Hey," I said. "Do I *look* worried?"

"*Yes,*" all three of them responded unequivocally.

"Wrong. This is my game face," I informed them. "I look like this to disarm my enemies."

Espie grinned. "You have a lot of enemies, Christopher?"

But she was the only one paying attention. I had the feeling Espie missed very little.

Anyway, who was I kidding? The only reason I wasn't worried right then was because I was exhausted and probably in shock. I thought longingly of my warm bed—if only I didn't have to journey cross the plains to get to it. I didn't fancy that long lonely walk across the muddy pasture—especially on my own.

Mindy pawed through the contents of her bag again. This time she was after one of those old-fashioned compacts that my granny used to use. I didn't think they even made those anymore. Fascinated, we watched her rub rouge into the apples of her cheeks without the benefit of a mirror. "How's that?" she inquired of the world at large.

"Uh..." *Perfect for this circus* was probably not what she wanted to hear.

Espie gave her the thumbs-up, black eyes dancing with unkind amusement.

Rita returned with Mindy's drink. "Anybody else want anything?" She seemed to be daring us.

I said, "I want a bottle of Bombay Sapphire, a large bottle of tonic water, a couple of limes, a bucket of ice, a tray, and a clean glass. Name your price."

She studied me with her gimlet eyes and then smiled a smile that warned of serious damage to my American Express card.

"That can be arranged, mister."

She departed once more. There was a volley of raucous laughter from the bar. Rachel straightened and said wearily, "My head is killing me. I'm going up to bed."

I glanced at my watch. Only ten o'clock. It felt much later.

"Sweet dreams," Mindy chirped as Rachel pushed to her feet.

Espie spoke in Spanish, and Rachel answered. That surprised me, although there was no reason that Rachel shouldn't speak Spanish. She was one of those overeducated, cosmopolitan types. She probably spoke eleven languages and had read all the classics. What really caught my interest was their tone of voice. I had only seen them bickering with each other, but Espie's tone was tender and Rachel's reassuring. The tone of old friends, sisters.

"See you in the morning," Rachel said to me.

"Night."

She turned and almost walked into George. He steadied her, apologized, and slipped into her seat. He, at least, appeared to be having a good time. His boyish face was relaxed and happy. Rachel walked away toward the lobby.

"There you are." Alcohol blurred the sharpness of Mindy's voice, but I could still hear the edge.

"I was going to go get my guitar," said George. "You want anything from the cabin?"

"It's getting late. I was thinking we should go to bed."

"It's not even midnight, Min."

"It's late for me," she said sweetly. "I have a long day tomorrow. This isn't a vacation for me."

The light went out of his face. He shrugged. "Fine. Whatever."

No one said anything as we watched Mindy gather her belongings. George stood silently by, his expression glum. "Good night, all," she caroled.

As we watched them heading for the lobby, Espie remarked, "Chico and the Mom."

My chuckle died as she mused, "I wonder if she did Peaches…"

"Are you serious?"

"Well, someone did her, right? That's what everyone's saying. Old Granny Goose was mad enough to kill last night." She seemed amused at the idea.

"Why?"

"Why do you think? Peaches never met a man she didn't like—or want."

"Oh."

"Yeah."

There didn't seem much to say after that. I was suddenly so tired I could hardly focus. I realized I should have asked Mindy and George to wait for me so that I didn't have to walk to the cabins on my own. Too late now.

"Looks like there may be room at the bar," Espie said.

I shuddered. If I never saw any of those people again, it would be too soon.

"Here you go," Rita announced, setting a tray with an unopened bottle of Bombay Sapphire, tonic water, and a couple of limes on the table in front of me. "There's an ice machine in the lobby."

"Thanks," I said, dragging myself to my feet. The tray looked like it weighed a ton.

"We'll see if you're still thanking me in the morning."

"All things in moderation," I informed her loftily. "See you both in the a.m."

"Bright-eyed and bushy-tailed," drawled Rita.

"If we're still alive," Espie added cheerfully.

* * * * *

I let myself quietly out the back, deciding it would be faster to cut behind the lodge. This or the front path, either way I'd be all by my lonesome. It was like they had planned the layout of this place after watching horror movies for a week.

It seemed years ago that I had crossed the wet-slick deck with J.X. and Edgar Croft.

I walked briskly down the cement path. The rain had stopped. The silence seemed absolute.

Somewhere to the left, an owl hooted, and I nearly jumped out of my skin, the bottles on the tray I carried rattling in alarm.

I walked on, less briskly. The sound of my footsteps on the path had a hollow sound—which matched the feeling in the pit of my stomach.

As I reached the end of the walkway, I heard a noise. I looked around, trying to identify the source.

There it was again. Small and furtive. Followed by the sound of a rolling log.

The woodpile.

I froze, my heart pounding hard.

Kneeling, I carefully lowered the tray with the ice bucket and bottles to the cement. As quiet as I tried to be, they sounded like alarm bells going off. I crouched there, breathing hard, waiting...

Nothing happened.

I didn't hear anything now. Could I have imagined it? Maybe it was a squirrel or a lizard with a taste for the nightlife.

I stood up, stepped past the tray, and sidled along the hedge until I reached the end. Cautiously I poked my head around, twigs pulling at my hair.

I had a quick view of the woodpile silvered in moonlight. There was no one there.

The next instant I was grabbed by the lapels of my Burberry, yanked out of my hiding space, and thrown to the ground.

CHAPTER TEN

Someone was howling—a thin, breathless cry that was, in fact, more breath than cry.

Me.

Far from splitting the night, my bleat barely carried three feet, so I had no trouble hearing my attacker's exasperated, "*What. The. Fuck?*"

I knew that voice.

I bit off the rest of my screech and sat up, wincing as pain shot up my spine. I was sitting in a puddle, ice-cold water soaking through my trousers. The last time I remembered being decked had been a playground rumble at Our Holy Mother. I'd been thirteen. My bounce had been better back then. Now I felt like I'd wrenched every muscle in my already worn-out body. And my back... I'd be lucky if I wasn't crippled for a month. I wiped the mud off my face.

"I am *so* going to sue your ass," I spluttered.

"Well, what the *hell* are you doing out here?" J.X. demanded.

No apology seemed forthcoming. Also, I couldn't help noticing, neither was help from the lodge. Were we too far away to be heard? Not a happy thought.

"What do you think I'm doing? I'm going to my cabin."

"Crawling on your hands and knees?"

"I wasn't *on* my hands and knees till you knocked me down."

"You sure as hell were skulking in the bushes."

"I heard something—you—and I was making sure it was safe."

He continued to stare down at me. I wished I could see his face. His motionless outline caused my scalp to prickle. Then he reached down a hand.

His hand was warm on my chilled one. Again I was aware of his wiry strength. He wasn't much taller than me, but he was in a hell of a lot better shape. He pulled me to my feet and dropped my hand.

"What are *you* doing out here?" I asked, uneasily rubbing the twinging small of my back.

"Grabbing a log for my fireplace." He reached past me and picked up a nice stout sawed-off limb. "It's going to be a cold night." He picked up another log. "Here's one for you."

"Thanks." I stepped out of range, trying not to be too obvious about it. Not that I didn't appreciate the gesture, but there was something unconvincing in his manner. What had he been looking for out here?

J.X. still held out the log. I took it gingerly.

"I'll see you to your cabin."

"Oh. Okay. Thanks." I remembered my minibar set up. "Hang on."

I limped back to where I'd set down the tray. Everything was as I'd left it. I lifted the tray and nearly dropped it. J.X. stood right behind me, log in hand.

I managed to save the gin. The tonic water, ice bucket, and glass slid off the tray and landed in the mud.

"What is it with you?" I demanded and thrust the log and the tray at him. I knelt, gathering up the fizzing bottle and glass. The scattered ice cubes winked dully in the pallid moonlight.

"What the hell is this about?" J.X. indicated the tray.

"What the hell does it look like? I'm planning to drown my sorrows."

"That's not going to solve anything."

"I'm not trying to *solve* anything." I added pointedly, "I'll leave that to the experts."

"It's your head," he said. "Come on." He put his hand under my arm as I started to rise, and I nearly lost the entire load again.

"Do you *mind*?"

"Sorry. Jesus, you're jumpy."

"I can't imagine why." I rebalanced and set off—limping—down the path.

"Do you really have a bad back?" he asked, behind me.

"No, it's just something I say to get chicks."

He didn't respond, but as we reached the edge of the meadow, he caught me up so that we were walking side by side. "This way."

I followed him down the dirt path that cut across the open field toward the cabins. The sodden clouds had parted, and a lackluster moon gilded everything in unnatural light. In the absence of the rain and wind, the stillness seemed uncanny.

Mostly to fill the uncomfortable silence between myself and J.X., I said, "There's something eerie about the stillness."

"It's the eye of the storm."

"You mean there's more rain on the way?"

"Oh yeah. We're a couple of hours away from another downpour."

"Great."

"Which is your cabin?"

"That one—with the lights on."

He said sharply, "Did you leave the light on?"

"Yes." I cast a quick glance at his silvered profile. "Why? You don't really think I'm in any danger, do you?"

"No."

"You could try to sound a little more convincing."

What he sounded was irritable. "You had to go around telling everyone Peaches had been murdered, didn't you?"

"That's it." I stopped walking. The glassware rattled to a halt with me. "We need to have this out here and now." I was talking to his back. "*Hey.*"

He kept walking. I had to trot to catch up—which irritated me further.

"Listen," I said, "I did not tell anyone *anything.* Peaches was everybody's candidate for unnatural selection. From the minute I said I found her in the woods, people were speculating about how she died."

"And you encouraged their speculation."

"I didn't. I didn't say anything one way or the other. I didn't *know* anything one way or the other. I still don't."

J.X. stopped walking. His voice was low. "We both know she was killed."

I swallowed hard. "Are you sure?"

He nodded.

"Did you tell the sheriffs?"

"Yep."

He started walking again. After a few seconds of thought, I tagged after.

As we reached my cabin, he asked, "You want me to take a look inside?"

I hesitated. If he was a homicidal maniac, this was his big chance. No one had seen us walk out here together. Certainly no one had responded to my shouts.

On the other hand, what if the homicidal maniac was hiding under my bed? I didn't feel up to dealing with it on my own.

I unlocked the door and pushed it open. The first sight to meet our gaze was my brand-new silk jockstrap lying on the floor next to the bed. Scarlet silk. I mean...

"I had no idea," J.X. murmured.

"You still don't."

He laughed, and I was abruptly reminded that this was not the first time he had been in my bedroom. I remembered some other things too—things I'd thought I'd forgotten: the smoky, sweet taste of his mouth, his husky laugh, his strength—and his gentleness. You don't expect gentleness from a twenty-five-year-old macho cop, but he had been...tender. Energetic, but tender.

I had handed him the drinks tray while I unlocked the door; now I watched him set the tray of gin and tonic water on the table by the wall. I opened my mouth to ask if he was married—but there is no way to ask that it doesn't sound like you have a personal stake in the answer. It's like asking a man if he's gay—which would have been my second question.

And while I had no personal interest in J.X. Moriarity, hearing him confirm tonight that he was straight would have felt like the very last straw.

So I watched him open the closet and push my few clothes aside. He stepped into the bathroom and shoved the shower curtain back.

I squatted down and looked under the bed. "All clear."

His expression told me that I was not taking this seriously enough.

He examined the window casings while I went to rinse my muddy glass out in the bathroom.

I sat on the bed and unscrewed the bottlecap. "Would you like a nightcap? I think there's a plastic cup in the bathroom. Or you can use the coffee pot to drink from."

He studied me.

"Look, Kit, I realize it's none of my business, but go easy on that stuff. You need to keep your wits about you."

"I'm never wittier than when I've had a few drinks," I informed him in my best Elsa Lanchester imitation. Not that he would have a clue who Elsa Lanchester was; she was well before his time. Well before mine, too, now that I thought about it, but the evening had aged me.

J.X. sighed. "I know you've had a rough day. But this is for real. If someone really wanted into this cabin, it wouldn't be hard to get inside."

"I'll sleep with one eye open."

"Better yet, sleep with that chair propped beneath the door handle."

Great minds.

"Okay." I held up the bottle. "Sure you won't have one for the road?"

He shook his head. "I need to sleep. I'm dead."

"Unfortunate choice of words." I poured gin in the glass. Studied the still bubbly tonic water. That bottle needed to be opened in the bathroom over the sink to minimize loss of vital fluids. "Sleep tight. Don't let the bed bugs bite."

J.X. opened the cabin door. He hesitated. "Steven can be a real asshole."

"There it is again, the keen eye of the master detective."

His mouth tightened. "Don't forget to lock this door."

I rose, went to the door. He stepped out, and I closed the door, sliding the bolt home. I leaned against it and closed my eyes.

"What is the matter with you?" I whispered.

Then I nearly jumped out of my skin as someone banged on the door. I backed away and called, "Who is it?"

"Me." The muffled voice was male.

Heart thudding, I got out, "Me who?"

"Kit!"

I recognized the exasperation. I unbolted the door and opened it.

J.X., looking unexpectedly self-conscious, pointed to a few cabins down and said, "Look, if something does...happen. I'm right over there. Cabin six."

"Within screaming distance," I observed.

"Uh...yeah."

"Thank you," I said. "I'll try not to take advantage of the situation. I know you need your beauty rest."

He gave a funny laugh, shook his head, and turned away.

"J.X.?" I said.

He stopped. I fastened my hand on the damp collar of his leather jacket and drew him through the doorway and back into the cabin. With my free hand I gave the door a shove. It snicked shut. J.X. reached back and locked it.

If they gave prizes at picnics for shucking your clothes fast, we'd have scored a jar of homemade preserves and a blue ribbon for sure. As it was, we had to be satisfied with our performance in the three-legged race, which somehow occurred as J.X. was struggling out of his jeans and I was dragging him to the bed. We collapsed on top of the calico bedspread, J.X. gracefully sprawled beneath me.

He was beautiful. I'd forgotten that about him in all those nasty online exchanges through the years. I gazed down at the strong, handsome lines of his face—dark eyes shining and a crooked white smile framed in the perfectly trimmed Van Dyke—took in the bronzed, muscular chest. Like rock...only not. His skin gleamed like brown satin, the small, flat nipples like dark copper pennies. I traced the left one with a fingertip. He closed his eyes, the lashes black crescents against his high cheekbones.

Reaching up, he locked his hand in the back of my hair, pulling me down. Our mouths met in a warm open kiss, and he tasted cold like the outdoors and the night, and he tasted unbelievably hot.

I kissed him hard, and he smiled against my mouth and rolled us over onto our sides. I knew I'd had way too much to drink because for once I wasn't worrying—wasn't thinking at all. No self-consciousness, no second thoughts... I was totally in the now, touching and tasting. I'd nearly forgotten how much fun sex was. How *good* it felt.

J.X. nibbled my earlobe, his breath gusting moistly into my ear, and I found that incredibly arousing. In ten years David hadn't thought to kiss that tiny hollow, or the one at the base of my throat, or my eyelids or—actually, David and I hadn't done a lot of kissing. In fact, I didn't care for kissing, really...

Except that J.X.'s kisses were getting me so hot and excited I wasn't sure my skin could contain all that light and energy buzzing inside me. I wrapped my arms around him, delighted when he reciprocated, pulling me tight to him with those hard, muscular arms.

He thrust against me, his cock poking me painfully in my belly, leaving that streak of sticky, and I thrust back, and it was a relief to let go, to bump and grind, to hump away like a pair of landed porpoises, to rut and root in the blessing and beauty of uncomplicated and impersonal sex. The bed thumped rhythmically against the wall of the cabin. I thought it might have been bouncing off the floor—I wouldn't have been surprised to hear the cabin itself was shaking beneath those rafters of moonstruck clouds.

It felt too raw and real to compare with…any memory, but I did remember something as we rocked in each other's arms, dicks rubbing enjoyably, skin flushing hot and moist beneath our hands, belly to belly, chest to chest, tangle of legs—I remembered the first time we had fucked he had come almost immediately. J.X. had been…so young. So tough, but so young. And every time we had fucked that long-ago weekend, he had shot his load fast and frantically—and it had embarrassed him.

And I had told him we just needed more practice.

My chest tightened with those unexpected memories, an unforeseen sentimental ache—or more likely I was too old for this and about to have a heart attack.

The good news was his technique had improved a lot through the years, and as harried and feverish as this was, it was a good long ride before it exploded in juddering, convulsive pleasure. Pleasure being one feeble word for that blissful sensation of physical release so intense it felt catastrophic.

We lay there catching our breath, relaxed and boneless in a hot and sticky tangle of limbs.

J.X. said finally, sitting up and raking a hand through his shiny black hair, "Well, that was a mistake."

CHAPTER ELEVEN

I sucked in a sharp breath and then let it out. "Thank you for saying so," I said coolly, and I sat up too.

There are few things more awkward than the moments after sex with someone you shouldn't have had sex with. No way was I going to sit here side by side making polite—or not so very—conversation with J.X.

I got off the bed, and he had the same idea. He rose and began pulling on his Levi's. He was still wearing one sock. One white boot sock, which seemed fascinating to me as I poured myself another couple of fingers of gin.

"You know what I mean," he muttered.

Does anyone ever really know what anyone else means? I said, "Sure." I unscrewed the top of the bottle of tonic water, and fizzy wet sprayed me in the face—which was really the perfect touch.

He didn't laugh, and neither did I. Actually, I don't think he even noticed. He buttoned up his shirt almost as quickly as he had unbuttoned it. I wiped my face on my arm, splashed tonic water in my glass, and drank it down fast. The burn nearly choked me, but I kept swallowing. When I surfaced, he had the door open.

"Lock this behind me," he ordered.

"*Oui, mon capitan.*" I came up close to him. He smelled like soap and sex, and he avoided my eyes.

"Good night," he said.

"Night," I returned. "Oh, and please don't forget to fill out our customer-satisfaction survey."

His eyes met mine. I could see he was about to say something, but then he changed his mind. He went out, and I closed the door behind him and locked it.

The rain was starting to fall again. The eye of the storm had closed.

* * * * *

I woke drenched in sweat, my heart thudding with the panicked memory of my dreams—nightmares. Or *was* it a nightmare? I stared into the darkness, listening.

The wind howled outside the cabin. Was it my imagination, or were the curtains by the window stirring?

I sat bolt upright and reached for the bedside lamp.

Mellow light flooded the room. No one stood over my bed. No one crouched in the corners of the cabin. No one was trying to pry open a window. The curtains trembled in the draft from the leaky window casement as the wind gusted outside.

I was perfectly safe, but my heart continued to race. I had a pounding headache and a mouth like cotton. One too many nightcaps had about capped *me*. I pushed aside the blankets and staggered across the chilly floorboards to the bathroom. I relieved myself, gulped down a couple of plastic cupfuls of tap water, and stumbled back to bed.

I needed Tylenol and an ice pack. I needed central heating and a stack of feather pillows. A full-time nurse wouldn't be a bad idea—a really handsome, muscular, tender—

The windows rattled as another gust of wind shook the cabin.

"That's it." My voice sounded very loud in the cabin, underscoring how alone I was out here.

It would take me less than five minutes to walk back to the lodge. Given the adrenaline and alcohol coursing through my body, I could probably make it under two. There would be ice at the lodge and headache tablets, and best of all, people. Lots of people—most of them probably still drinking at the bar.

Shuddering at the thought of any more alcohol, I climbed out of bed, pulled a sweater and jeans over my pajamas, slipped on my Reeboks and coat, and grabbed the poker from the fireplace.

I was slightly drunk, slightly sick, and totally annoyed. God help the homicidal maniac who got in my way.

I opened the door to the cabin, and the wet wind hit me with a cold slop in the face. I don't do dark and stormy. I particularly don't do it at three o'clock in the a.m. But what was the choice? Rose-tipped dawn was hiding out in some warmer clime. Overhead, the thunderous black cloud cover looked like upside-down mountains, like the world had flipped over—or maybe that was my stomach.

I started walking, picking my way through mud and rocks. The lights were out in all the other cabins, and it was impossible to see through the wall of dense hedges and trees whether any windows were still lit in the lodge. The barren landscape stretching before me had an otherworld, wind-scrubbed look. I dodged a tumbleweed rolling past.

Maybe this wasn't such a great idea. But the remnants of the nightmare still clung to me, and I didn't want to sit in that drafty cabin with my head killing me, afraid to fall asleep.

Anyway, I didn't believe that I was a real target, despite J.X.'s dire warnings about keeping my mouth shut and my eyes open. It's not like I knew anything that I hadn't immediately spilled to everyone who would listen. What would be the motive for getting rid of me? The fact that J.X. assumed I would automatically be marked for murder probably had more to do with J.X.'s feelings than the killer's.

But I didn't want to think about J.X.

Screw him.

Oh. Right.

I occupied myself by trying to walk in a straight line. Yep, I was definitely still feeling the effects of alcohol. It didn't help that the wind was blowing against me the whole way.

Despite my earnest effort, my wilderness trek took more than five minutes.

I assumed the back door to the lodge would be locked, although it hadn't been locked when I had slipped out a few hours earlier. I decided to go for the front entrance. I was convinced that someone was sure to still be in the bar. That was the way it worked at every other conference I'd ever attended.

The cowbell chimes were jangling as I marched up the front porch stairs.

I tried the front door. It was locked. I remembered George shoving the bolt home when we had arrived that evening, so that was no surprise. I pounded with my poker.

Waited.

Be patient, I told myself. Someone is bound to hear you.

I banged again. The poker dug some chunks out of the wood, and I eased off.

Stepping back, I studied the long line of the building and tried to determine where the bar was in relation to the front of the building.

It occurred to me that there were no lights on. Anywhere. Not in the entire building.

They were all in bed before daybreak. And they called themselves *writers*?

Amateurs.

Now what? I tried to think. Admittedly, my powers of reason seemed slightly dimmed. My head felt like it was being used for an anvil. *Boom, boom, boom.* Was that a hangover or high blood pressure reaching critical mass?

I stumbled down the porch steps and walked around to the back of the lodge. It seemed a very long way.

A dark and wet and silent long way.

Not that darkness or wetness or silence ever did anyone any harm—which is what I kept telling myself as I walked, feet pounding the pathway. The night seemed to swallow the sound of my footsteps, which is why when I heard something—a furtive noise from the patio around the corner ahead of me—I froze.

What...was...that?

Metal on cement. The scrape of a chair? Who the hell would be sitting out on the patio in this weather at this time of night?

I opened my mouth to call out—but something stopped me.

I listened.

No voices. Nothing but the lonely sound of the wind through the aspens. *And yet...*

Something changed. The stillness took on a listening quality. I felt with uneasy certainty that my approach had been heard, that someone was standing around the corner waiting for me—even as I stood waiting, heart banging away against my ribs, sweat chilling on my skin.

I took a soft and careful step backward.

A funny shiver ran down my spine. My bad feeling suddenly gave way to a wave of sick fear.

Instinct? Alcohol? Or sheer cowardice?

I turned and sprinted back down the path the way I had come.

Pausing at the point where the walkway branched off, I braced my hands on my thighs and gulped in air. I really needed to get back into shape—if it killed me.

I listened.

Anything?

Nothing.

I was being a total goof. And yet...the night seemed *too* quiet. There was something unnatural about the silence. Something alert. Attentive.

And standing out here on this walk, I was completely exposed, completely without protection. I looked around myself and spotted the old vine-covered arbor a yard or so down the other walk. Since it was the only real concealment in sight, it wasn't much of a decision.

I ran down the other walkway and slipped into the pitch darkness of the arbor. I waited. The wind filtered through the vines and latticework, cold breath on the back of my neck.

Footsteps were coming down the path. Brisk steps but... quiet. Not stealthy, but not the normal beat of approaching feet.

I flattened myself against the vines, my fingers sweaty on the warm metal of the poker. Even assuming I could manage to clobber someone with this—was I ready to bash someone's head in?

What if someone wrested it out of my hand and used it to bash *me*?

The footsteps paused. A silhouette loomed at the mouth of the tunnel. Huge, black, menacing. It seemed to block the entranceway. My heart stopped—which was all right because time stopped with it.

I didn't move, didn't breathe, didn't blink.

My hand gripped the poker so hard my fingers ached.

I waited for what seemed a lifetime, and then at last the silhouette withdrew. The footsteps moved softly away.

I expelled a long shaky breath.

What the hell had that been about? Why hadn't I spoken up? Why had I acted like a...a criminal? Like *I* was guilty? Like *I* had something to hide? Talk about paranoid. Talk about too much imagination.

But I wasn't talking. I was still standing there very quietly, barely breathing, waiting.

And waiting. I waited until I was damn sure he was gone. Then I gave it another five minutes.

It began to rain again. The drops slipped through the vines and lattice and fell in wet plops on my head.

And still I waited, shivering with nerves and cold.

Finally, when I was too miserable to hold out any longer, I crept out of the arbor and took a look around.

No sign of anyone. I scanned the empty pasture.

There was nowhere to hide on that empty flat stretch of land—that was the good news. The bad news was that in seconds *I* would be crossing that empty flat stretch with nowhere to hide.

I started running, pounding across the sodden weeds, trying not to sprain an ankle or fall in the mud—because how damsel in distress would that be? I zigzagged across the field, hopping puddles, managing not to trip in any ground-squirrel holes.

There was a bright side. Assuming I lived through this weekend, I was probably going to see some serious weight loss. I hadn't had this much physical activity in years.

As I reached the cabins, I veered to the left, making a detour toward J.X.'s. Number six he'd said. It sat still and silent in the pattering rain.

I banged on the door.

No response.

I whaled away with the poker a couple of times.

Nothing.

Not again. What was the *matter* with these people? Were they all wearing earplugs or what?

J.X. couldn't be that deeply asleep. No one could.

I had a sudden unwelcome memory of his face half-buried in a pillow next to me...

I mean, for crying out loud. I was having more flashbacks than a Vietnam vet in a seventies' action flick. The minute I knew J.X. was totally unavailable I couldn't stop obsessing about him. What the hell was my *problem*?

"Moriarty," I yelled.

Nothing.

He wasn't inside. He couldn't be. No one could sleep through the ruckus I was making.

Was J.X. the person who had followed me into the arbor?

So much for my survival instinct. If J.X. was wandering out here somewhere in the night, it was because he was doing a spot of off-duty investigating. I had never been in any danger. Not for an instant.

Right?

The rain was coming down hard now, plastering my hair and soaking my coat.

I turned away and walked slowly back to my own cabin.

CHAPTER TWELVE

Morning always comes too soon when you've spent the night acting the part of a character in a Thorne Smith novel. Sometime after dawn, I cracked the window shades of my eyes, promptly pulled them closed again, rolled out of bed, and crawled into the bath where I suffered the tortures of the damned—the damned silly—for the next forty-five minutes.

When I finally tottered back into the bedroom, clean and relatively sober, it was about eight o'clock, and while the thought of breakfast made me feel faint, the idea of central heating and hot coffee was enough to get me into my clothes.

Or whosever clothes these were. I peered blearily at a pair of Armani jeans that had been artfully bleached and beaten (*why?*) and a waffle crew sweater in a suitably muted gray. I felt too weak to comb my hair, and I didn't trust myself with a razor; clean clothes seemed enough of a concession to civilization and polite company. Not that a mob of writers bent on furthering their careers could be mistaken for polite company.

I managed to dress without incident and opened the door onto a bleak autumn morning. The rain had stopped, but that appeared to be more like the storm pausing to draw a deep breath than any actual break in the dialogue of bad weather. Large brown ponds dotted the meadow, clumps of scrub and weeds glistened in the feeble silvery light.

I glanced over at cabin number six. No sign of life. But just in case J.X. happened to be staring out his window, I strode off across the pampa, Burberry flapping about me, trying to exude brisk confidence and cheerful sobriety.

It was probably a reasonably convincing performance from behind, but I was panting and sweating by the time I reeled onto the front porch and tried the heavy wooden door. To my teary-eyed relief, it swung open, and I slipped inside the lodge.

The smell of coffee and cooking breakfast hit me from down the hallway—along with the din of glad voices—and after an uncertain moment while my guts struggled to make sense of all that had befallen them, I headed for the dining room.

It was packed. Wall-to-wall chicks. Most of them in pink. For an instant I suspected a bout of delirium tremens.

"Family seating," Rita informed me, as I stood there weaving with indecision.

Family seating? Then why wasn't everyone decently buried behind newspapers and coffee cups?

I considered foraging in the vending machines, but Rita planted her hand in the middle of my back and urged me forward with an unexpectedly strong push. "There's an empty seat over at the table by the window."

I thanked her and made my way to a crowded table. The inhabitants looked up with the sharp-eyed interest unattended men always garner at these things. They introduced themselves, I promptly forgot all their names, and I introduced myself.

"Christopher Holmes?" a lanky gray-haired woman asked. "Don't you write that pet-sitter series?"

I controlled my irritation. "I write the Miss Butterwith series," I said. "She's a—"

"Oh my gosh," said the youngest of the group. "Miss Butterwidth!"

"Butter*WITH*," I corrected.

"I used to read those when I was a kid. I *loved* them."

"Thank you," I said weakly. Since she was about J.X.'s age, I assumed she didn't mean literally *a kid.* Or maybe she had me confused with Agatha Christie. Or maybe she was simply being polite. I picked up my menu and hid behind it while they resumed their conversation—the main topic of which seemed to be J.X. How charming he was, how handsome, how modest—

What did that girl mean she *used* to read my books? Did that mean she felt she had outgrown them? I stared unseeingly at nauseating descriptions of pancakes and omelets and corned beef hash.

The topic of J.X. continued unabated around me. How funny he was, how helpful, what a good writer, how successful—had they mentioned how handsome he was?

On and on and on.

"Too bad he's married," my former fan chirped.

I stayed still behind my menu.

"The rich, handsome, polite ones always are," someone said.

"Or gay," someone else chimed in, and they all tittered.

I put my menu down, and they stopped chuckling. I said, "Do you think the bar is open? I'd kill for a Bloody Mary."

At the table next to us a woman was saying loudly, "Don't forget the three *E*'s of modern publishing: ebooks, erotica, and elves…"

"You could ask," one of the women said. I glanced around for a waitress, but they seemed to be in short supply.

"The buffet is over there," the chirpy young one put in, pointing across the room at a long table laden with chafing dishes. "The eggs Benedict are pretty good."

I swallowed hard. "Thank you."

They launched back into further discussion of J.X. I couldn't decide which I found more nauseating on top of a hangover, J.X. or eggs Benedict. I broke in, "So did any of you know this Peaches Sadler?"

There was an awkward pause.

"We knew *of* her," the gray-haired woman said.

The young'un said, "She didn't hang with people like us. She stuck to her own circle."

I was thinking pentagram. Probably inverted. I asked, "Her own circle?"

"Oh, you know. The superstars. J.X. and Steven Krass."

One more mention of J.X. and I was going to run amuck. The gray-haired woman interjected, "Buzz Salyer. Mindy Newburgh, I mean."

But another woman shot this down. "Not these days. She's not part of *that* group."

I felt an unworthy stab of relief. Once I would have been part of that group, and no one wants to wander off into exile by his lonesome.

"Speaking of which," the gray-haired woman said, checking her watch, "we're going to miss our workshop."

They began pushing away their plates, tossing napkins on the table, shoving chairs back.

At my inquiring look, the young one informed me, "Steven Krass is holding a workshop on the Top Ten Things Editors Hate."

"Ah," I said. "Colored fonts, my-mother-loves-my-book—"

"They don't like colored fonts? Have you taken his workshop before?" She seemed genuinely shocked.

The others shepherded her off. Briefly, there was peace. The waitress showed up, filled my coffee cup, and instructed me on how to partake of the joys of the buffet. I sipped my coffee and stared out the rain-fogged windows at the gloomy day—what I could see of it through the steam and mist.

The table rattled as someone took a chair on the other side of that linen no man's land. Espie Real deposited an enormous plate of food on the table and grinned at me.

"You look like death warmed over."

"Hey, it's what's for breakfast." I nodded at her plate.

She laughed. "Rough night?"

"I've had rougher."

"I bet." She heavily salted the piles of eggs, bacon, French toast, hash browns, and creamed chipped beef.

I shuddered inwardly—and outwardly. "You're not attending Steven Krass's workshop?" I inquired.

She had taken a forkful of eggs and potato and God knows what else, but she withdrew it intact in order to answer me. "Ha ha."

I stared, fascinated, at the mini mound of food wobbling on her suspended fork. "That's right," I said. "You're not a fan."

"No. I'm not a fan." She gave a sly look. "Maybe we should start an un-fan club; what do you think?"

"I think I'm a charter member." She seemed pretty frank. I asked, "So what was the beef with you and Peaches?"

She snorted, shoveled in the forkful of food, and chewed. I didn't think she was going to answer, but she swallowed finally and said, "You know her big breakout book?"

I must have looked blank, but the fact was I'd never heard of Peaches Sadler until—cue the theme from *Psycho*—she came slashing after me with her poison pen.

"Poké Stack."

I was still lost.

Espie brushed my ignorance aside. "Anyway, it's really a chicks book. Sort of a noir foodie romance."

"With that sexy chick-lit sensibility," I suggested.

"Yeah. Anyway, that was *my* book."

"*Poké Stack* was your book? You mean she ripped you off?"

"It's called *plagiarized*," she said flatly. "Yeah. We were both clients of Rachel's—well, hell. We were *friends*. The three of us. That's why I never saw it coming."

"What happened?"

"She and Rachel were kinda…" She raised her eyebrows suggestively and shoveled in more food. She ate like people in prison movies eat—sort of hunched over her plate and scooping bites up quickly between words.

"Rachel?"

She guffawed at my expression. "You don't get out much, do you?"

I felt that was rather beside the point. "So Rachel let her see your manuscript?"

She shrugged. "She saw it. Let's leave it there. Rachel never meant for it to happen, I know that. It's Krass's fault."

"It is?"

"This was back when he was Senior Editor at Gardener and Britain."

"Right," I said. Gardener and Britain was a small, well-respected press known mostly for literary mysteries.

"Well, he'd already bought my book, *Hot Sauce*. But then he's porking Peaches, yeah?"

"Uh...yeah." And Peaches had been porking Rachel and Krass? Yeesh.

"And along she comes with her version of my book, and he buys that and never notices—or just doesn't give a shit—it's the *same* book."

"You're joking."

"No, sweet stuff, I'm not joking. It's the same fucking book, names changed to protect the guilty. And Krass buys it and spends a shitload of money to promote it, and when I point out to him that it's my book, he basically tells me to keep my mouth shut about it or it will be the last book I write for Gardener and Britain—and maybe anyone else."

"And what was the justification for that?" I asked.

"Oh, you think there's a justification for that?" she asked hotly, glaring at me.

"No, of course not. I mean, what justification did Krass give you?"

"That the publisher had spent a lot of money and it was embarrassing to everyone involved, and the best thing would be that I let it be."

"And did you?"

She stared at me, eyes very bright, the tattooed teardrop black against her skin. "Yeah, I did. I talked it over with Rachel, and we decided it was the best move."

"What happened to your book? *Hot Sauce*?"

"It was published. It had a tiny print run, no promotion, and it sank like a stone."

"And no one commented on the similarities between your book and Peaches'?"

"Nobody *read* my book." She looked at her watch. "Shit, I gotta give a workshop on Writing Through Violence."

She jumped up and took off across the dining room, causing people to stare after her.

"Something you said?" Rita inquired, refilling my coffee cup.

"She's late for a workshop."

"These people ever do any writing, or do they just talk about it?"

I shrugged.

Finishing my coffee, I wandered off to see what I could find out about the possibility of getting back to civilization that day.

The lodge seemed relatively quiet with the majority of people in workshops or talking in small groups. I spotted my breakfast companions in a huddle at a table in the bar.

"How was the workshop?" I asked.

The perky girl said, "Steven Krass never showed up. He blew us off."

I couldn't say that surprised me. It sounded like his style.

"Any word about when we might get out of here?"

They all shook their heads. I spotted J.X. coming in the side door and excused myself. The last thing I felt up to was making polite conversation with J.X.

I didn't have a destination in mind, so I headed down the hall and went into the first open doorway. It seemed to be some kind of reading room or library. There were a number of knotty pine shelves stacked with books—mostly paperbacks—a couple of low rough-hewn tables littered with magazines, and a few comfortable chairs.

In one of the comfortable chairs was Debbie Croft, the daughter of the house. She appeared to be crying over an issue of *People* magazine.

I couldn't imagine what drove her to tears. Another wardrobe malfunction? Another substance abuse hospitalization? Another debut album from a celebrity who couldn't sing to save her life? Whatever it was, I didn't want to know.

And it appeared Debbie didn't want me to know. She looked up, saw me, and threw the magazine aside. Then she was on her way out of the room with some muffled comment I didn't catch.

Since I didn't know what else to do with myself, I sat down, picked up the magazine, and studied the glossy layout. The usual suspects behaving predictably. Then I blinked. Second photo from the top. Tom Hanks and Rita Wilson at a Literacy Fundraiser in San Francisco. And in the background stood bestselling crime author J.X. Moriarity and bestselling author and columnist Peaches Sadler. Peaches had her red-taloned hand fastened on J.X.'s sleeve, and she was beaming at him with an expression that was anything but fraternal.

I examined them. If I knew anything about body language—and thanks to *Miss Butterwith and the Body of Lies*, I did know a fair bit—there was quite a lot of sexual interest on the part of Peaches Sadler. J.X. was harder to read because he was partially turned away, smiling at someone off camera. But his body language conveyed…a certain level of comfort.

Relaxation. He certainly didn't *mind* her hanging on his arm and gazing soulfully up at him.

It didn't matter to me, naturally. It was merely a point of interest. Academic interest.

I tossed the magazine aside and walked down to the front desk to see if anyone had any information on when we might escape this hellhole, but once again it was deserted.

Feeling more and more restless, I wandered into the large meeting room with its panoramic view of the vineyards and the mountains wreathed in mist. Tables had been set up everywhere so that people could sit and chat in small groups.

I didn't see anyone I knew, and I wasn't in the mood to make new friends. I decided to return to my cabin.

Leaving through the back entrance, I walked across the rain-slick wooden deck, down the stairs, and started through the maze of metal tables and chairs. Preoccupied as I was, I didn't notice there was someone sitting at a table until I was a few feet away.

I halted. The rain ticked down on the metal tabletops, bouncing away like grain. Two tables from me a man was slumped over. I saw a black jacket and blond hair. His face was hidden in the curve of his arm—as though he were crying. Water sheeted off the table, reinforcing the idea. But he wasn't crying, although perhaps he should have been—what with that axe crunched in the back of his skull.

CHAPTER THIRTEEN

I was all out of dramatic reactions. All out of any reaction at all. Mostly I felt…tired.

Two bodies in two days? Could I be dreaming? Or how about a nice ordinary psychotic break? Wasn't that a lot more likely than this blood-spattered indication that I was spending the weekend with a serial killer?

I couldn't seem to tear my gaze away. I couldn't seem to make sense of the big picture; it was all little details: the gold Rolex ticking away on his wrist, the gray roots of his sodden blond hair, the pink tinge to the water pooled on the table.

Steven Krass.

Even though I couldn't see his face, I recognized the burly set of his shoulders, the expensive watch and signet ring, the thick bull's neck. The axe was new, but I can't say it didn't suit him.

Catching the echo of that thought, I realized that I was probably in shock. Not that I was going to pretend that my antipathy for Krass had changed because he'd found lodging in that cabin in the sky, but I didn't approve of murder on general principles. Not even of people who seemed to go around begging for it.

My next thought, oddly enough, was of J.X. Irritating bastard he might be, but he at least would know what to do about this. It was nothing personal. I was thinking strictly of his professional expertise and savvy—not the warm strength of his arms or the muscular hardness of his chest. Because I had no intention whatsoever of throwing myself in his arms. None. Even if he had been in range.

I glanced around, just in case, and was astonished to see that there *was* someone in range, though not J.X. In fact, it appeared to be Little Red Riding Hood—further confirming my suspicion that I was enjoying a particularly vivid nervous breakdown. But after a few seconds the costume resolved itself into a red raincoat, and the face and body reconciled themselves with Rachel's stricken features.

We stared at each other and neither of us said anything, which seemed, on reflection, unusual.

"Did you see what happened?" I asked at last.

She shook her head.

"It must have happened in the night. The blood has mostly washed away."

She put a hand out and hung onto the side of the building, as though feeling faint. A feeling I sympathized with.

"We have to get someone," I said. "Do you want me to go, or do you want to go?"

The problem was abruptly taken out of our hands when someone began to scream from the deck above. I turned, and a girl dressed in pink was having hysterics. She kept pointing at me—or perhaps Krass—and shrieking, but I couldn't make out a word of it. Not that I needed to; I got the gist. And so did everyone in earshot. In a matter of seconds the deck was crowded with people all expressing horror and shock in various tones and pitches, and J.X. was pushing his way through the pink mob and coming swiftly down the steps.

I was relieved to see him. He didn't seem to share my pleasure.

"What the hell happened?" His face was unusually pale, all sharps and angles as he got to me. He reached for Krass's leather-clad arm, feeling for a pulse apparently, which I thought indicated a nice optimistic streak.

"I don't know. I found him like this," I said.

He straightened, pinning me with a look. His eyes seemed almost black. "What were you doing out here?"

"I was walking back to my cabin."

"Why would you come this way?"

I stared at him. "I don't know. I guess because I was standing by the back entrance when I got the idea." I began to get angry. "You can't seriously think *I* had something to do with this?"

He hesitated.

I said hotly, "In case it's escaped your attention, *Dick* Tracy, he's been dead for hours."

He had to have seen that—even I had noticed that much—but he continued to scrutinize me with that fierce consternation. The rain ran down our faces as we glared at each other. I looked past him at Rachel.

She was gone.

Now that was weird.

"Two bodies in two days?" J.X.'s voice was hard. "I know, given the stuff you write, that probably seems perfectly reasonable, but in real life it's a little hard to swallow."

I opened my mouth to let him have it, but I was forestalled by the arrival of Edgar Croft.

"Good God Almighty," he said, staring down at the grisly table arrangement. "What in hell is going on around here?"

"You've got a homicidal maniac on the loose," I replied, although the question was probably rhetorical. I sneered to J.X. "And no, I'm not laying the groundwork for my insanity plea."

"What's that?" Edgar asked.

"Nothing," J.X. said. "Kit's kind of shaken up."

A sudden gust of wind tipped a line of patio chairs clattering over like a row of dominos and sent a couple of tables scraping back a few feet. J.X. and Edgar looked at each other, and I knew what they were thinking. No police helicopter was touching down here anytime soon.

"Christ," J.X. muttered, raking the wet hair out of his face. "We've got to secure this crime scene somehow." He turned to me. "Go inside and ask Rita to have everyone go to their rooms or cabins. You wait in the bar for me."

"You've got to be kidding me."

Given the grimness of his expression, he wasn't kidding.

"You honest to God think you're going to be able to confine this crowd to their rooms? And then what? Send the murderer to bed without supper?"

He continued to try and bend me to his will with the sole power of his Magnetic Gaze.

I said, "You're going to question them one by one?"

"Unfortunately, we don't have a drawing room to gather the sus—"

"Oh, go to hell." I turned and went up the stairs to the deck, and after a hesitation, the crowd which had fallen uneasily silent made room for me. "We're supposed to go inside and leave it to the professionals," I announced irritably.

To my surprise, they actually did begin filing back inside. To the questions thrown my way, I kept shaking my head and saying, "You know as much as I do. I just walked outside and found him."

I got a fair bit of sympathy for that, but I also got some skeptical looks. I wasn't clear if the skepticism was due to my high rate of dead-body discovery or the suspicion I knew more than I was telling.

It took a few minutes, but I found Rita standing at the giant misty picture windows in the main meeting room, gazing down on the gruesome scene below. I explained what J.X. wanted, and she raised her eyebrows.

"How does he think I'm supposed to enforce that?"

I shook my head. "All you can do is tell them he's acting in absentia of the sheriff's department."

Shaking her head, she bustled off to send everyone to their rooms. I could hear the protests from down the hall. I couldn't blame them. It was probably the first genuinely interesting thing to happen on site since the conference began. I continued to gaze out the window, watching J.X. and Edgar conversing. It looked to me like they were going to be a while.

I left the meeting room. The halls and rooms were empty with the exception of the dining room where staff was still clearing away the breakfast debris and setting up for lunch. Upstairs it sounded more like a beehive than ever, voices buzzing behind every door.

Every door but one. I knocked, and Rachel called, "Come."

I opened the door. She was at the window again, smoking. "What's going on?" I asked.

She raised pencil-thin eyebrows and blew out a long, perfect series of smoke rings. No dragon lady ever did it better.

"What were you doing out there? Why did you disappear like that?"

"Does J.X. want us milling around?"

"You know what I mean."

"No I don't." She met my perplexed gaze coolly.

I tried to look at it from her POV, but I don't do omniscient very well. She had been standing where no one from the house or deck could see her, so unless I mentioned it, it was unlikely anyone would know she had been there—stumbling upon the body around the same time as me. But while I could understand her reluctance to place herself at the scene of the crime, was there a valid reason *not* to? I was coming under special scrutiny for having been in the wrong place at the wrong time. Wasn't it only fair for Rachel to fess up to the same ill fortune?

Slowly, I asked, "Are you expecting me to keep the fact that you were out there a secret?"

She lifted a shoulder. "If no one knows I was out there, they can't ask me about you."

"About *me*? What about me?"

She gave another one of those maddening shrugs.

"For your information, he was probably killed in the middle of the night—" I broke off, remembering my own nocturnal adventures which had conveniently escaped me until now. I remembered the strange sounds and the uncanny feeling that had gripped me as I walked down the path to the back of the house. If I had rounded the corner to the patio, would I have found Krass's body—would I have found Krass's murderer waiting for me axe in hand?

My knees suddenly gave out, and I had to sit on the edge of Rachel's bed and take a few deep breaths as I recalled those muffled footsteps following me to the arbor—the shadowy figure that had waited there, listening.

"What's the matter with you?" Rachel demanded. "Are you having a heart attack?"

She probably didn't intend it to sound like an accusation. And just what I needed, a reminder that I had now reached the age when everyone assumed signs of distress indicated impending coronary. I shook my head.

"It's probably reaction. Put your head between your knees."

Like at my age my spine had that much give and play left? Did she think I was a yogi? Gumby?

As I sat there huffing and puffing, I noticed that Rachel's nightwear was one of those sleep-shirt things emblazoned with the figure of Sailor Moon. Somehow I'd have guessed something in traditional silk brocade with a mandarin collar and a hem stained with the blood of rejected authors and other peasants. Not that I—God strike me mercifully blind—had been dwelling on the image of what Rachel did or did not wear in the sack. It was the incongruity of it. It seemed so...un-Rachel. This half-formulated idea distracted me enough that I quit hyperventilating over my narrow escape and sat up.

"Espie told me how Peaches Sadler plagiarized her novel to get her first big break."

"Plagiarism!" Rachel gave a harsh laugh. "Plagiarism doesn't cover it. She duplicated the entire damn novel. She merely changed the names."

"I can't believe no one caught it."

"Nobody *read* Espie's novel. As for Gardener and Britain, they invested a lot of money in launching Peaches. And the book hit the New York Times Bestseller List within a couple of weeks.

From their perspective there was no advantage in revealing the truth."

"No advantage? What about the advantage to Espie—the person who actually wrote the bestselling novel?"

"Christopher." She looked at me with a kind of pity. "They did try to make it up to Espie. They contracted two more of her books. The books didn't do anything. And it wasn't anything to do with Peaches or Krass because they'd both moved to Wheaton & Woodhouse by then."

"How can that be? How could Espie's book—her skill—be bestseller-worthy when it was written by Peaches but not when it was written by Espie?"

"*Because*," she barked. "As I keep *striving* to bear upon that blond head of yours, it's not merely the *writing*. It's the whole fucking *package*. It's the look, it's the platform, it's the overall marketability. It's how you interact with fans. Christ on a crutch. I had to use a crowbar to get you to leave your bleeding house. And, yes, I'm sorry about the—the breakup, sorry that David was such a bastard, but anyone with half a brain would have seen him for the lecherous lout he was long before he ran off with that twink you called a personal assistant."

I blinked at her while she continued to yap at me like a Pekingese after too many generations of inbreeding. When she finally wound down, I said, "Leaving my *package* out of it for the moment, I do not believe that the hook is much more important than the writing. And neither do you. And secondly, it sounds to me like both you and Espie have a pretty good motive for wanting to whack both Peaches and Satan Krass."

Her eyes bulged—which is really not that easy with Asian eyes. "*Me*? What possible motive could I have?"

"For one thing, after he dissed you last night you were saying what a pity it was no one had brained him. *And* you were behaving in a most sinister fashion asking whether I thought it was true that Krass knew something about Peaches' murder."

She opened her mouth, but I kept going. "Also, it's very obvious that you had an...um...complicated relationship with Peaches. She'd betrayed your trust over stealing Espie's manuscript—oh, and while we're on the subject of bad taste in lovers, *hello*?"

Rachel had the grace to look sheepish.

"You were overheard arguing with Peaches the night before she died, and then you're discovered skulking around the scene of Krass's murder. If this was a movie, believe me, you would be the killer."

"Are *you* accusing *me*?" she screeched.

"I don't care if you killed him or not. You're my agent. And a great agent at that. That bloodthirsty streak is part of what I pay you for. Just tell me so I don't put my foot in it when J.X. whips out his rubber hose." I paused. "Uh...I mean..." I coughed. "Oh, and also please don't try to kill me because I know your guilty secret. Because that is really going to put a strain on our professional relationship."

"Are you done?" she asked with great restraint.

"Pretty much. Yes."

"I didn't kill Peaches Sadler or Steven Krass."

"If you say it, I believe you."

"I *do* say it."

"I believe you."

"I don't want anyone knowing I was out on the patio because, as you say, it probably looks suspicious, and it's true that if someone started digging, it would rake up all that old history—which would not be good for Espie or myself."

I translated "not be good" to mean "would indeed uncover motives for murder" for herself and Espie. I said, "Okay. I'll do the gentlemanly thing and try to protect you. What the hell *were* you doing out there this morning?"

Her eyes shifted from mine. She said uncomfortably, "I went for a walk."

"What?"

"I know. But it's true. I woke up with a headache, and I thought…maybe a walk before it starts raining again…"

"Where did you walk?"

"I walked down to the vineyards and looked at the buffalo."

"They have buffalo in the vineyard?"

"Of course not. The buffalo are in the pasture—" She gave it up. "I was on my way back to the house, and I decided it was faster to go in the back way, so I cut around the side of the house and there you were."

"I was walking back to my cabin."

"I don't care what you were doing," she said. "I don't care if you did knock off Krass. Even if I didn't hate his guts, you're my client after all. Not that it wouldn't make one hell of a sensational real life—"

"He was probably killed in the middle of the night," I interrupted.

"Well, then." She shrugged.

I glanced at the clock on the nightstand and remembered I was supposed to be waiting meekly in the bar for Field Marshal Moriarty. "All right, then," I said. "Mum's the word."

CHAPTER FOURTEEN

J.X. was not in the bar when I arrived. I coaxed a gin and tonic out of Rita and was halfway through it when he finally showed up looking grim and wet. He asked for a towel and ordered a Jack Daniels.

When he sat down across from me in the booth, his damp hair was glossy and spiky from its recent toweling. His face was flushed with the cold and his exertions. His gaze was as hard as tiger's eye. I had an uncomfortable—and unsettlingly vivid—memory of what it had felt like to be in his arms again, the silkiness of his beard as his mouth found mine, and how soft and dark his eyes had seemed gazing—

"All right," he said, jolting me out of my thoughts. "From the top."

"Are you a top?" I asked innocently. "I did wonder because you're pretty aggressive once you get g—"

His color went from a healthy honey-brown to a dusty brick color. "Yeah, you're a shoo-in for class clown, Christopher," he said thickly. "And you're looking pretty good for prime suspect too."

That brought me back to earth fast. "How do you figure that?" I demanded indignantly. "You know as well as I do Krass had to have been killed during the night—or maybe in the early hours of the morning. I didn't get that good a look at him."

"This isn't one of your books, Christopher. It's not an academic puzzle. A man has been killed. Someone in this house killed him."

"That lets me out. I'm staying in the cabins." He was staring at me with disbelief. I said shortly, "All right. I talk too much when I'm scared, and yes, I am scared." I found it ridiculously difficult to meet his eyes. "Look, I walked over for breakfast, that's all. I'm not taking part in the conference. I never intended to. My sole purpose for being here was to talk to Krass." I drew a deep breath. "Well, you saw how that went down."

J.X. didn't say anything, and I couldn't look at him. Once I had been the golden boy, the rising star on the mystery scene, and he had been an eager and admiring acolyte. He had thought I was wonderful; my predilection for spinster sleuths and cats notwithstanding, he had wanted—well, better not to think of that. Now he was the blazing success story, the boy wonder rocketing to the top, while I was the aging has-been. The wax had melted off my wings, and I was plummeting toward obscurity and the remainder shelf.

"I finished breakfast, and there was no reason to hang around. If you want to know the truth, it's humiliating. Everybody in the fucking place knows what happened." I sighed. "I couldn't face running into Krass again. I decided to go back to my cabin and hide out until the weather cleared enough for me to get out of here."

"Kit…" The reluctant sympathy in his voice was more than I could handle.

I talked over him quickly. "I went out the back way because I was standing right there when it occurred to me I didn't have to hang around pretending to be a good sport and providing Krass with another target. That's it. I walked outside, started down the patio, and I saw him."

"Why didn't you go for help?"

"I...I was going to." I did meet his eyes then. "I was shocked. I know I write about this stuff, but it's startling when you come face-to-face with it in real life."

His expression was sardonic, but he didn't stop me.

"I couldn't have stood there for more than a minute. Maybe two before that chick started screaming."

J.X. said without inflection, "The girl who screamed said that you were standing there talking to the body."

My jaw dropped. Casting my mind back, I realized what J.X.'s witness must have seen and the interpretation she had clearly placed on it. Did I give Rachel up, or did I continue to cover for her? I said, "It wasn't much of a conversation. I think I was probably saying something like, oh shit, what do we do now?"

He said gravely, "She said she thought she heard you say, *are you going for help, or am I?*"

I couldn't help it; I started to laugh. Granted, it was probably close to borderline hysteria. I got myself under control enough to inquire, "And what did Krass say?"

"It's not funny, Kit."

"It's *kind* of funny," I pointed out.

"Was someone else there?" J.X. asked. "Was there someone standing on the walkway out of view of the deck?"

"You were there. Did you see anyone?"

He didn't respond, viewing me meditatively. "Did you touch Krass?"

"No." That I could answer with confidence.

"Did you lean over his body to try and get a look at his face?"

I shook my head.

"Then explain to me what this was doing underneath Krass's body." He set a tiny platinum and diamond ear stud on the table between us. It sat winking in the muted light like an unlucky star.

Instinctively, I put a hand up to my ear. The lobe was bare. I hadn't bothered with fripperies that morning.

"It's yours, isn't it?"

"I…think so," I admitted. I couldn't seem to tear my gaze away from the earring.

"I recognize it as the one you were wearing when you arrived here yesterday."

"You noticed my *earrings*?" I asked blankly.

There was a hint of color in his face. "You never used to wear jewelry." He shrugged. "Yeah, I noticed it." His voice was hard when he continued, "Where did you lose it?"

"I lost one in the woods."

"One?"

"There were two of them. I lost one thrashing around the woods, and I took the other out."

"Where? When?"

"I don't remember."

"Is it in your cabin?"

"I don't know," I said. At his obvious exasperation, I added, "A lot of stuff has happened to me since I arrived here. I think I took it out when I showered last night."

"Why would you take it out?"

"Because I'd lost the other one? I don't know. I didn't think about it." A question occurred. "Was I wearing it last night at dinner?"

He swept the stud off the table and back in his pocket. "I didn't notice. I was pissed off with you because you went around telling everyone Peaches was murdered."

"I did *not*."

"I thought you did," he qualified. He narrowed his eyes. "I don't think you were wearing it. You looked really nice in that gray shirt, by the way."

Color warmed my face. "Thanks."

He finished his Jack Daniels and set the glass down. "Look, here's the way it shapes up. You found both bodies—that's not good. As you know, since you've harped enough on it in those books of yours, discovering a body generally puts a person in a suspicious position. On top of that, you had an unfriendly history with Peaches—"

"I never met her!"

"And you were overheard threatening Steven Krass."

I nearly dropped my glass. "I *what*?"

"You said you didn't want to drink with him because you'd be tempted to poison him."

"I was kidding. Sort of. That's not the same thing as threatening—let alone trying—to do it."

"But do you understand the way it sounds?"

"Yes, and I don't think it sounds suspicious."

"Then you've got your head stuck in the sand."

"Well, that's better than some places I've stuck it."

He bit his lip, and I thought for a minute he was going to laugh. However, he said, "Kit, you've got to take this more seriously."

That did it. "J.X., do you honest to God think I murdered anybody?"

He gave me a long dark look and then shook his head. "No. It's obvious Peaches was killed Thursday night. And I sure as hell can't see a way you could have lured her away from the lodge or snuck in and kidnapped her."

"So it's a matter of logistics? Thanks for your faith in me."

"Give me a break," he retorted. "Miss Butterball is supposed to be some kind of detective idiot savant, right? You ought to know by now all kinds of people commit murders. And let's not forget the fact that you're a selfish, callous bastard, which, right there, are pretty good traits for a murderer."

That time I did drop my glass. It fell to the table, and ice spilled out on the carpet. I managed to get out, "No, how could I forget that. I'm a *selfish, callous bastard*? How the fuck dare you?"

"Hey, if the condom fits…"

I was gasping as though he'd slugged me in the guts—which is actually how it kind of felt. "What, I'm supposed to have taken advantage of your boyish innocence, is that it? If anybody rushed anybody into it—"

He shrugged. "Ancient history," he said easily. "It gives me insight into your character, that's all. Anyway, we can verify your alibi for Peaches' murder based on your plane flight manifest, the car rental info, credit card trail—that kind of thing. And since these murders are almost certainly linked together, if you're cleared of Peaches' homicide, it's unlikely you'll be nailed for Krass's, although your motive is stronger and there's more evidence—"

I don't think I heard half of it. I was sitting there stricken with memory, with the fact that he believed…whatever the hell it was he believed about that long-ago weekend.

There was a pause while he waited for me to respond to something he'd asked me. I said haltingly, "Listen, J.X., if I...if I did anything to hurt you, I apologize. That was not my intent. For reasons I won't bore you with, that weekend meant a lot to me—"

He laughed, not very kindly. "Hey, believe me, I got over it a long time ago. And even if I was carrying some grudge, which I'm not, I wouldn't stand by and let you be framed for murder."

I repeated stupidly, "Framed for murder?"

"Have you listened to anything I've said?" he asked impatiently. "That earring didn't happen to land underneath Krass's body. If you didn't drop it, then someone planted it. Someone is trying to frame you for murder."

CHAPTER FIFTEEN

It took Rachel a few seconds to answer the door.

"Bloody hell, Christopher," she exclaimed, stepping back as I pushed my way inside her room. "What's the matter with you?"

"I know you're trying to frame me for Krass's murder."

She shrieked, "*What?*" in much the tone the empresses of old used when the only chocolates left were the marshmallow-caramels.

"I left that goddamned ear stud here when I showered after I first arrived."

She was staring at me as though convinced I was insane.

I said clearly, "I left it on the glass shelf in your bathroom. So don't give me that look."

She continued to give me that look.

"Why are you doing this to me?" I demanded. "What did I do to you? You want me to write a damned regency demon P.I. thing, I will. I'll even throw in a werewolf. Just...stop."

She whipped around and went to the dresser, sifting through the debris of jewelry, bottled water, receipts, and assorted cosmetics. "It's not here!" she exclaimed. She turned around to face me. "I put it up here in this glass so it wouldn't get lost."

"Are you sure it's not there?" I joined her at the dresser, and we both sifted through the pile of junk. There was no water glass—empty or otherwise—and while there were plenty of earrings, none of them was mine.

"It was here," she insisted. "I did see it in the bathroom on the shelf, and I picked it up."

The fact that she admitted seeing the earring calmed me way down.

"Was your room cleaned today?"

"If you can call it that. They made the bed and brought clean towels."

"Maybe the maid took it."

"She must have." She was eyeing me with speculative amusement. "Did you really think I'd framed you?"

"Hey, you're not in the clear yet." I was thinking rapidly. If Krass had been killed and my earring planted during the night, no maid was responsible for clearing away that glass and stud. "Do you know who cleaned your room?"

"Probably the kid. What's her name? Donna?"

"Debbie."

"Right. She did it the morning before."

I said suspiciously, "If I tell J.X. you had my earring, you're not going to do something weird like deny it, are you?"

"Why would I?"

"I don't know. It happens a lot in old mystery novels."

"You read too many old mystery novels," Rachel informed me. "You need to read some Kate White or M.J. Rose." She thrust a stack of paperbacks at me.

"You just don't want to have to carry these back on the plane." I headed for the door. "I'm bringing J.X. back here, and I want you to tell him the truth."

She stared at me and then smiled a slow, evil grin.

"Very funny," I said and slammed out of the room.

* * * * *

I found J.X. in the lobby. He had the front door open, and he was speaking to Rita, who was behind the front desk. At the sound of my footsteps, he glanced around and, if possible, his expression grew even grimmer.

"I thought you said you were going back to your cabin."

"I was," I lied. "But then it suddenly occurred to me what I did with that other earring."

"And what was that?"

"I left it in Rachel's room. I took it out when I showered after I first arrived here. She remembers seeing it. In fact—" I turned to Rita. "Who cleaned the rooms this morning? Rachel says she left the earring in a glass on her dresser."

Rita's hatchet face grew sharp enough to chop wood. "What are you implying, mister?"

"I'm not implying anything. I'm wondering if the earring got picked up or thrown out by accident, that's all."

"Kit."

"Nobody picked up any earring by accident or any other way."

"Well, couldn't you ask whoever did the rooms?"

"*Kit.*"

I turned impatiently. "What?"

"I need to talk to you." There must be something to that whole cop mystique because although I was certainly older, at that flat, authoritative tone I suddenly felt like I was being summoned to the principal's office.

I said, "But don't you think we should find out what happened to that ear stud?"

"I'll look into it for you. Come on." He held the door to the lodge open.

I couldn't read his expression at all as I stepped outside, but the very impassivity of his features made me uneasy.

"What's wrong?" I asked.

"I'll explain it to you on the way to your cabin."

We went down the wooden steps and crossed the yard, and I threw a couple of uncertain glances J.X.'s way. His profile looked older, resolute—Ernest Shackleton preparing the *James Caird* for launch.

"What is it?" I asked.

He looked at me then. "You were seen last night."

"I was…seen?" Recollection hit. I could feel myself changing color. "Oh. I was going to tell you, but you brought up the earring and I wanted to settle that before I told you something else that was liable to seem incriminating."

"For Christ's sake. You didn't think the fact that you were trotting around this place about the time Steven bought it was something you needed to mention up front?"

"Yes. I did. But I also knew how it was liable to look."

"What the fuck were you doing outside at three in the morning?"

The harshness in his voice took me aback. "What I wasn't doing was taking my little axe and giving my editor forty whacks." There was no softening, no understanding in his face.

He looked...stony. I realized I was in serious trouble, and the fight drained out of me.

"I woke up, and...oh hell. I felt like shit. I needed Tylenol and ice and...company."

"Company?"

"What the shit is so strange about that? It's a writing conference, for God's sake. If you ask me, the strange behavior belongs to these so-called writers who went to bed at midnight. I thought the bar would still be open. I was...nervous out here on my own."

Zero comprehension on his face.

I stumbled on, "But when I got to the lodge the lights were all out and the doors were locked. So...you have to understand. I'd had a lot to drink after you left."

There at last was a flash of acknowledgment.

"You drink too much."

"I know." I made a face. "Anyway, I wasn't thinking too clearly. I thought maybe I could get in the back way. I didn't realize they locked the place down at night."

He snapped out, one word at a time, "There is a killer on the loose here, Christopher. Of course they locked the goddamn place down. Are you telling me you don't remember I told you to lock yourself in last night and not open the door to anyone? What did you think I meant? Don't open to Girl Scouts selling cookies? Don't open to the Jehovah Witnesses? Don't open to trick-or-treaters?"

"I wasn't thinking clearly."

I watched him courageously struggle to overcome the desire to say, *I told you so!* "Go on," he managed between clenched teeth.

"Before I got to the back patio I heard…maybe a chair being dragged or a table being dragged across the cement. Anyway, it was weird enough that I stopped to listen." I swallowed dryly, remembering the sour taste of my fear. "I…something about it…I can't explain it, but I suddenly lost my nerve."

He was watching me closely, his eyes narrowed as though trying to determine if I was telling the truth or not.

"I ducked into the arbor. I waited there, and then I heard footsteps. Someone—I couldn't see who—came to the mouth of the arbor and stood there waiting and listening. Then he went away. When I was sure he really was gone, I ran back to my cabin."

Whatever he saw in my face must have convinced him I wasn't fabricating this.

He said quietly, "Jesus. Do you realize how close you came to dying last night?"

I nodded sheepishly.

We were nearly to my cabin now. J.X. sighed.

I tried to read his expression, but it was a closed-casket viewing.

At last he said, "Look, I believe you. I don't think you killed Peaches or Steven, but…"

"But what?"

"That's my own personal belief. There's enough circumstantial evidence to arrest you right now."

"You can't be serious."

"I am serious." He looked serious, true enough. "And a number of people are already asking that you be locked up until the sheriffs can get through."

I stopped walking.

"What? Who? *Whom?*"

"It doesn't matter. People are scared, and right now you look like the most obvious suspect."

"That's ridiculous."

"No, it's not." He met my gaze and repeated steadily, "No, it's not. You had history with both victims, you discovered both bodies, you were heard threatening one of the victims, you were observed on the scene at the time of the murder, and your earring was found at one of the crime scenes."

I regret to say that I lost all semblance of dignity. I quavered, "Am I going to be arrested?"

"I don't know," he said honestly. "I think there's a good chance of it. In the meantime, I've promised to lock you in your cabin."

I couldn't even get my mouth under control to form the words. I stared at him.

"I'm sorry," J.X. said. "I meant what I said. I don't believe you killed anyone, but I have to do what's best for everyone, and if isolating you out here makes everyone feel safer, that's what I need to do."

For one frightening instant I thought I might start crying. Thankfully, anger kicked in and saved the shredded tatters of my pride. "Wait a minute. First of all, who the heck is this witness who supposedly saw me running around last night? Maybe *that* person is the murderer?"

"I don't think it's very likely, but I'm keeping an eye on him."

"Him. Him who?"

He hesitated.

I said with great, if wobbly, dignity, "You're locking me up on this person's say-so. You at least owe me the courtesy of telling me his name. I mean, what happened to my legal right to face my accuser?"

"I'm not shipping you to Alcatraz, Kit," he said patiently. "It's just till the storm clears tomorrow. We'll bring you meals, and I see you've got books to read."

We both stared at my armload of pink and red book covers. I looked away, clenched my jaw hard, sniffed harder.

"Hell," J.X. muttered. "George Lacey saw you."

"What was he doing up at that time of night?"

"He and Mindy have one of the front bedrooms. He said he heard you pounding on the door with a poker, but by the time he got downstairs you had gone."

"So for all he knows I went back to my cabin."

Still patient, J.X. said, "He didn't say he saw you kill Steven. He said he saw you running around at what was the approximate time of the murder."

"Well, for that matter," I said tartly, "you were running around at the approximate time of the murder too."

He went very still. "What are you talking about?"

"After I left the arbor, I went to your cabin, where I whaled away with my trusty poker—to no avail."

To my unease, he couldn't seem to come up with an answer. I hadn't really suspected him of killing Krass or anyone else, but the way he stood there looking sort of blank and discomfited threw me.

"Where were you?" I asked.

He seemed to snap out of whatever was mesmerizing him. "I did leave my cabin," he admitted. "I went down to the ice-house to check on Peaches."

"*Why?*" It seemed like such a gruesome thing to do. Brave, but gruesome. And rather unnecessary because it wasn't like Peaches was trying to escape.

"I don't know." It was his turn to look sheepish. "I had an uneasy feeling. This is a weird setup."

"Again, the keen eye of the Master Detective," I said bitterly, and I marched on to my cabin.

As we reached my door, he said, "May I have your key?"

"Do I have a choice?"

"No."

"It's in my back pocket."

He slid his hand in my back pocket and felt around for the key.

"Other pocket," I said tightly.

"Sorry."

He retrieved the key with a minimum of caressing my ass, and unlocked the door. I went past him and threw the stack of paperbacks on the neatly made bed, turning to face him.

"When are my mealtimes, or do I rattle my water glass against the prison bars when I'm hungry?"

He sighed. "Your meals are the regular mealtimes. Look, I'm not enjoying this any more than you are."

"That's very easy to say on the other side of the bars."

"You know, you really are a bit of a drama queen, Kit."

"And you really are a bit of an insensitive, unimaginative, arrogant, fascist prick."

His mouth compressed, his eyes darkened.

I added, "And I hope I broke your heart all those years ago."

"You did," he said evenly. And with that he stepped outside the cabin and shut the door.

I was still standing there with my mouth open as I heard the key turn in the lock.

CHAPTER SIXTEEN

The funny part was, I had been on my way back to my cabin when I discovered Steven Krass's body, so why was I now prowling the interior of the log cabin, muttering to myself, and returning to the front window every few steps to gaze across the empty field at the rooftop of the lodge?

It was all about freedom of choice. And I currently had none. Also no TV, internet, or telephone. What was I supposed to do to amuse myself for the rest of my stay here at Bates Motel? Wait for the power and heat to go off? Wait for the lynch mob to show up?

When I had worn myself out pacing—which didn't take long given how out of shape I was—I flung myself on the bed and picked up one of the candy-coated novels Rachel had thrust upon me. A short time later I wondered if it was reasonable to consider suicide half an hour after incarceration.

Oh, the books weren't that bad. Really. But once again it was borne in on me why my beloved Miss Butterwith was getting so severely dissed by the handful of mystery fans still reading print. There were no elderly botanists in this pastel selection of crime fiction. No, the sleuths were wedding planners, fashion reporters, hairdressers, yoga instructors, and chicks with no visible means of support at all. They were young and mouthy and inordinately concerned with fashion and their love lives. You've come a long way, baby? Full circle in fact.

I could only take so much of it before I decided I'd prefer to read the instructions on the back of my multitude of grooming products. And, in fact, I was figuring out how to use something called "Shea Butter Ultra Rich Hair Cream" when someone scared me out of a week's worth of growth by rapping sharply on the cabin window.

I yanked back the plaid curtains and returned the favor as I was wearing some kind of dark blue facial mud mask in addition to the pale blue hair mask. Mindy Newburgh's eyes went enormous behind the rhinestone glasses, and she fell off the milk crate she was standing on to peer in my window.

"Are you all right?" I called, trying to squint down past the sill.

She picked herself up and climbed back on the milk crate. "Christopher Holmes, what on earth are you doing in there?"

Other than the Peeping Tom thing, she was starting to remind me more and more of my own grandmother. Or perhaps Miss Butterwith.

"I'm killing time," I replied through the glass. "And, for the record, that's the *only* thing I've killed since I got here."

Wasted would be a better word for it.

"You look like you belong in that Blue Man Group."

"Maybe I can find work with them after I get out of prison."

She made a tsking sound. "That's actually why I came down here. I wanted to apologize for Georgie. He'd told J.X. about your midnight escapade before I had a chance to stop him."

"I didn't kill anyone."

"I know that, silly. You couldn't hurt a fly."

Actually I was pretty good at pinging flies right out of the air, but I tried to look appropriately harmless. "Someone's trying to frame me."

"It's not George." Mindy wobbled on the milk crate. "He felt that it was his duty to tell what he saw. It's nothing personal, kiddo. George doesn't have a lot of imagination."

I was about to take issue with that statement, when she added, "Anyway, if you *did* whack Steven, you did us all a favor."

"I appreciate the support, but I didn't kill him."

"I suppose not. You couldn't have killed Peaches, and it's obvious the two murders are connected."

"What's the connection, though?"

"I think Steven saw whoever killed Peaches."

"What makes you think so?"

"Remember last night in the bar when we were all at the Wheaton & Woodhouse table...?" She trailed off awkwardly as it occurred to her why I had been at the Wheaton & Woodhouse table last night.

"Vaguely," I replied.

"Steven was an asshole," Mindy said. "For the record." Her breath steamed the glass between us.

"For the record, thank you. What did you see last night?"

"It's not that I *saw* anything exactly, but didn't you think Steven was challenging someone when he was talking about anyone who had information about Peaches' murder needed to come forward?"

"He was challenging J.X."

Mindy nodded solemnly.

If I'd been standing on a milk crate, I'd probably have tumbled off it. "You don't think *J.X.*...?"

"If Steven was killed because he knew something about Peaches' death, well, I happened to overhear J.X. and Peaches arguing the night before she was found murdered."

"About what?"

"I didn't hear it all. But she called him queer."

"Isn't"—I caught myself in time—"that something?" I managed.

"I think J.X. probably is..." Mindy wobbled her hand indicating AC/DC—and nearly fell off her pedestal again. "He and Peaches definitely had a thang goin' on."

I can't tell you how disturbing it is to hear an apple-cheeked granny utter the words "thang goin' on."

"Definitely? I thought he was married?"

"What's that these days?"

Well, she was talking to the right person now. I concurred bitterly, and Mindy said, "Peaches was not above telling J.X.'s wife out of spite. She was a *very* spiteful person."

"How do you know?"

"I know," she said, "because she came on to Georgie, and that was simply to prove to me that she could get anyone she wanted. Of course Georgie wasn't having any of it."

My mud-coated face was starting to crack. "Of course not."

"She also tried to convince Steven to let her try her hand at writing a new series of thrillers about a divorced Jewish female assassin."

"I thought you already—"

"Exactly."

"And was Krass entertaining that idea?"

Mindy's expression changed. I think it belatedly dawned on her that she was building a nice motive for murder for herself. "Of course not. It gives you an idea of the kind of person Peaches Sadler was. Absolutely ruthless. She and Steven were two of a kind."

I thought this over slowly as the wind shook the window in its frame. "So you think Krass was killed by J.X.?"

Mindy shrugged. "I don't know, but who's better placed to hide evidence and control the investigation? And he did lock you up, which really wasn't necessary in my opinion."

"I appreciate that."

She had a point, although I couldn't really see J.X. losing control to the extent that he would resort to murder. Not that I really knew that much about him—nor did he rank high on my People I'd Like to Know Better list.

The rain was coming down harder now. Mindy's nose was as pink as her cheeks. She looked skyward and then peered at me through the glass. "Is there anything you need?"

"Paper, pens, ice, another blanket, coffee…"

The top of her head disappeared from sight while I was still talking.

I spent another very long hour washing off all the gunk I had applied, pacing the room and listening to the rain, and trying to outline my ideas for a Regency P.I. novel with a pencil and the single sheet of stationery supplied by the lodge. The lack of paper wasn't a problem because I was out of ideas not long after I wrote the words *London 1815.*

When someone pounded on my cabin door shortly before lunch, I jumped to my feet in the hope that the killer had finally arrived to put me out of my misery. The key scraped in the lock, and the door swung open. A tall figure filled the frame. At first

I thought it was J.X., and I was very irritated at the way my startled heart sped up.

"I thought you might be getting chilly down here," Edgar said, holding out a carrier of wood.

I was pretty damn cold by then, so I did appreciate the thought.

"You do know how to light a fire?" Edgar asked.

"Well...I'm used to the gas kind, to tell the truth."

I appreciated the fact that he didn't so much as roll his eyes. I sat on the bed so he could see how non-threatening and harmless I was, and he carried the wood in and laid the fire. By the time he stood up again, it was crackling merrily and already starting to throw off a little heat.

"Rita's getting your lunch ready to bring down now."

"Thanks."

"There are candles and matches in the desk drawer if the power goes out."

"Please tell me the power isn't going out."

"We've had a couple of flickers today."

"Great."

He nodded, polite but distant, and headed for the door. He paused on the step as though about to say something. Or maybe he was waiting for me to say something, but I had no idea what to say. *I didn't do it!* They all said that, right?

Edgar went out and locked the door, and I did a couple more turns around the room. I felt increasingly trapped and desperate. It was silly because I was doing exactly what I'd have done by choice. It was the knowledge that I *didn't* have a choice. That I couldn't leave—and that my peers believed I had killed another person.

It was incredibly depressing.

There was a rattling sound outside the door and another thump.

"It's open," I called, to be funny.

The key turned over, and once again the door swung open. This time to reveal Rita, holding a rolled blanket beneath her arm, stooping down to pick up a lunch tray.

I said, "I'd offer to get that for you, but I don't want you to mistake my enthusiasm for lunch for a jailbreak."

She gave a dry cackle, which I was grateful for. "That old lady friend of yours gave me a list of things you need." She lugged the tray over to the desk and deposited it there.

It was a very nice tray. She had loaded it up with sandwiches and cookies and chips and pieces of fruit. There was an ice bucket and a yellow legal pad and a couple of pens.

"Somebody's going to bring you down an old coffee maker if we can find one," she informed me.

"Thanks," I said, and I really was touched. "What's going on up at the lodge?"

"What do you think?" she asked dryly. "They're talking. That's all those folks do."

"Has J.X. questioned everyone?"

She snorted. I couldn't tell if that meant he hadn't bothered now that I was incarcerated or that it had proved a total waste of time.

I sat down at the desk and unwrapped a corned beef on rye bread sandwich. All at once I was starving. Nerves. What I actually needed was sleep, and I was too wound up to close my eyes.

Rita tossed the extra blanket on the foot of the bed.

"I can't say either of that pair was any loss," she said. "Whoever did away with 'em did a community service in my opinion."

"Krass was pretty rude last night," I agreed around half a sandwich.

She gave another of those sharp laughs that sounded like something breaking off. "Yep, he had a real way with him, didn't he? Well, I guess he shot his mouth off one too many times."

She gave me an expectant look, and I said thickly, "I didn't kill him. Really."

"Sure." She nodded agreeably. "Not that I blame you. I don't see how you could have killed Patty Ann, though."

"Who's Patty Ann?" The body count was climbing alarmingly, and I say that as someone who never wrote less than three murders a novel.

Rita burst out with more of that raspy laughter. "Patty Ann Stewbecki. The one calling herself"—Rita donned her version of a snooty English accent—"*Peaches Sadler.*"

"You knew Peaches?"

"Honey, she grew up in these parts. You didn't believe all that crap in those magazines, did you? All that stuff about growing up in New England and being a debutante and going to...where the hell was it? What's that famous women's college?"

"Wellesley, Vassar, Smith, Bryn Mawr...?"

"One of them." She waved the Seven Sisters off like Pig-Pen brushing at the fumes. "It was all crap. She grew up right down the road. She was a few years behind me in high school. Hell, she dated my brother. What a pill she was. And then she comes along with her airs and graces, acting like she's never had to eat in a dining room with other people or lay that bleached blonde head of hers on cotton sheets."

"Was she complaining about the maid service too?" I tore open a bag of chips.

"No." Rita snapped that one off. "She couldn't have been sweeter to Debbie, but that wasn't anything about Debbie or her being able to write stories. That was Patty Ann getting back at *me*."

I crunched chips and contemplated. Debbie was the kid. Edgar and Rita's daughter—though she looked more like a granddaughter. I remembered her grief and worry when she had escorted me to my cabin last night. Debbie had said something then about Rita and Peaches quarreling.

Neutrally, I said, "Why do you think she'd want to do that?"

"She didn't need a reason." Rita said wearily, "Some people are shit stirrers by nature. They just can't help poking their sticks into other people's business, and sometimes what they stir up is a nest of rattlesnakes."

I thought I might get further if I tacked to the left. "Is Debbie a good writer?"

Rita's hard face softened. "She's pretty good. She doesn't write about the kind of crap Patty Ann did, though. Sex and more sex. She's a good kid."

"She seemed shaken up yesterday."

"Of course she did. Who wouldn't be shaken up by a murder happening in your own backyard?"

"Did Patty Ann have any old enemies around here?"

Rita gave me a long look. "Honey, enemies are all she had. People like that? Even their friends hope to one day see them fall flat on their faces."

CHAPTER SEVENTEEN

I was dreaming about David.

We were arguing—nothing new there—but even in the dream, angry though I was, I had a sense of loss. A sense of the waste of it—the waste of what had once been real and genuine and good between us. Love. Yes, we had loved each other once, and after love had gone, I still had tried to hang on. Maybe David had too. There had been plenty of affairs—even before we made our relationship official with a commitment ceremony—but he had never wanted to end *us*. Not until Dicky Dickison.

Something had changed for us both with Dicky. Maybe this time it really was love for David. Or maybe I had run out of lies to tell myself. Or the energy to keep lying even if I could have come up with a story I could believe in.

In the dream, for the first time, I accepted that it was my failure and my loss—that I was alone now because of the choices I had made along the way. For starters, always choosing career over relationship. Was that because I'd known in my heart it was going to end this way? Everyone else had known. Maybe even David had known. But we had stuck it out for ten years. I might have stuck it out forever. Not because I still loved David or forgave him, but because my life was my work. I could shut David and his dick...er...Dickys out because my true life companions were Miss Butterwith and Mr. Pinkerton.

But in my dream it was hard to turn my back on David. Hard to walk away. Hard for David too because he came after me saying softly, "*Kit...*"

A gust of frigid air across my face. I unstuck my eyelashes, itched at my nose. That was funny. I never remembered David calling me...

"*Kit?*" a familiar and unwelcome voice demanded in my ear.

I sat up fast, the lousy mattress and my back both protesting the incautious move. I regret to say that the sound that issued forth from my lips was closer to girly squeal of terror than manly shout of outrage, but either way it worked and the sinister shadow looming over me backed up hastily.

"Why didn't you answer me?" J.X. demanded.

At the same time I was yelling, "What are you doing in here?"

"I knocked and you didn't answer. I called to you three times." J.X. now stood a safe distance at the foot of my bed. He was wearing some kind of olive green rain poncho and a cowboy hat—and they suited him ridiculously well despite the fact that both hat and poncho were soaked.

"I couldn't hear you over the rain," I accused, untangling myself from the extra blanket.

"Or the snores."

I kicked free of the final folds of wool. "That's right. I wore myself out running amuck and killing people last night."

He looked heavenward—reminding me of those somber portraits of saints right before their heroic breasts were riddled with arrows. "Look, I already said *I* don't think you—"

"I don't give a damn what you think. Why are you here?"

"I came to take you to dinner."

"Ha! Flattering though that is, I'm not in the mood. However, if you're willing to wait till I get out of prison in twenty years or so..." I rolled off the bed and staggered into the bathroom, slamming the door behind me and cutting off whatever his answer might have been.

When I emerged shortly thereafter, relieved and refreshed, he was sitting on the foot of the bed, his booted foot keeping time to an inaudible tune.

"Did you have a nice day?" I inquired more civilly. "Because I didn't."

"I don't see what could have been so bad about it," J.X. said. "It looks to me like you spent the afternoon napping and eating and reading. It's certainly nice and warm in here."

"You can skip the hard sell. 'The caged bird sings with a fearful trill.'"

His brows drew together. "Tell me you haven't been drinking."

"I haven't even had a cup of coffee since breakfast."

He said placatingly, "Well, see, I'm going to escort you up to the house for dinner. You can have all the coffee you like."

"Why the day pass, Marshal Dillon? Don't tell me all the decent law-abiding folk have run out of things to talk about?"

He didn't answer directly, his glance falling on the yellow legal pad which I had been using to jot down my thoughts and notes on the murder before I fell asleep. In the tone of one trying hard to change the subject to more pleasant matters, he said, "Were you working on your new project?"

"Yes." I reached for the pad. "Some of us can't get away with recycling old police reports. We actually have to make things up."

"I'll say. Including police procedures."

"Police procedure is different in Britain."

"You're not kidding. And it's especially different in St. Mary's Mud or wherever you set those things." He had picked up the pad before I could, but something—probably his own name—caught his eye, and he pulled the papers back and began to read.

"Do you mind?"

I didn't quite dare grab the thing out of his hand, and he ignored me. As he read, his expression grew noticeably grimmer.

At last he looked up. "What do you think you're doing?"

"Preparing my defense. If I'm going to be arrested, I'm sure as hell going to supply the local cops with plenty of other possible scenarios."

He nodded to himself, then ripped the sheets with my notes off the pad, folded them, and stuck them in his pocket.

I gaped at him as he handed me the blank pad back. "What the hell do you think *you're* doing?"

He was watching me with an oddly serious expression. "I can't figure you out, Kit. You're so clever in some ways. And in other ways you're like the boy who was raised in a bubble. Has it occurred to you that one reason I've got you sequestered here is for your own protection?"

"No. That still hasn't occurred to me."

"Then think about it for a minute. For whatever reason, whoever killed Peaches and Steven wants you blamed for his—or her—crimes. Maybe you happened along at the right time. Or maybe it's personal. Maybe someone here specifically wants *you* to take the rap for these homicides."

"How could it be personal? I don't know anyone here except you and Rachel."

"You know Mindy."

"*Mindy?*" He thought Mindy was trying to frame me?

J.X. said patiently, "I'm just *saying*, it might not be a coincidence that you're being implicated in these crimes. It may be personal. If that's the case, even if it's not the case, the best way to defuse this guy—"

"Or gal."

"Or gal—is to let them believe that their plan is going ahead without complication. If you appear to be a good fit for scapegoat, there's less chance they might feel any need to…"

"To what?" I stared at him. "To *kill* me?"

"I don't know." His dark eyes were very serious as they met mine. "This is what I keep trying to tell you. We don't know why they've targeted you. You need to be careful."

"Well, I'd prefer not to be so careful that I end up doing time for a murder I didn't commit."

"Once you get out of here, you and your attorney can start putting together your defense. Hell, you might not even be arrested. But for now, keep a low profile."

"How the hell lower can my profile go?" I objected. "I'm stored out here on the back forty. The only people with lower profiles are the ones rooming in the icehouse."

"Kit."

"All right." I whirled away and strode up and down the floor in front of the fireplace. "So you don't want me to ask any questions about the murder. You don't want me writing down my theories. You want me to sit here like a good little patsy."

"You got it." He smiled, that wry white curve lightening the haughty lines of his patrician features. He glanced at his wristwatch. "And I want you to throw a coat on so we can get up to the house and have dinner."

Still blinking in the reflection of that bright charm, I grabbed a fresh pair of corduroy jeans and a clean sweater and modestly retreated to the bathroom to change. When I reappeared in yet another overpriced ensemble—this time in Ralph Lauren black cords and an emerald green chunky ribbed mock turtleneck—J.X. stared at me and said awkwardly, "You look nice."

"I've been having beauty treatments all day."

He laughed.

"You think I'm kidding."

I shrugged into my coat, and we went out into the rain-swept night. The rain flew in our faces in peppery blasts; the wind seemed to yank the breath right out of me.

Still, as we plowed our way upstream across the pasture that now resembled swampland, I found air enough to gasp, "What have you found out so far?"

He threw back, "I haven't found anything out so far because I'm not investigating."

"What do you mean, you're not investigating? I thought you used to be some kind of hotshot police inspector?"

J.X. said tersely, "I'm not a cop anymore, and I'm sure as hell not an amateur sleuth."

"You're trying to tell me you're not looking into this at all?"

"That's exactly what I'm trying to tell you. We're trapped here with someone who shows every sign of being totally ruthless when it comes to protecting his or her self. Poking into this could be hazardous to your—to anyone's—health."

"So you do think Krass's murder is related to Peaches'?"

I stumbled in a gopher hole, and he put his hand out to steady me. He was slender, but he was wiry and very strong. "That's pretty much a no-brainer. Steven sat in the bar that night hinting he knew something about Peaches' murder. That was tantamount to announcing to the world at large that he had information that could destroy her killer."

"That's what I thought too."

"That's what everyone thought," J.X. said dryly. "Which is why he should have kept his mouth shut. There's no proof that he did know anything. Being Steven, he could have thought it was funny to stir everyone up."

I thought about what Rita had said about Peaches being a shit stirrer. I remembered what else she had said.

"What did you argue about with Peaches the night before she was killed?" I asked.

"None of your business."

He'd said it without missing a beat. It sort of irritated me. "What did you pick up beside Peaches' body when we were by the shrine?"

He shot me a quick look. "I have no idea what you're talking about."

"After you and Edgar carried Peaches to the truck, you came back and looked around where the body had lain. You knelt down and slipped something in your pocket."

He put his hand on my arm and stopped walking. I stopped too. I couldn't see his expression at all beneath the brim of the cowboy hat, but I could feel his warm breath against my face.

He said softly, "You're not a very good listener, Christopher," and placed his hands on either side of my head. There was nothing threatening about it. In fact, I sort of thought he was going to kiss me. As cold as his hands were, they were still warmer than the wind and rain sleeting against my skin. He was brushing his thumbs lightly against my cheekbones, the most insubstantial of caresses. It gave me funny chills, my skin seeming to tingle where he touched me.

He leaned forward and, his mouth a kiss away from mine, whispered, "Do you know how easy it would be for me to kill you?" His hands slid down to encircle my throat, and his thumbs rested delicately over the hollow at the lowest part of my neck.

The hair on the back of my neck rose. I stood very still while the pad of his thumb brushed the pulse pounding away in my throat.

"This is a pressure point. If I strike you hard here, I can knock you cold or kill you. It's one of several ways I could take you out. I know a dozen different strikes and choke holds. I could say you attacked me and I tried to subdue you and it went wrong."

Belatedly, I knocked his hands away and planted my own in J.X.'s chest—hard. He rocked but didn't take so much as a step back. Even in the darkness I could see the white glimmer of his smile.

He asked conversationally, "You think you could outrun me or overpower me out here? Why don't you try it?"

I started to shake with tension. "What's your point, asshole?"

"My point," he said curtly, "is that you don't know who to trust. Which means you can't afford to trust anyone, so you can't—*cannot*—keep asking these questions. You're going to get yourself killed. I can't think of any other way to say it."

"I got the message. I didn't think I had to pretend with you." I started to turn away, but he caught my arm.

"Kit, you have only my word for it that I didn't kill Peaches or Steven." He let go of my arm, adding, "If you think about it, I'm one of those people who might feel they have a personal grudge against you."

I opened my mouth, but for once words deserted me.

J.X. turned away and started walking. After a pause I followed.

Glancing at me, he said, "A key fell off my fob; that's what I was looking for on the ground where Peaches was found."

Neither of us said anything else until we reached the lodge.

CHAPTER EIGHTEEN

You know in movies where something embarrassing happens and the sound falls off and everyone in the scene stares at the hapless focus of the camera's zoom? Well, that was me walking into the dining room at the Blue Heron Lodge that evening.

The noise level, which had been subdued compared to the previous evening, dropped off to nothing, and every head in the place seemed to turn my way. I tried to tell myself they were really looking at J.X., but there was no admiration in the faces directed toward us.

The one that hurt most was Rachel, who looked right at me, and then dropped her gaze to her plate.

"We'll sit over here," J.X. said, nodding to a table for two wedged by the window. I nodded, moving blindly, and he rested his hand on my lower back. I'd have taken it as a gesture of support if he hadn't spent the last few minutes demonstrating the numerous ways he'd like to kill me.

We took our seats, and the people at the surrounding tables made ostentatious effort not to look our way. Debbie appeared with menus, handing me mine without looking my way. I began to understand why that shunning thing was such an effective punishment—even on someone as generally antisocial as me.

I ordered a G&T, ignoring J.X.'s look of disapproval. He ordered coffee. Debbie retreated, and J.X. said, "It's an awkward situation. Don't take it to heart."

"*Moi?*" I bit out. "Far from minding, I'm delighted. You've solved my career problems for me. I'm going to sue your ass when I get out of here and take you for every dime you have." I stared out the window and got a nice reflected snapshot of my white, furious face and every other head in the dining room turned my way under the impression I couldn't see them.

My eyes blurred. I blinked hard, aware that J.X. was staring at my profile.

"Kit," he began gruffly.

I turned to face him. "You know, it's bad enough to have to sit here like I'm the main exhibit in a zoo. I don't feel like making polite conversation with the keeper."

He flushed, and his jaw tightened. "Suit yourself," he clipped out. "I was trying to be nice."

"I can see that. And it's hard to think of anything nicer than being locked up in the stockade all day and then having someone threaten to kill you."

"I didn't threaten to kill you."

Now that got some interested looks—quickly concealed.

J.X. lowered his voice. "Jesus, you're a baby. I've done all the apologizing and explaining to you that I'm going to do. You got yourself into this. If you want to sit there and sulk, be my guest."

Debbie reappeared with our drinks, saving me from having to answer, even if I could have. Maybe I wasn't being very reasonable about the situation, but...it wasn't an easy situation to be reasonable about.

J.X. ordered the salmon. I said I wasn't hungry.

I said it politely, by the way, but J.X. muttered, "Oh, for God's sake. He'll have the salmon too."

Debbie departed, I sipped my drink, and J.X. stirred sugar into his coffee. I watched the room mirrored in the dark window. The other diners seemed to be losing interest in us.

"Are you really going to write a series about a Regency P.I. demon?"

J.X. was smiling a little, his eyes teasing, and I realized that he was one of these unbearably irrepressible types who got over their anger quickly, forgiving and forgetting—occasional death threats aside.

"No," I said repressively. I couldn't help adding, "Anyway, the P.I. is not a demon, her boyfriend is."

"Ah." He sipped his coffee. "Can I make a suggestion?"

"Could anything on earth stop you?"

"No."

"Be my guest."

"Why don't you write about something you know?"

"Because I write mysteries—and we can't all be cops."

"We can't all be elderly spinsters with cats either."

"So what do you suggest? I join the police force? I kill someone—oh, wait. You think I did."

He didn't rise to the bait. "I'm not saying you have to live it to write it. That's biography, not fiction. I'm saying there are some young guys who could write believably about a repressed English spinster and her horny tomcat—you're not one of them."

"Wh-wh-*what?*"

He met my aghast stare calmly. "You heard me. Oh, you write one hell of an amusing mystery, but there's not one shred of anything real or meaningful in it. Those books are just witty, academic puzzles."

"How very *dare* you!"

To my mounting outrage he continued to smile at me, his expression quizzical. "Come on, you know exactly what I mean. You've been cranking those things out in your sleep for years now. I'm not saying they're not clever. I can never figure out where you're going with them. But there's nothing real in them. There's nothing of you in them."

"How the fuck would you know whether there's anything of me in them or not? You don't *know* me."

"I thought I did once."

I opened my mouth to deliver the obvious and crushing truth, but somehow I couldn't. Somehow, remembering how... sweet he had been all those years ago. Not in a sappy way. He had been a tough, savvy young cop sort of awed to find himself with a book contract and rubbing shoulders—and other things—with the mystery elite. And every time his eyes met mine that long-ago weekend there had been a look that said he thought I was wonderful. And when we had made—fucked—there had been something alarmingly close to tenderness—

But why think of that now? What was the point? It was painful remembering.

So I swallowed the cruel words, and I stared out the window at the black rain washing away the world beyond this dining room.

"Why don't you write about something that matters to you?" J.X. asked.

"You think Regency period demons don't matter to me? You really *don't* know me." I raised my brows mockingly and sipped my drink.

Debbie brought our salads then, and the conversation was limited to passing the salt and pepper and me ordering another drink.

We had worked our way to dessert and the dining room was largely emptied when Espie stopped by our table, pulling up a chair.

"Please don't talk to the prisoner, ma'am," I drawled.

She guffawed. "Yo, esse, if you offed that pair, you'll be getting a commendation from the writing community."

"I'll look for it with my next royalty check."

J.X. gave another of those long-suffering sighs. I said to Espie, "For the record, I didn't kill either of them."

"I believe you," she said easily. She nodded at J.X. "He believes you. He told us all he'd lock you up if that would make everyone feel better, but it didn't look to him like you could have done it."

I threw J.X. an uncertain look. I couldn't bring myself to say thank you, although I was grateful for this unexpected show of support.

"Did he tell you they found a rain slicker covered with blood in the Dumpster behind the patio?"

"No, he didn't," I said, my gratitude fading as quickly as it had flared. J.X. was looking at Espie with resignation.

"It was from the closet in the lobby. That means anyone could have taken it."

"Anyone in the lodge," I said.

"Right."

I said tightly to J.X., "But not me because I wasn't in the lodge, and you know damn well I wasn't wearing it or carrying it when I went back to my cabin last night."

He said evenly, "How many times do I have to tell you that I don't think you killed anyone?"

"He thinks I did it," Espie told me.

"Did you?"

"Nah. I've had the prison experience. Been there, done that, and I have no intention of ever going back."

"What were you in prison for?"

"I killed my boyfriend." She chuckled at my expression. "It was an accident. Sort of. He was cheating on me, and I chased him with my car. I hit him accidentally on purpose, if you know what I mean." She tapped the side of her head as though to indicate *non compos mentis*. "I was seventeen. You know what *that's* like. Anyway, I did my time. And I am a *very* safe driver these days."

J.X. looked unamused. Once a cop, always a cop. I said, "What would your motive be this long after the fact?"

"Revenge. We Latinas are known to be very hot-blooded."

"That's very hard to make fly in fiction, let alone real-life crime."

"Doesn't mean it couldn't be true."

The dining room lights flickered and went out.

CHAPTER NINETEEN

"Now's your chance to make a break for it, Christopher," Espie announced into the shocked silence seconds before everyone began talking at once.

"Don't even think about it," J.X. stated clearly over the rising babble.

Reaching for my glass, I replied irritably, "Where the hell would I go?"

We weren't in total darkness due to the candles on each table, but it was certainly very murky, and the remaining diners were gloomy outlines against the uncertain backdrop of candlelight. I could see a lot of shining eyes and shining teeth.

J.X. rose and requested that everyone stay in their seats.

"He's very good at this kind of thing," Espie said to me.

"Yes, he's a real loss to the crossing guard division."

She chortled. J.X. ignored this interchange. "Stay put. I'll be right back," he said, and we watched his tall shadow moving through the dining room, reassuring people as he headed for the entrance.

Espie and I abruptly ran out of things to talk about. We sat silently listening to the conversation around us—louder than usual as people instinctively raised their voices as though the darkness was a sound barrier.

"They were saying earlier that it happens out here a lot during the winter…"

"It seems kind of a coincidence…"

"This is bullshit about not being able to get a refund…"

"Maybe she tried to blackmail the wrong person…"

I glanced around, trying to see who had made that last comment, but although I could narrow it down to one of the two large round tables behind our own, I couldn't pinpoint it. I hadn't recognized the voice, and none of the weirdly highlighted faces at the table looked familiar.

Turning, I tried to find Rachel in the gloom, but it looked like she had already left her table.

I said to Espie, "How's Rachel doing?"

"Fine."

"Kit." I started as J.X. materialized out of the shadows. "Come with me."

I rose, excusing myself to Espie, and followed him across the assault course of chair backs and chair legs and purses. We reached the hall. It was darker here despite the sparsely placed emergency lights.

J.X. pushed my coat into my arms, and I put it on automatically. "What's going on?" I asked.

"Come on," he said, turning away. He had a high-powered flashlight, and the beam lasered its way down the hall to the front door. I matched J.X.'s long strides past the Indian baskets and long wood-framed mirror. As we reached the front door it swung open, and a frigid blast of icy rain gusted in with a tall figure in a cowboy hat.

Edgar Croft looked mighty cold and mighty grim.

"Someone's been fooling with the generator," he told J.X.

"Sabotage?"

"Looks that way."

"Can you fix it?"

"We can try." He ducked out into the wet darkness.

J.X. turned back to me. "I don't want to leave you on your own. That's why I'm dragging you out here. You understand?"

I nodded. I felt his unease plainly. If he was seriously worried about my taking off on my own, he could relax. No way was I about to brave the elements—let alone a possible stray murderer.

He stepped outside the door, and I followed, turning my collar up against the blast. Tracing Edgar down the porch, we squelched after him across the muddy yard. It was bewilderingly dark—even the lodge vanished into nothingness a few steps away from its porch—only the windblown cacophony of the chimes giving away its location.

We dodged dripping tree branches, and J.X.'s flashlight picked out a small shed like a tiny log cabin. The door stood open, and a feeble light shone from within. We crowded inside and studied the large blue and silver Yamaha generator.

Edgar was quietly but fluently swearing as he examined an empty propane bottle. "Someone's drained the tank on the generator and emptied all the fuel storage containers."

"Will it run on gasoline?" J.X. asked.

"It will, but even if we emptied every vehicle on the place, we'd only have a couple of hours' worth of fuel. This little girl drinks it up like soda pop."

"Then we better save that option until we really need it," J.X. said.

"Exactly what I was thinking."

"How long does the power usually stay out?" I asked.

Edgar shook his head. "It depends. Sometimes the power company gets right on it. But in a storm like this...nobody is going to be repairing lines tonight."

"The storm can't last forever."

Edgar and J.X. exchanged looks. J.X. said, "There's supposed to be another front moving in on the tail of this one. It might not materialize, but if it does, we could be cut off for another day."

"Nobody's going to starve, and nobody's going to freeze," Edgar reassured. "We've got food and fresh water stored, we've got kerosene lanterns, and we've got plenty of wood to burn."

I couldn't help pointing out, "You've also got a murderer running loose."

"No one's forgetting that," J.X. said warningly.

Edgar took his hat off and slapped the generator with it, giving vent to more quiet but heartfelt swearing, the gist of which seemed to be That Damned Woman. I took it for granted he meant Rita—my jaded view of marital unions, I guess—but J.X. said, "Are you talking about Peaches?"

"That's right," Edgar said. "If that bitch hadn't come around here, none of this would have happened."

Not that I was exactly donning sackcloth and ashes for Peaches, but I didn't see how the storm of the century could be blamed on her.

"That bitch was trouble from the minute she showed up," he concluded.

I said, "She was originally a local girl, wasn't she? Did you know her back when she was Patty Ann Stewbecki?"

Edgar gave me a long, grim look. "Yeah, I knew her," he said at last. "Every boy around here knew her. And despite the fancy clothes and the fancy hairstyle and the fancy fingernails and the fancy name, she hadn't changed any."

He gave J.X. what they used to call "an old-fashioned look," and J.X. said, "Hey, not guilty."

Edgar shrugged, clearly not believing him. "Well, I don't want to speak ill of the dead." As though he hadn't spent eight and a half minutes cursing Peaches to Kingdom Come.

I said, "Steven Krass seemed pretty fond of her."

Neither J.X. nor Edgar had an answer. We filed back out into the blustery wet, and Edgar locked the door behind us. Unspeaking—the wind would have swallowed our words in any case—we trekked back to the lodge.

Rita and Edgar gathered everyone in the main meeting room and doled out candles and matches and extra blankets. They reassured the conference attendees that power outages were nothing new in these parts, and that everything was under control.

"What about him?" one young woman said, pointing at me. She looked vaguely familiar. I thought she might be the one who had screamed for help after I discovered Krass's body on the patio. She seemed, in my opinion, prone to hysterical outbursts.

J.X. said reassuringly, "Mr. Holmes will be staying out in his cabin."

There were murmurs of approval. I opened my mouth to point out the obvious, that the generator had been sabotaged by someone who wasn't me since I'd been locked up all day, but catching J.X.'s eye, I subsided. I understood why he didn't want the attendees aware that the generator had been sabotaged, but I would have preferred not to star in the role of bogeyman. There were approximately fifty loudmouths in attendance who were going to leave this conference convinced that I was a homicidal maniac. Like my career wasn't in enough jeopardy as it was.

The meeting disbanded, and the chicklets retreated to their rooms, clutching their candles like heroines in gothic novels, casting me disapproving looks as they queued past.

I made my way over to Rita. "Did you have a chance to find out anything on that earring I was asking about?"

She gave me a blank look. "What earring?"

"The earring that was in a glass on the dresser in Rachel Ving's room."

"I don't know what you're talking about."

I tried for patience, but I know I sounded agitated. "I was asking you about it this morning—right before I was dragged off to quarantine."

"Do you know how much has happened here since this morning?"

"This was important, though. This could help prove—"

J.X.'s hand fastened around my arm. "Time to go," he said, and despite the brisk tone, he was glowering at me. I was tempted to dig my heels in then and there, but the bitter awareness that he could put me in a headlock and drag me off—and was probably looking forward to doing so—forced me to give in with good grace.

Or at least give in.

He towed me right out of the room and down the hall to the heavy front door.

"Listen," I gritted through my teeth, freeing myself at last. "I understand about not antagonizing this killer, but I don't want to spend the next twenty years rotting in prison for a crime I didn't commit. That earring is vital to my defense."

"If you're dead, you won't need a defense." He thrust my still-damp coat at me.

I shrugged it on, saying, "You're going to great pains to make sure I can't talk to anyone or build any kind of case that could help me."

"So you know, I already asked the kid, Debbie, about the earring."

"What did she say?"

He said calmly, "She said the glass was on the dresser, but it was empty."

I stared at him. "That can't be right."

"I'm just telling you what she said. So you see, there's no point going around blabbing to people that you think you're being set up. You're not going to get the answer you want, and you're liable to draw the wrong attention."

I was silent as he hauled open the door. In fact, I couldn't think of a damn thing to say all the long trek back to my cabin. The night seemed eerily black and silent, the rain pattering steadily and the squishy thump of our boots the only sound as we walked. The perfect circle of J.X.'s flashlight beam bounced merrily ahead of us, highlighting puddles and clumps of weeds. Our breath smoked in the air. The cabins rose out of the light-less night. Dark windows and smokeless chimneys. About as uncheery a destination as could be.

J.X. unlocked my cabin door and pushed it wide.

I stepped inside and waited for him to lock me in and leave me alone in the woodsmoke warmed dark, but he stepped inside too and shut the door behind him.

Still saying nothing, he set the kerosene lantern he'd brought from the house on the table and lit it. The flame guttered and then lit, throwing crazy shadows across the rough wood interior.

"Why don't you pour yourself a drink?" he said as he moved to the fireplace.

"I thought you said I drank too much."

"You do, but tonight you're entitled to have a drink. One drink," he added. "You can pour me one too."

I didn't bother pointing out that this would make it my third drink of the evening; he knew as well as I did. Maybe he hoped I'd drink myself into a stupor, and anything that might shut me up for the night was worth a try. "To what do I owe this honor?" I asked bitterly, but I poured us each a slightly flat gin and tonic while he rekindled the fire in the fireplace. When the fire was crackling brightly, I handed him his drink.

He took the glass, sipped it, set it aside, and took my glass from my hand. I looked at him uncomprehending—and more uncomprehending as he put his arms around me. I stood there rigid as a plank of wood as he held me, and it gradually dawned on me that he was simply hugging me. A simple, uncomplicated hug. When was the last time that had happened to me? Against my better judgment I found myself hugging him back, taking the unexpected comfort gratefully.

Against my ear J.X. said gruffly, "Hey. I know you're scared. I give you my word I won't let you go to jail for something you didn't do. Okay? Can you trust me a little?"

I couldn't rely on my voice, so I settled for nodding, resting my forehead on his shoulder. He was that disconcerting bit taller than me. David had been two inches shorter, so this unexpected dynamic threw me.

He said, still husky-voiced, "First and foremost, I want to keep you alive."

I nodded again and then pulled away, keeping my head ducked so he couldn't see my face because it really was too ridiculous getting choked up over the idea that someone cared if I lived or died. Not that there were people lining up, exactly.

He picked his glass up, staring at the fireplace. The fire threw shadows across his bearded face. I sat down and pulled my boots off.

Tossing the rest of his drink off, J.X. said, "I should let you get some sleep."

He set the glass on the desk and headed for the door. "Don't drink any more tonight."

"Are you going back to the lodge?"

"For a while. But I'll sleep down at my cabin."

I had the impression that was supposed to reassure me. And I suppose it did on one level. It's not like I relished the idea of being the only living soul this far from help. If the killer did come after me, J.X. had already demonstrated what a jam I'd be in.

He scrutinized me. He dug in his pocket. "I won't lock you in tonight, but for Christ's sake keep the door barred. Don't leave this cabin unless it's actually on fire. Do you understand me?"

"*Ya voll, mein commandant.*" I saluted, then grabbed hastily at the key he tossed my way.

He opened the door, and I said, "Was it something I said or something I didn't say?"

"What's that?"

"Someone waiting for you in your cabin? You're in quite a hurry."

He didn't move a muscle.

"Did I really break your heart?"

J.X. said, "I was pretty stupid back then. I probably deserved to have my heart broken."

"Come here," I murmured. "Let me kiss it better."

* * * * *

I didn't want to be alone, that was all. This wasn't about anything but expediency, but I was already getting to know the taste of him, the texture of his skin, the sounds he made. I liked that he was calm and quiet in the face of my hunger, giving what I needed, giving generously, and taking without greed, appreciating as he went.

The light from the fireplace cast an arc over him, an old-gold nimbus behind his head as he bent over me, and he was so beautiful it took my breath away. My hands shook, sliding up beneath the warm cotton of his shirt, pulling him down till our mouths met.

Yes, he'd learned a lot over the years. His lips were sweet and coaxing and wicked all at the same time, and though I had told myself I was in control here, I opened right up to him, murmuring acquiescence, liking the taste of his desire.

He pushed up on his arms, the ropes of muscle delineated by the shifting shadows, and he was smiling, but it was a knowledgeable smile—the vulnerable boy was long gone, and I felt regret for that. Regret that I hadn't cherished that boy.

"You're very beautiful," I said.

His lips—well-shaped and rather sensual—curled cynically.

"You do talk too much, that's a fact." His mouth covered my own again. So many kisses after scarcity.

I rested my hand against the side of his face, feeling the silk of beard and hair, the smoothness of his bare skin. My tongue prodded his mouth and he let me in, his tongue lazily pushing and then twining with my own. I'd forgotten how pleasurable kissing—just kissing—was.

And how pleasurable it was to be naked with someone again, to feel warm skin gliding on warm skin, the different textures of bone and muscle and hair. Our hips moved together, cocks rubbing against each other, thrusting with urgent playfulness that gradually gave way to something less playful but still unselfish, ungrudging. His mouth closed on my left nipple and sucked, and I arched up against him, fingers sinking into his back muscles.

"That's...nice," I got out.

J.X. raised his head. "*Nice?*"

"Nice is highly underrated."

He chuckled. He lowered his head again, licking and then teething very gently, and his dark, shining head moved to my other nipple. I moaned, and he smiled against my chest. It was too good to bear. I tugged at him, and his mouth reluctantly loosed the oversensitive nub. He resettled against me as though we were locking into place. Lock and load...

Oh God, the feel of bare skin from belly to thigh as we rocked against each other, harder, faster, fiercer—I could feel that heat shivering through me like wind shaking dry grass, setting it alight...setting a match to me...all that energy coalescing into—

What if we did it for real? Fucked for real?

Would he let me? Or would I have to—? The idea of letting him was unexpectedly...tempting.

But I let the thought go because that was getting complicated, and the last thing I wanted was complications. Simple, quick, warm relief. That's what this was about.

His skin was gleaming with sweat, tinted amber, and his heart was banging hard against my own as we thrust and tussled our way to a sudden, pumping, slick release…desperate friction giving way to the slip and slide relief.

There it was…there…that spate of wet heat and snapping energy, a fireball blazing through nerves and muscles and razing everything in its path, setting the fields of gold on fire. Summer once more.

CHAPTER TWENTY

When I finally marshaled my scattered forces, we had caught our breaths again and were dozing side by side, arms brushing but otherwise not touching. I turned my head on the pillow and studied J.X.'s face. His eyes were closed, although I knew he wasn't sleeping.

He had disarmingly long eyelashes.

As though feeling my gaze, he opened his eyes, slanted me a look. I waited for another comment about how this had been a mistake, but maybe he thought that went without saying.

With my usual flair for pillow talk, I said, "So why don't you wear your wedding ring?"

He didn't blink, didn't move a muscle. I wasn't sure he'd even heard me, although given the fact that our noses were inches apart, I didn't see how he could have failed to. At last, he said evenly, "Would it have mattered to you?"

"Not if it didn't matter to you. Why should it?" Nobody was faithful, right? No such thing as fidelity anyway. Wasn't even a realistic expectation, and only fools let themselves get hurt.

He said as a statement, not question, "Because this is just sex."

"Right." I said it, but I can't say I felt any great confidence as the word left my mouth. Sometimes I wonder if anything is "just" sex. There are ramifications for everything we do, and I didn't like that particular glint in his eyes. Maybe it was the uncertain light...but I didn't think so.

I was disconcerted to hear myself add, "Isn't it?"

"It is for me."

That was blunt enough, and it's not like I was asking for it to be anything else, so I'm not sure why I felt that barb working its way up through my guts toward my heart.

"So...what's the deal with you? You're bisexual? You were going through one of those heterosexual phases?"

He said calmly, "I don't feel a need to explain myself to you. I'm not asking you any questions, am I?" He sat up and reached for his boxers which were lying beside the bed. I felt taking time to don underwear showed a certain level of maturity, and I accepted that the ardent boy I had once known was truly gone.

All the same, I pushed up on my elbows, watching him dress. "You can if you want to."

He gave me another of those brief gleaming looks. "It doesn't matter to me anymore."

"Ouch."

"Hey, you asked."

Watching him fasten the fly of his jeans, I observed, "The fact that you still seem resentful of something that happened over a decade ago might lead someone to think that you still have feelings for me."

"I have feelings for you," J.X. said. "I feel that you're an egotistical and self-centered prick. But you're a good fuck. I feel it would be a shame not to take advantage of that." He shrugged into his shirt, his eyes meeting mine steadily, unselfconsciously.

I was the one coloring. To my astonishment, I heard myself confess, "I was scared."

He raised his brows politely. The Grand Inquisitor allowing the convicted a last word.

I said, "The weekend of the conference I'd come home from a book tour to find my lover in bed with a neighbor. I thought it was over between us, and I...was in a lot of pain. It was not my intention to hurt you." I grimaced. "You probably kept me from chucking myself out of a hotel window that weekend."

He did the buttons of his shirt swiftly, eyeing me without interruption.

"But when I went back home, David apologized. He begged for another chance."

"And you didn't have the balls to explain that to me? You couldn't take a couple of minutes to answer my emails or phone calls and tell me the truth?"

I put my face in my hands and groaned. "I know. I *know.* I'm sorry. I know I treated you badly. I was a shit."

"Past tense? You still *are* a shit, Christopher." He even smiled, though it was rather derisive. He picked his jacket up from the floor near the door and pulled it on. "Only this time around it's David you're treating badly, not me. Because I don't give a damn."

He zipped his jacket, opened the door, and said, "Lock this behind me."

With that he was gone, and I leaped across the chilly boards to slide the bolt and sprint back to the warmth of the bed. I huddled into the bedclothes and listened to the beat of the rain—and the echo of J.X.'s words.

It sank in on me that I still hadn't really managed to tell him the full truth—that I had been too gutless to allow myself further contact with him because I wasn't sure I could end it. I'd liked him a lot. So much so that I'd been in danger of falling hard for him that weekend. For a kid five years younger than me. An ambitious newbie. A cop. He'd scared me in so many ways it wasn't funny. Meanwhile there was the devil I knew. David. David, who was so sincerely sorry, and so determined to make it up to me, and so safe, and so familiar. And we'd already paid for the commitment ceremony.

I had never been very adventurous. Hell, admit it. I was a fucking coward. Which is why I wrote mysteries about a geriatric gumshoe and her furball feline.

I watched the firelight flickering across the open beams of the ceiling. Did I owe J.X. that truth? He'd pretty much made it clear he didn't give a damn one way or the other, and me still harping on it might, in fact, lead someone to think that it was *I* who had feelings for *him*.

Did I?

I mean, surely I had enough wrong in my life without looking for more trouble?

But…it had been extraordinarily pleasant to be held, to be kissed and made love to—because that's what it had felt like. Like J.X. was making love to me.

On that strangely soothing thought, I fell asleep.

My dreams were not soothing, though. I found myself trying to explain my bad decisions to Steven Krass, who ridiculed them—and me—while he stood at a potbellied stove cooking flapjacks for everyone at the lodge. Even Peaches was there, looking disturbingly dead in her plum-colored pajamas as she sat at a long picnic table with the other guests. I looked down the row of familiar—and unfamiliar—faces. Even Edgar, Rita, and Debbie were seated, scarfing down flapjacks like there was no tomorrow. *One of these people is a murderer*, I thought in my dream. And then, in that way dreams can seem suddenly portentous, I thought...*where's J.X.?*

I jerked awake. It took me a few seconds to place where I was, my first impression being that I had fallen into a Very Special episode of *Little House on the Prairie*. The room was cold and smelled of old wood fires and recent sex. The rain continued its unceasing drum on the roof. I rolled over to look at the clock, but there was only blackness where the face of the clock should have been. I remembered that the power was out.

I snuggled into the blankets and wished that J.X. had stayed the night. It would have been warmer with him. Oh hell, it would have been better all around with him.

By the way, where the hell did he get off giving me attitude about David when he was married himself?

Only this time around it's David you're treating badly.

My eyes flew open. J.X. thought David and I were still together. I lay perfectly motionless absorbing this. No wonder he didn't have the highest opinion of me. Not that he was in any position to be making moral judgments, but...

Yeah, that made a difference. A big difference. To both of us. I threw the covers back and rolled out of bed, feeling around for my clothes. I dragged a heavy sweater over my nakedness. Finding my wristwatch on the night table, I pressed for the luminous dial. One o'clock in the a.m.; J.X. had said he was going up to the lodge, but he would be back in his cabin by now.

I stumbled around, nearly falling over my suitcase, and then rifling through its contents for a dry pair of jeans. I found the jeans—and clean socks—dressing unsteadily in the darkness. Feeling my way back to the night table, I groped for the key J.X. had tossed to me. I inadvertently swiped it off the table surface and then spent several minutes feeling for it under the bed.

At last I had the key, and I clambered to my feet and found my coat, which was still damp from my last sojourn hours earlier. I pulled it on and let myself out. The door about tore out of my grasp in the gale.

The irony was it was lighter outside my cabin than it was inside. I could see J.X.'s cabin a few yards down. Smoke wafted gently from the chimney, white against the stormy sky. I locked my cabin and sloshed my way down to J.X.'s.

I knocked on his door.

Nothing.

I turned my collar up and knocked harder.

The eternal silence of the grave…

Now why the hell did I have to think of that now? I cast an uneasy look over my shoulder and slammed my palm against the rough door a few times.

Nothing. This was getting monotonous.

I tried the door, and to my surprise, it swung open. Not sure why I was surprised since doors always swing open in mystery novels…it's simply that real life is rarely as accommodating.

I called, "J.X.?"

There was a fire burning in the fireplace, sending shadows licking across the floor. I could make out the outline of the bed. It was empty. There was a suitcase sitting open on the desk. I stepped inside the cabin. I could discern the outline of the bathroom door standing wide open. He wasn't in here. The bed was rumpled but still made.

Okay. Well, he hadn't been home when I called last night either. Maybe he was checking on the icehouse guests again.

Or maybe not.

Why the hell would he leave his cabin unlocked?

By the dying firelight I could see there was something black and shiny lying on the floor. For one lightheaded moment I feared it was a puddle of blood. Then I realized it was a large black trash bag.

Now why did that trigger an easy recollection?

Where had I last seen a trash bag?

Edgar handing J.X. a black trash bag in which to wrap the sawed-off oak limb that had been used to hit Peaches.

I crossed to the fireplace and looked in, but all burning wood looks pretty much the same once it hits the point of turning into a bed of orange coals.

Looking around, I made out the glint of a flashlight on the bed table. I picked the flashlight up and examined the interior of the trash bag. There were bits of pine needle and tree bark. J.X. was burning the murder weapon.

My legs seemed to give out, and I dropped down on the foot of the bed. Mystery writer though I was, I couldn't come up with a single innocent reason for such a thing.

Unless…

Unless J.X. wasn't burning the murder weapon. Unless someone else was burning it…

Where *was* J.X.? Why hadn't he taken the flashlight with him? Why would he leave his cabin unlocked?

I shone the flashlight around the empty room and noticed something I had missed before. J.X.'s jacket was hanging on the back of the chair tucked in the desk.

I crossed over to the desk and touched the jacket. The leather felt cool and mysteriously, strangely alive. It also felt slightly damp because he had been wearing it earlier, and I couldn't think of a single good reason for him not to be wearing it now since he clearly was not in this cabin.

Too much imagination is part of the mystery writer' job description, but this time my brain was presenting me with a series of facts that I could not—refused—to make sense of.

Because it did *not* make sense. No murderer would be crazy enough to tackle J.X. What would be the point of doing such a thing?

Or was the point turning to cinders in the fireplace right now?

I stared unseeingly at the red ribs of the wood in the grate. Attacking J.X. did not make sense, but neither did it make sense that he had gone off without his jacket and flashlight—leaving his cabin unlocked.

Well, but maybe he had another jacket and another flashlight. And maybe he had only stepped away.

Stepped away where?

But if someone had attacked J.X.... Say it. If someone had killed J.X., where was the body? Why hide his body when the killer hadn't hidden anyone else's? Why hide evidence of this crime?

Because there was no crime. Because J.X. had gone out voluntarily.

After destroying evidence in a murder investigation?

Who was in better position to do so? He had argued with Peaches the night before she was killed, and he declined to say why. He was clearly leading a sexual double life. Krass had taunted him in the bar.

Well, maybe he hadn't specifically taunted J.X., but he had been taunting the murderer, hadn't he? And then he'd wound up dead too. And J.X. certainly had the insider's track on the Murderer's Things to Do List. And he'd been quick to shut me up every time I tried to defend myself—he'd got me isolated out here—

Now I was scaring myself. If J.X. was the killer, I did not want to be discovered standing here watching the evidence against him going up in smoke.

I headed for the door, checking on the stoop and making sure the coast was clear. The row of cabins stood silver gray in the night, and the world smelled of mud and rain and woodsmoke. The rain had dwindled to a misty drizzle. I squelched hastily back to my own cabin and let myself inside. I locked the door behind me and went to the window where I stood watching the darkness, wondering what I was waiting for.

I was still waiting when morning came.

CHAPTER TWENTY-ONE

They were not happy to see me at the lodge.

Velma—Debbie, that is—would probably have slammed the door on me, but I got my boot through the opening between door and frame when she cautiously looked out. I grabbed the edge of the door and thrust it back, and she staggered a few steps. Her eyes were enormous behind the glasses.

"I need to talk to your dad," I told her. "I'll wait here, but go get him now."

"What the hell is going on now?" Rita appeared with a stack of much-laundered towels in her arms.

"He got in," Debbie quavered, making it sound like one of the undead had slipped past the garlic wreath on the door. Come to think of it, I felt like one of the undead. Lack of sleep and a permanent state of chills was beginning to affect my normally sweet disposition.

"Is J.X. here?" I demanded of Rita.

"The cop? I think he had breakfast, didn't he?" She looked at Debbie who shrugged. "Or maybe that was yesterday. Why?" Her gaze fairly crackled with suspicion and hostility.

"Is he here *or not*?" I yelled, and they both jumped.

I could hear doors banging open from upstairs and voices rising as the hens woke up to the fact the fox was inside the fence.

Edgar strode down the hallway toward us. "Something wrong?" He looked around as though expecting to see J.X. on my heels.

I said, "I think something's happened to J.X. He's not in his cabin."

Edgar turned to Rita. She retorted, "How the hell should I know? He was in and out all day yesterday, poking around places he had no business poking."

"What makes you think something happened to him?" Edgar was frowning, but there was none of the alarmed distrust of his womenfolk.

See, real mystery writers would rather die than ever use the words *I have a bad feeling,* so I launched right into my reasoning: the unlocked cabin, the bed that hadn't been slept in, the jacket and flashlight left behind, the burned murder weapon.

The three of them listened dumbfounded as I concluded, "I checked his cabin again on the way up here this morning, and he's still not there."

"How'd you get out of your cabin?" Rita inquired.

"He left the key with me last night."

"Why would he do that?"

Edgar glanced at her and nodded, considering. "Sounds like maybe he was planning to disappear and left the key so you could get out if you needed to." Adding, in case I'd missed the point, "Since he wouldn't be around."

I hadn't thought of that, and it did give me pause. I shook my head. "I don't think so. Why wouldn't he take his jacket and flashlight?"

"Maybe he had another jacket and flashlight," Edgar said.

"How many people bring two jackets to a writing conference? And the flashlight would be one of your own. Did you give him another flashlight?"

Edgar shook his head slowly.

"Why should we listen to you?" Debbie said shrilly. "You killed Peaches and Mr. Krass."

Her mother shushed her, her harsh face softening fleetingly. That kid was certainly the apple of Rita's eye. I wondered briefly how far Rita would go to protect her baby. But protect her from what?

"I did not kill anyone," I said, snapping out each word for the benefit of the ladies lining up on the staircase to gawk down at us. By then I was all out of patience. "If I had, I wouldn't be up here now pointing out that J.X. is missing."

Rita said, "You might. Maybe you overpowered him last night and killed him too. We have only your word for it that he gave you that key."

"If I'd killed him, why would I—"

"To try and fix yourself an alibi," a male voice interrupted loudly. The four of us looked toward the crowded staircase as George Lacey made his way down the steps. "To try and throw us off the track," he continued, reaching the bottom and joining us. He was still fastening his belt, in his great hurry to drop the noose over my head.

"You weren't *on* the track," I said. "You're not even on the field. Hell, you're not even in the goddamned *ballpark*." I turned back to Edgar. "If I had anything to do with this, why would I tell you all that the murder weapon has been burned? I'd have replaced the real thing with a log from the pile out back. Only four of us knew about the branch that was used to kill Peaches— you, me, J.X. and the murderer."

Edgar gave me a long, thoughtful look.

"I'm telling you, something has happened to him. And the longer we wait—" To my amazement, I couldn't finish it. Couldn't put it into words. Could barely stand to think it. "We're wasting *time*," I pleaded.

"All right," Edgar said at last. "You've convinced me. Give us a chance to get organized here, and we'll split up in groups and see if we can find him."

"Aren't you forgetting something?" a new voice chimed in triumphantly. We all turned back to the staircase to see Mindy Newburgh wrestling her way through the pink flock. It had to be sleep deprivation, but I began to feel like I had wandered into the last half of *Murder by Death*. Not a film I ever cared for.

"What?" the Crofts and George asked on cue.

Mindy reached the bottom slightly breathless and slightly disheveled. "All of this makes perfect sense if...*J.X. is the murderer*." She paused as though waiting for the accolade. The others exchanged dubious glances.

I said, "Yeah, but he's not, so let's not waste any more time. We're not playing Clue here. People are dying."

"You don't know he's not the killer—unless you're the killer yourself," George announced triumphantly.

"Exactly," Mindy purred.

"Elementary, my dear dingleberry. *Not*." If only I'd had those laser contact lenses installed, the pair of them would have vanished in a blaze of cinders. I focused on Mindy, who really should have known better. "You know what, Min? Not only are you off your rocker—literally—can I say for the record that I can't—and never could—stand your work? And you know why? Putting aside the fact that you write the lamest male characters ever to swagger through a mystery novel—and if Buzz Salyer is supposed to be heterosexual, I'm a prima ballerina—you have zero understanding of human nature and the way the world works."

She spluttered. "Well, you're a fine one to talk. I don't think you've ever *met* a genuine old lady, let alone managed to write a convincing one."

"Folks," Edgar interrupted, "I think we're getting lost here." He nodded at me. "I agree with Christopher. I don't think it's very likely that J.X. killed anybody, and there does seem to be something strange about his disappearance. So let's all get dressed, and we'll start having a look around."

Some of my tension eased. At least I would have some help now. This place was too big and too spread out for me to try and search on my own.

Rita said reluctantly, "There's coffee and pastries being served in the dining room."

I nodded and made my way down the hall while a couple of the ladies on the staircase voiced their doubts about letting a dangerous character such as myself roam freely.

Espie joined me not long after I'd sat down with a cup of lukewarm coffee to stare moodily out at the foggy landscape.

"You must think he's dead," she said cheerfully. "I could hear you screaming all the way upstairs." She laughed gloatingly. "Man, I loved what you told Dork and Mindy. *Dingleberry.* I didn't think you had it in you."

"He's not dead."

"Oh ho," Espie said after a pause. "So that's the way it is?"

I looked at her. "He's not dead, that's all. If he was dead, the killer would have left him where he killed him. There would be no reason to hide his body."

"You don't know where he was killed."

I said fiercely, "He wasn't killed."

"Okay, esse. Okay." She was still grinning, but her gaze was measuring. "So what do you think happened to him?"

"I think he opened his cabin door to someone he knew—or thought he knew—and that person overpowered him—"

"Which means another guy."

"—or forced him to leave at gunpoint."

She considered that. "I guess it's possible. Nobody has been shot so far, though."

"Or knifepoint or axepoint or pitchforkpoint. I don't know. But forced him to walk away without his coat and flashlight."

"It could be, but where is someone going to stash a full-grown dangerous dude like J.X.?"

"That's what we're going to find out."

"It would be easier to kill him."

I gave her a long look, and she shrugged. "I'm just saying."

"Well don't."

She laughed. "This is a different side of you, Christopher. I like it." She proceeded to attack the mountain of food on her plate, and I drank my coffee and stared out at the fog-enveloped world.

The room slowly filled, the tables a safe distance from my own being the most popular choice in real estate. This morning everyone was keeping their voices down, possibly in an effort not to further agitate me. I could feel a lot of curious glances shooting my way. I didn't care.

"Where do you know Rachel from?" I asked finally, as Espie shoveled down the mountain of food to a molehill.

"She's my agent," she said thickly.

"No kidding. So you've known each other a long time?" I was sure they did. I wanted to hear her answer.

"Sure." After a hesitation, "I was her first client."

"I thought Peaches was?"

"No. Me, then Peaches. Then Sylvie Archer."

"Archer committed suicide, didn't she?"

Espie lifted a negligent shoulder. So much for Archer. "Then she took you on." She shook her head.

"What?"

"Just the money you both made on that old lady and her cat."

"Hey. I loved writing that series."

"Yeah, but Granny Goose was right. That Miss Buttercup was not like any senior citizen I ever met. I liked the cat, though. And the police inspector—although I gotta tell you, Christopher, that guy was *flaming*."

I scowled at her over the rim of my coffee cup, but she was unperturbed. "You should just come right out and write a gay mystery series."

"When did Rachel first sign you? If you were her first client that must have been…fifteen, twenty years ago?"

"Sixteen. What's with all the questions?"

"I'm just curious."

"You see where your boy J.X.'s curiosity got him."

Edgar walked into the dining room and called for everyone's attention. He gave an abbreviated version of what was going on, approaching it from the unlikely angle that J.X. might have fallen and broken a leg while wandering around the night before. He said we were going to start combing the property and checking out the outlying buildings in groups of four, and he asked for volunteers.

After much shrugging and exchanging of looks—and a few pertinent questions—we got a pretty decent show of hands. In fairness, most of these women had not come dressed to do anything but talk in civilized surroundings, and they had neither the outerwear nor the shoes for a serious manhunt. Or at least not the kind Edgar was proposing.

But he did get over half of them willing to look for J.X., which further proved how popular J.X. was given the fact that a lot of expensive footwear was going to be sacrificed on his behalf.

"What about maps?" one woman asked.

"There's no point handing out a bunch of maps," Edgar replied. "You can't see five feet in front of you. Keep one of your group on the road or the path you're using at all times." He gave a few more directions about where to go and what to do if they found J.X., and then everyone trotted off to change into warmer gear.

Joining me and Espie at the table, Edgar said apologetically, "I can't let them go very far in this fog. We're liable to have more people lost."

"I know." The main reason I wanted them all out there was because if J.X. was still alive—and I refused to think otherwise—the murderer was not going to risk going near him with all these chickadees wandering around. "Were you able to radio the sheriffs?"

He shook his head. "It's an old set. We were lucky to get through the first time. I'll try again later."

"Am I still under house arrest, or can I join in the search?"

Edgar wiped a big hand across his face. "I can't see any point in not letting you help look for him. I don't think anyone's going to want to team up with you, though."

"I'll keep you company." Espie reached across and patted my hand. She had strong hands.

"Then can you go get changed?" I requested. "We're wasting time."

Her brows lifted, but she rose. As she left the room, Edgar said, "The more I think about it, I'm wondering if he did leave of his own free will."

"What do you mean?"

His expression was uncomfortable. "He seemed like a pretty tough hombre to me. Savvy. I don't think it would be so easy to take him unawares. It's possible that he deliberately left his jacket and flashlight behind to make it look like he was attacked."

I rejected this theory immediately, but—that was emotion, not logic. I forced myself to consider dispassionately what Edgar was saying. "He wouldn't get far without a coat or a light in this weather. It was like a hurricane out there last night. He'd risk dying of exposure."

"Maybe he'd rather risk that than prison. Ex-cops don't do well in prison from what I hear."

Again, I had to sit on my angry rebuttal. "Could he make it out on foot?"

"No." Edgar's eyes met mine. "But he might not believe that. He's not local. He might think he could make it."

I nodded, mulling it over. "Do you know what J.X. and Peaches argued over the night before she died? I heard they had a pretty loud difference of opinion."

"I don't have any idea."

"Did he come back up to the house last night?"

Edgar had to think before he answered. "I don't remember seeing him. He said he was coming back...but things were a little hectic."

That was one word for it. It certainly described what had been going on in my cabin.

And remembering that, I said, "I didn't get the feeling last night that he was planning on going anywhere."

Edgar didn't twitch a muscle. "Appearances can be deceiving." He added, "Maybe you saw exactly what J.X. wanted you to see."

CHAPTER TWENTY-TWO

As Espie seemed to be taking her sweet time getting ready, I left the dining room and went upstairs to knock on Rachel's door.

"Enter," her voice commanded distantly.

"Sorry to disturb you, Your Majesty," I said, shutting the door behind me. "I wondered if you'd reconsidered your decision to let me hang in the wind."

She jumped about a foot—and so did I, never having seen her without makeup before. The thin Sailor Moon T-shirt wasn't doing either of us any favors.

"What are you doing out?" she demanded.

I seemed to get that a lot lately.

"I'm on parole. Time off for good behavior."

"*That's* hard to imagine," she said, recovering a little of her old charm. "Why are you here?"

"You're my agent. I thought maybe you could give me some advice on what to write while I'm in prison. You know, what's hot, what's not—no pun intended."

"You're not going to prison."

"You're right about that because you're going to tell me why you killed Peaches and what the hell you did with my earring."

"I told you what I did with that bloody earring," she roared. Personally I thought it was a little odd that she focused on the second half of my comment, but clearing myself was my main concern. Well, second main concern.

"The kid swears up and down that the glass on your dresser was empty."

"She's lying!"

"Why would she?"

"Why would I?"

"Because you're trying to frame me." I said it quite reasonably since we'd been over it before.

She refuted my hypothesis quite loudly, reminding me more of Yoko Ono with every screech. She concluded the opera with, "And I already *told* J.X. I'd had the bloody thing, but it was lost. Ask him. Ask him."

"I can't ask him. He's missing."

"He's missing what?"

"Everything as far as I can make out." I stared at her suspiciously. "How did you not hear that piece of news? The entire lodge knows. Where were you when everyone else was trying to crowd into the lobby?"

She whipped away to the nightstand and held up a black sleep mask and earplugs. "I didn't sleep last night."

"Not a good time to admit that," I told her. "Someone made off with J.X. in the middle of the night."

"Made off with him?"

"He's gone. And I don't think he went voluntarily."

She stared at me aghast. "What is going on?" she whispered.

"My best guess? We're being picked off one by one *à la* Agatha Christie." I don't think she even heard me. I was watching her expression very closely.

"This doesn't make any sense."

"Is there a part of it that *does* make sense?" I inquired. "If so, you should tell me now before you're knocked off as well. Because as far as I can see, nothing so far has made sense—except that I think Peaches was trying to blackmail you."

That was a total shot in the dark, so I was startled—but gratified—to see her turn the color of wallpaper glue. "How... do you know that?" she breathed.

"I know eveeryting and noooting," I told her grandly. I was kidding because I was afraid she was going to faint, and no way could I scrape her off the carpet. She stared at me with empty eyes, and I said, "It's something to do with Espie's book, isn't it?"

She answered mechanically. "Peaches wanted a look at it."

"She wanted..." The light went on. "She wanted a look at Espie's *new* book?"

She nodded.

"She was going to steal Espie's new book?"

Another of those nods.

"But...I mean, Jesus, couldn't she steal from someone else for a change? Or. Here's a wild idea, couldn't she write her own damn book?"

Rachel said dully, "She hated Espie. I think it gave her a special thrill to know she was robbing her. And, no, she couldn't write. Not like Espie. Nothing she wrote on her own—assuming she ever did write anything on her own—did what *Poké Stack* did. That book put her on the literary map. As this next one is going to do for Espie."

"So you didn't let Peaches see the manuscript?"

"I told her—" She cut herself off.

I decided to circle round. "And that's what you were arguing about that night?"

"Yes."

"How did Peaches find out about the manuscript?"

Rachel winced at some memory. "Espie was boasting about it the night we arrived. It's going to auction. Two major houses are bidding for this manuscript."

I felt a sharp stab of jealousy. I'd never had a book go to auction. I ignored the green monster in the room and asked, "Does Espie know Peaches was blackmailing you to get a look at her manuscript?"

"No."

"Are you sure?"

"I didn't tell her."

"Would Peaches?"

"Not unless she wanted to commit suicide." Her eyes widened. "Oh my God."

"What?"

"Oh. My. God." She was staring at me in a kind of horror.

"What? *What?*" I yelled, looking around. Expressions like hers usually herald someone getting bitten in half by a giant ant or spider.

She said faintly, "I know what I did with your earring."

I blinked at her, trying to reconcile this with the unimagined horrors that I had, in fact, been imagining.

Rachel was on her feet, dragging her purse out from the side of the bed and pawing through it like she'd missed her last dose of Dr. Jekyll serum. "Oh my God," she said again, and pulled her wallet out.

She ripped open the wallet, dug frantically inside, and held up...my earring.

"I put it away for safekeeping," she said into my stupefied silence. "I remember now. I was afraid the maid wouldn't notice it in the glass and might accidentally throw it away, and I didn't want to mix it in with my jewelry."

I stared at her, then reached out and took the small winking stud. For a time I stared at it.

Rachel was still babbling guiltily. "With everything going on, it utterly skipped my mind. The only thing I remembered was putting it in the glass…"

So if the stud I had been wearing when I reached the lodge was now in my hand…that meant the earring found beneath Steven Krass's body was the earring I had lost in the woods.

I fastened the stud in my ear, thinking all the while. Once again I remembered J.X. kneeling down to pick something up. He had said it was a key off his chain, but there was nothing to substantiate that. For the first time I seriously contemplated whether there was anything to Edgar's theory that J.X. had deliberately disappeared.

Actually, from a mystery-writing standpoint, it looked pretty good. The old murderer-pretending-to-be-a-victim ploy. I'd used it successfully twice myself. Once in *Miss Butterwith's Double Trouble* and once in *Dead Weights for Miss Butterwith.*

But what possible motive could J.X. have for killing Peaches? Krass, yes, that I could see. His comments at the table that night had seemed to be largely directed at J.X. I hadn't taken them seriously—I don't think anyone did—because being an ex-cop J.X. was pretty much above suspicion. Which was ironic considering his own work was full of corrupt and crooked cops.

Okay, to be fair, it wasn't simply J.X.'s former line of work. He was…nice. A nice guy. Smart, talented, handsome, funny, and…nice. True, he was also married and screwing around which sort of undercut his nice-guy standing. Did his screwing around make him vulnerable to blackmail? Because it was sinking in on me that extortion was Peaches' modus operandi—and had probably gotten her killed. Although it was kind of hard to picture. Blackmail wasn't the motive it was back in the Golden Age of mystery. And what was Peaches blackmailing J.X. *for*? From all indications she wasn't short of cash, and she could hardly pass one of J.X.'s hardboiled cop thrillers off as one of her own.

"What's the matter?" Rachel asked. "I thought you'd be relieved."

"We have to find J.X.," I told her. "Get dressed. I need your help."

* * * * *

Through the white emptiness we could hear voices distantly calling out to each other while the other searchers slowly and painstakingly worked their way through the outlying cabins and sheds.

Rachel and Espie were stumbling along at my heels, both of them grumbling about their feet hurting before we had gone more than a few yards. Not that I could really blame them, my blisters had blisters following that forced march up from the bridge the afternoon I'd arrived. I ignored the scrape and sting.

"We're not going to find anything in this fog," Rachel informed me.

"You're just giving the murderer a good excuse to be wandering outside," Espie put in.

I said, "If he hasn't killed J.X. already, there must be a reason. If we could figure out what that reason is, maybe we can head him off."

Neither of them answered. Instead I heard some splashing sounds behind me followed by cursing. I decided to let them catch up with me in their own time.

J.X.'s cabin loomed out of the fog. The windows were dark, the door swung silently open when I touched the handle. Not that I had expected to find J.X. sitting inside, but the chill silence that greeted me was depressing. I went to the chair where J.X.'s jacket hung and checked the pockets. They were empty. So what had he done with the notes I'd jotted down yesterday on the legal pad? He'd had them folded in his pocket when we went to dinner.

I began to go through his things slowly and methodically. Where was the earring he had found under Krass's body? Had he hidden it for safekeeping? It didn't appear to be anywhere.

He was doing quite well for himself judging by the quality of his clothes. Very different from when we had first met and his wardrobe had seemed to consist of Levi's, white shirts, and a leather bomber jacket. One thing hadn't changed. He still packed as neatly as if he had to pass government inspection, but the garments he now packed were…well, actually for the most part he was still packing jeans and white shirts. The difference was the jeans were now made by Marc Jacobs and the white shirts were by Armani. He'd tossed in a couple of lambswool sweaters and a few silk T-shirts, and there was a gorgeous black wool suit by Carlo Pignatelli hanging in the little closet. If I didn't know how well his books did, I'd have been highly suspicious.

As it was, his deepest darkest secret appeared to be…shoe trees.

There was also the fact that there did not seem to be any indication of his married life. I'm not sure what I expected. A silver framed photo of the missus and the kid? There was nothing. If I didn't know better, I'd have said this was the suitcase of a happily single male.

"What are you doing?" Rachel demanded behind me. I managed not to start—but it wasn't easy, clutching J.X.'s Calvins. I unclenched my hands from his snowy boxers and glanced casually over my shoulder.

"I'm searching his things."

"You can't do that."

"He searched mine, I'll guarantee you." Although what deductions he could have drawn were beyond me—seeing that I hadn't even picked most of what I had packed, let alone worn it. I was kind of a jeans and T-shirt guy myself.

"He's searching J.X.'s things," she informed Espie as she staggered up to the doorway.

"Tell me he's got some good blow. A couple of OCs. I'll even settle for half-smoked leaf."

"He's clean," I said like I was starring in a 1970s cop drama. And he *was* clean. He even folded his dirty laundry.

"What exactly are you looking for?" Rachel demanded. "Clues?"

"Red herrings?" Espie offered. "They'll be stinking by now, esse."

"I don't know. But I can tell you what I'm not finding—and that's anything to do with the murder. The branch, log, whatever you want to call it that was used to clobber Peaches came out of the woodpile back behind the lodge, but it went up in smoke last night. My earring is missing. There's nothing here relating to the murders at all."

"Why do you think he'd be keeping anything in his cabin?" Espie asked curiously. "Wouldn't he leave that stuff locked in the lodge safe?"

"He's an ex-cop. He doesn't trust anyone."

In an effort to get the torture over with as soon as possible, Rachel began checking behind the pillows on the bed, feeling between the mattresses. She worked fast and efficiently. I was impressed and left her to it while I went in the bathroom and checked the orderly row of grooming products. John Varvatos aftershave, deodorant, and fragrance. Baby shampoo. Manual razor and an electric trimmer. Electric toothbrush. Mini floss and cute little bottles of mouthwash.

"I thought we were looking for J.X?" Espie called. "I can tell you right now, he's not here."

The bathroom light suddenly came on.

"Oh, thank God, the power's back," Rachel cried from the other room.

"Halle-fucking-lujah," Espie said. "Can we go back to the house now and get warm? I'm tired of freezing my ass off so Christopher can paw through J.X.'s underwear."

I stared unseeingly in the silvered mirror over the sink. He could be anywhere. Tied up in a barn or buried in the vineyard. How the hell were we going to find him?

Gradually my face came into focus. I looked like a stranger. Pale, drawn, blond stubble, bleak, red-rimmed eyes... I looked old. I looked like a guy who had lost everything that mattered.

CHAPTER TWENTY-THREE

I stepped out of the bathroom and said, "I want to try the icehouse."

Rachel and Espie exchanged looks. "Where's that?" Espie asked.

"Down the road a little. Behind the trees, I think."

"You *think*?"

"Look," I said, "I know you're tired and your feet hurt, but I don't believe we should split up, and I want to check the icehouse. I think J.X. might be stashed there."

Rachel said uncomfortably, "But isn't that where...?"

"Yes. That's where they're storing Peaches and Krass. Which is why I think it's a great hiding place. No one is going to go poking around in there." No one except J.X., who had admitted to investigating the icehouse the night before last.

Espie stared down at her mud-caked shoes and then stared at me. Rachel looked about as woebegone as I'd ever seen her.

She sighed. "Right. Well, I suppose it's my fault you're in this jam. If I hadn't insisted on dragging you up here—"

"That's right," I told her. "And don't think because you're admitting this now that I'm not going to throw it up at you in future arguments." I trailed them out into the swirling mist.

"I can't believe this shit. It's like we're in that episode of the *Twilight Zone*," Espie was grumbling as I shut the door to J.X.'s cabin and took the lead, starting relatively briskly off toward the dirt road—or what I hoped was the direction of the dirt road.

"A regular pea souper," Rachel agreed.

"Is that what they call it where you come from, *querida*?" Espie asked dryly.

Rachel didn't respond.

We could still hear our fellow searchers calling out to each other in the cotton wool silence.

"You sure we're going the right way?" Espie asked after a time.

"Yes," I lied.

We continued our way down the uneven dirt track—or what I hoped was the dirt track—avoiding the puddles and rain-carved furrows the best we could. The farther we walked, the fainter grew the voices behind us.

"I don't like this," Rachel said. "What if we can't find our way back?"

"There it is," I said with relief. I could make out the roof through the eddying mists. "Rachel, you stay on the road here. Espie and I will go check the building."

"How did I get elected action hero?" Espie objected, but she followed as I lengthened my strides.

The building rose in front of us, weathered with time and silvered by the rain. It was a single-story windowless structure built into the hillside behind it. Rain dripped in slow loud plops from the eaves. The double doors were chained and padlocked.

I'd figured on the padlock. I hadn't figured that there would be no windows or any way to see inside. I walked down the side of the building. No windows. No side entrance. I walked back and explored down the other side. Same story. No windows, no side entrance. I came back to the double doors and contemplated them.

"Bloody hell," Rachel called. "I can't see either of you now."

"We're right here," Espie called back. "We got a little problem." To me, she said, "You ain't going to break that padlock, esse. It's got a steel shroud around the hasp to keep people like you and me out."

She'd read me right; I had been searching the ground for something I could use to smash the lock. She was also right about the padlock. The only way in would be to break the chain, and the links were heavy steel—shiny and new.

"Edgar think he got a pair of zombies in there?" Espie remarked, picking up the heavy links and giving them an experimental tug.

I swore and banged on the splintering face of the door. "J.X.?" I yelled. "Are you in there?"

Espie and I listened tensely. The doors creaked in a phantom breeze, the rain dropped in heavy splashes from the roof.

"If he's *not* in there, I hope nobody else answers," Espie whispered.

I pounded on the door. "J.X.?"

I could hear Rachel pacing uneasily a yard or so away.

"J.X.?"

"You're creeping me out, man," Espie said. "He's not in there."

"He might be unconscious."

"Then he's not going to answer you."

I slammed my hand against the door in frustration one final time. "Okay. I need to get Edgar to open this goddamned building for me."

"Now you're talking," Espie approved. "Let's go back to the lodge. Maybe there'll be some good news. Or some hot coffee. I think they waved the pot this morning over a match."

"What's going on?" Rachel shouted. "Are you both all right?"

"Yo!" Espie yelled back. "We're fine." To me she said almost kindly, "Come on, Christopher. If he is in there, the faster we get back to the lodge, the faster you can get to him."

She was right, but I had a horrible feeling as we turned and made our way back to the road. I was convinced that J.X. was in there and that if we left him now, we were leaving him to die.

But there was no way to get inside the damned building...

I stopped walking. "I'm going to wait back at the icehouse. When you get to the lodge, tell Edgar to come down and unlock the doors."

"You can't stay down here by yourself," Rachel shrilled. "What if the killer comes after you?"

"Why should he? He wants me to be blamed for the murders. He can't very well kill me."

"He can if you make too much of a nuisance of yourself."

Espie said, "I don't know if anyone still thinks you're the killer after the hissy fit you threw this morning."

"Sometimes in a room full of women you have to raise your voice to be heard," I said with dignity.

"Raise your *voice*? You raised the roof. And then you got in a catfight with—"

"All right, all right." I said to Rachel, "Anyway, I'll be fine. The place is crawling with searchers right now."

"Who can't see five feet in front of them," Espie pointed out. "Don't be stupid, homeboy. Do you see any searchers around here?"

By now they each had hold of my arms—it didn't help that they seemed to want to drag me in different directions. I shook them off. "Look, enough talk. I let him down once. I can do this much for him."

Neither of them said anything.

"All right," Rachel said finally. "We'll be as quick as we can. But I think you're *mad.*"

I was already heading back to the icehouse.

Their voices—and uncomplimentary opinions of me— faded into the mist. And I knew they were right. This made no sense at all. If I couldn't get into the building, then how would the killer get past the chains?

Unless the killer was Edgar. Or Rita. Or Debbie.

I considered this as the ramshackle structure materialized before me again.

Edgar would certainly be a physical match for J.X. He knew the lodge and was best positioned for moving and hiding bodies. And he'd be the best bet for disabling his own generator—especially since the generator hadn't been damaged, just a lot of fuel wasted.

I considered the disabling of the emergency generator. Come to think of it, what had been the point of that? Someone wanted us without power...why? We already couldn't get out. Contact with the world beyond the lodge was sketchy at best. Someone wanted us to eat cold food and drink cold coffee? Someone wanted us to go without heat? Someone wanted the lights off at night? Bingo. Someone wanted the cover of darkness. Because something had been planned for last night. J.X.'s disappearance. But was it voluntary or involuntary?

I believed it was involuntary, but...was that because that was what I wished to believe?

I leaned against the rough wood face of the building, huddling deeper into my coat. It was Northern California, not Alaska, for God's sake. Why the hell was it so cold? And so *quiet*...

I tuned out my uneasiness. So...Edgar. He had the means and probably the opportunity, but it was very hard to see Edgar in the role of ruthless murderer. For one thing he seemed too calm, too practical. This kind of murder was a crime of desperation, surely?

I mulled that over. Actually there were three—two—different murders to consider. There was Peaches' murder, which seemed to have been the best planned out. Meaning, whoever had killed her had time to cart her body off to the woods and hide her. Her belongings had been packed, creating the illusion that she had left voluntarily. And if the bridge hadn't washed out, and I hadn't come stumbling along, that facade probably would have held up for at least a few days—maybe even a few weeks. Long enough to better conceal the body and belongings.

One thing was for sure, whoever killed Peaches was pretty coolheaded. They'd have to be, to calmly pack up her belongings and then cart body and suitcases off to the woods.

That meant having access to Peaches' room. Granted, he—or she—would have that after they'd killed her. They'd also need access to one of the lodge vehicles—but I'd already noticed that the truck and van keys were kept in a key box behind the front desk. If I'd noticed, safe to assume plenty of other people had too. The killer would need to know about the shrine in the woods, right? But the shrine in the woods was mentioned in the lodge brochure as a hiking destination.

So...not necessarily someone from the lodge. Not by any means. Besides...what would the motive be? Debbie had clearly adored Peaches. Rita had loathed her, but loathing was still a long way from removing someone from the face of the planet. Edgar...it was hard to read Edgar. He mostly seemed to view Peaches as a pain in the ass.

Motive. That was the hard part because aside from Debbie, the only person who seemed to feel much affection for Peaches had been Krass.

Man, it was taking a long time for Edgar to show up. I rubbed my hands up and down my wool-covered shoulders and walked the length of the icehouse a couple of times to try and keep warm.

Krass. His murder seemed much more like a matter of expediency. He had seen something that made him suspicious—he couldn't have known for sure who killed Peaches because he'd surely not have been stupid enough to meet that person alone behind the lodge that night. Assuming that was what had happened. Whoever killed Krass, in my opinion, had killed him out of fear of exposure. So the key to the murderer still lay with figuring out who had a strong enough grudge against Peaches to risk killing her this weekend.

Because that was the other key consideration—timing. Why this weekend? If it was someone who knew and loathed Peaches, why now? Why not wait? Killing her at Blue Heron Lodge guaranteed a small pool of suspects, which upped the chance of getting caught.

There must have been some urgency for getting rid of her now. Why?

I turned my collar up and considered the time-honored tropes of mystery fiction. Pregnancy. Peaches was pregnant with someone's baby. That let Edgar out, but what about George and J.X.? J.X. had apparently been seeing Peaches socially, so it was a possibility. Mindy kept George on a pretty tight leash, but that didn't mean he never slipped his collar, and he'd certainly been quick to try and get me lynched for the murders.

Or what about this...what if Peaches was actually Debbie's biological mother and she had come to claim her this weekend? Even if she hadn't come to claim her...I could see Rita wiping Peaches out without thinking twice to protect Debbie.

Yeah. I liked that. I liked it a lot better than the notion that Peaches and J.X. were having an affair.

My thoughts were interrupted by the squishy thud of approaching footsteps. I waited, eyes searching the swirling brume.

I saw his cowboy hat first, and then Edgar appeared out of the fog. Belatedly, it occurred to me that if Edgar *was* the killer, I had placed myself in an extremely vulnerable position—although if Edgar was the murderer, even he must be getting uneasy about the unsightly body buildup.

His greeting was prosaic enough as he held up a key ring. "Your friends told me you think the cop might have been dumped in the icehouse."

"I know it's a long shot."

"Son, it's no shot at all. You saw the chain on the door. I locked that padlock myself yesterday morning after we put your editor in there. Nobody could get inside."

"Where do you keep that key ring?"

He hesitated. "In the front desk drawer."

"Someone could have taken them, then."

He stared at me. I couldn't tell if he was mostly exasperated or confounded. "All right," he said at last, in the tone of one humoring an unreasonable but loyal customer. "Let's have a look." He picked up the chain and inserted the key in the padlock.

I realized I was shaking with nerves and cold as I waited for him to twist the key, wriggle loose the shank, and pull the chain free. It slid clanking to the ground, and Edgar hauled open the heavy door. The hinges groaned.

"Watch where you step," Edgar warned me. "There's a wooden walkway around the spring. It's not in great shape these days." He ducked inside the door, and I followed him cautiously.

Edgar switched his flashlight on. The wan beam swept across the still, ink-black water and poked into the cobwebbed corners. Two long motionless tarps lay side by side on the ground beside the walk. I felt the hair rise on the back of my neck.

The smell of death mingled with dank water. My stomach roiled unhappily. I was glad I hadn't had anything to eat for breakfast.

"Seen enough?" Edgar asked somberly.

"How deep is the spring?"

I felt his stare. "You've got quite an imagination," he said. "It's about twelve feet deep."

My footsteps echoed hollowly as I picked my way down the wooden ties that formed the walkway. Kneeling, I peered into the pool. It was black, fathomless. I couldn't see anything in those jet waters. I dipped my hand in. Ice cold. I pushed the water aside, trying to see through the murky wet. Yeah. Nice try.

I rose painfully, my back protesting all this unaccustomed physical activity. If I managed to survive this weekend, I was going to make getting back in shape a priority. I said, "Can you shine the light over here? I want to check who's wrapped in these tarps."

The silence that followed was one of the loudest I've ever heard.

At last Edgar said, "You think the killer tossed one of the bodies in the pond and wrapped Moriarity in a tarp? Why not throw Moriarity in the pond?"

"Because maybe he's not dead." I cautiously approached the first mound of tarp. I'm not going to pretend I was filled with anything but dread. Thanks to too many scary movies, I wouldn't have been surprised if a hand had suddenly shot out of the wrappings and grabbed my ankle. Well, maybe I would have been surprised, but mostly I'd have been too busy shrieking.

I said with a steadiness I didn't feel, "Maybe the killer is keeping him alive for some reason."

"What reason?"

Edgar's footsteps came down the wooden walkway. The flashlight beam spotlighted the top of the nearest tarp.

"I don't know." I said, "Maybe J.X. has some information he needs. Or maybe the killer is leery of killing a cop. Or an ex-cop. I'd be. Cop killers don't do so well. Or...maybe I have to believe that he's still alive."

"I didn't think you two got along," Edgar said after a pause.

"We don't."

When I didn't say anything more or make another move, Edgar said grimly, "Be my guest."

I bent over the long tarp and pulled back one dusty edge. Steven Krass. Steven Krass with an expression straight out of a horror movie. I swallowed hard and covered his face again.

I stood up feeling weirdly lightheaded.

"You okay?"

"Fine," I got out. I walked around Krass to the other neatly wrapped mound. I bent and jerked back the flap. Wrong end. But maybe that was a blessing. Her feet looked like wax in the dingy light. The toe ring glinted dully. I tossed the tarp back over her and straightened, hand pressed to the small of my back.

"Seen enough?" Edgar asked politely.

I nodded. Words were beyond me.

CHAPTER TWENTY-FOUR

The first person I ran into when we got back to the lodge was Mindy Newburgh. She saw me and sniffed, heading for the staircase.

I went after her and said, "Mindy, I owe you an apology. I was rattled this morning, and I said some things I didn't mean." Not the things I'd said to her, but no point rubbing salt in the wound.

She paused on the lower steps and looked me up and down disapprovingly. "You were hysterical this morning."

"I know. I'm sorry. Murder accusations before I've had my coffee make me cranky."

She said patiently, "I wasn't accusing *you* of murder. I was accusing J.X. of murder."

"I don't like that a lot better, to tell you the truth."

"Well, if I'd realized at the time that you had one of those unrequited things for him, I'd have…I suppose I'd have tried to be more sensitive. Really, I don't know what I'd have done, Christopher, because it's perfectly obvious J.X. is the culprit and now he's made his escape."

"He hasn't made his escape. He's the killer's latest victim."

"Nonsense. There's absolutely no sign of him, and we all spent the morning searching the grounds."

How quick everyone was to turn the minute one of the herd showed weakness. Was the pack mentality programmed in? I protested, "But what would his motive be?"

"It's perfectly obvious that he and Peaches were having an affair. I think he wanted to break it off, and she threatened to tell his wife."

Could that possibly be grounds for murder in this day and age? True, I'd used it a few times in books, but I'd also used the blackmailed-for-being-homosexual and, except in the case of politicians and public figures, that motive had pretty much rusted to a standstill.

"Do you have any proof he was having an affair with her?"

"When you get to be my age, you have a sense for these things."

Was that like the sixty-seventh sense? Given the tripe Mindy wrote, I found it hard to believe she had the faintest notion of how people actually related to each other in the real world. Unless I was missing my—admittedly cynical—guess, she was holding the luscious George in thrall by the purse strings. Which reminded me.

"You said Peaches came on to George. Was that here at the lodge?"

Her eyes were very hard and very bright behind the pink rhinestone spectacles. "Yes, it was here. But don't try to drag Georgie into this mess. He told her to stuff it."

It took supreme effort, but I let that last comment go. Instead, I said, "Did he tell you about it, or did you happen to overhear them?"

"He came straight to me and told me all about it," Mindy said. "And I gave that little bitch a piece of my mind then and there."

"Then and there where?"

"I went right to her room and told her what I thought of her behavior."

"And what did she say?"

Mindy's cheeks grew pink. "She pretended to laugh it off, but I know those words struck home."

I don't think even Mindy believed that charming fantasy, but I nodded politely.

"She had somebody with her, though," Mindy said suddenly, frowning. "There was a man in there with her. I just thought of it. She was holding the door half-shut so that I couldn't see past her, but I saw a pair of men's boots by the foot of the bed when she first opened the door."

"Did you recognize the boots?"

Mindy made a tsking sound that reminded me strongly of Miss Butterwith. "I don't look at men's *feet*." She made it sound slightly lurid.

"What kind of boots were they? Cowboy boots?"

"I don't...I don't remember. I didn't really notice. I only glimpsed them."

Wouldn't cowboy boots stick in her memory? They were pretty visual. "What night was this?"

"Thursday." Her eyes were narrowed, thinking back. "It wasn't Georgie, obviously. And it wasn't Steven because he was still in the bar."

"What time was it?"

"Late. After eleven."

Only here in Westworld would eleven be considered *late*. I had to admit that this was an interesting development. There was no proof that the man with Peaches had killed her, but at the same time no one had rushed forward with the information he'd been boinking the deceased the night of her death.

"So you see," Mindy said. "Everything indicates J.X."

"Or Edgar." For that matter, Rita wore rugged work boots. Not that I thought for one instant that Rita and Peaches had put aside their differences for some sizzling sheet time. And frankly I wasn't discounting Gorgeous George merely because Mindy alibied him.

"Edgar!" Mindy chuckled. "Edgar was the one man here absolutely impervious to that slut's charms. I don't think he even knew she existed."

I said, "I thought George was absolutely impervious to her charms?"

Mindy's smile faded. Her eyes were cold. "I was not including George, naturally." She looked at the pink rhinestone watch on her wrist. "Look at the time. I wanted to get my seven pages in this morning."

She bustled up the staircase, and I headed for the main meeting room. The conference was now officially over, but since we were all stuck for the time being, the room was crowded with small groups of chatting women. I didn't see anyone I wanted to talk to, and I backed out again.

I tried the dining room next, but it was empty except for the couple of staff members setting up for lunch. I had better luck in the bar where I found Rachel and Espie drowning their sorrows over glasses of wine that looked large enough to be water tumblers.

"Hoo boy, Christopher, you have got to hear this," Espie greeted me when I poked my head through the doorway. She beckoned me over, and I slid into the booth beside Rachel.

She nodded cordially to me and said on a little gust of wine breath, "Don't give up, Christopher. Don't ever give up."

Being the amazing master detective that I am, it took me about two seconds to deduce they were both drunk off their butts. At eleven thirty in the morning, no less. And people said *I* drank too much.

"Go get a drink," Espie commanded. "You gotta hear this."

"And it'll go down better if I'm drunk?"

They both giggled maniacally at that, and I slid out of the booth and went over to the bar where Rita was wiping glasses. She gave me a dry look—the only dry thing in the room at that point.

Ordering a brandy, I carried it back to the table.

They both watched solemnly as I took a swallow. Then Espie said to Rachel, "Tell him."

"You tell him," Rachel said, recalcitrant all at once. In all the years of our association I'd never known her to be remotely tipsy. The weekend's fallout had resulted in some stimulating moments.

Espie leaned across the table and whispered, "There is a rumor going around..." She started laughing, unable to finish. Fascinated, I studied the crinkling tattoo tear by her eye as she soundlessly giggled.

"Holmes and Moriarty," Rachel said, losing patience. "Christopher Holmes and Julian Xavier Moriarity. Someone finally noticed your last names, and the rumor going round is that this is all some kind of battle of wits between you and J.X." She met Espie's eyes, and they practically fell across the tabletop laughing.

When I had recovered enough to respond, I said, "Can't these morons spell? His name is M-o-r-i-a-r-i-t-y not M-o-r-i-a-r-t-y."

For some reason that struck them as even funnier.

"Holmes and Moriarity sitting in a tree, K-I-L-L-I-N-G," sing-songed Espie. Rachel bent over the table, her nose just missing the fogged surface as her head bounced with giggles.

"Dear God," I murmured.

"Elementary, my dear Holmes," gulped Espie.

I swallowed the rest of my brandy and rose. "Is there any word from the sheriff's department? When are they sending help? We've been cut off for three days."

"Two and a half," Rita said from behind the bar.

All at once I was very tired—and fresh out of ideas. I left Rachel and Espie cackling to themselves and wandered down to the reading room. The kid, Debbie, was in one of the overstuffed chairs reading furtively. She sat bolt upright when I walked in, and I saw the title of the paperback she held. *Some Like it Haute* by Peaches Sadler.

She moved to make her escape. I said, "Can you not run away? I swear to you I had nothing to do with anyone's death. I'm as scared as you are."

She sank back in her chair, eyeing me warily. "Then why does everyone think you did it?"

"They don't. Now they think J.X. did it."

I could see by her expression that she had heard that rumor. She scoffed. "No way. He's not the type."

"Ouch. But you think I am?"

She smiled reluctantly, although her gaze was still doubtful. "He got along with everyone. He was nice."

"Yeah, he was." My throat closed up, and I had to look away. It had to be the lack of sleep, but for a second I couldn't say anything.

Still observing me in that frank way adolescents do, she asked curiously, "You were good friends?"

"I don't know what we were," I admitted tiredly. "But I'm not going to sit here while…"

My voice trailed because that's exactly what I was going to do. I had no idea of how to proceed from here. I was so far out of my depth the sharks were nibbling my toes.

"Are you crying?" she demanded, shocked.

I straightened, wiping hastily at my eyes with the back of my hand. "Allergies," I told her. "Can I ask you a kind of weird question? Can you think of any place around here someone might…try to hide a body?"

I risked a glance. Debbie looked more sympathetic than shocked. She shook her head. "We searched all the cabins and sheds and the garage."

"It's such a big place."

"Yeah."

"Did you grow up here?"

She nodded.

"It's kind of lonely, isn't it?"

She seemed amused. "It seems that way because we're cut off now, but I used to go to the local high school. It's only an hour by bus."

"You don't go anymore?"

She laughed outright at that. "How old do you think I am? I'm in college now. Or at least I was. I'm taking a semester off."

"Oh?"

She made a little face. "I'm trying to decide what I want to do. College bores me."

"Maybe you're taking the wrong courses."

I spoke absently, but she responded immediately, "That's what I think. Mom and Dad want me to take business and hotel management."

"Ah."

"But...I mean, I love it here, but..."

"You don't want to spend the rest of your life running the Blue Heron Lodge?"

She nodded sheepishly.

"What did Peaches think about that?" I inquired. "You said you showed her your work?"

"I *did*?"

"Maybe it was your mom." I watched her expression. "She said Peaches was very encouraging."

"Mom said *that*?" Debbie gazed at me, puzzled.

"She did, yeah. Well, maybe that was a mother's pride talking—"

"No, Peaches was great," Debbie said quickly. "She said wonderful things about my writing. She said I should be writing full-time, not standing behind a check-in counter."

"Ah." I began to understand some of Rita's fury. "Well, you could do both, right?"

"Not really. Peaches was saying that in order to write, you had to have something to write about. Life experiences."

I knew where this was going. "And Peaches didn't think you could get life experiences here or in college?"

"She said college is for the people who want to teach, not people who want to *do*."

Peaches was a freaking idiot. I said mildly, "Don't you need to learn *how* to do something before you start trying to do it?"

She shook her head. "The best way is to jump in and start doing it. That was what Peaches said."

"Yeah, well, judging by the number of drownings each year, I'm not sure that always works."

Debbie frowned disapproval at this heresy. I said, "So did Peaches have a suggestion about how you could get life experiences?"

"She thought I should move to New York because that's where the publishing industry is centered, and maybe I could get a job as an editor's assistant somewhere. She said she'd put in a good word for me."

I swallowed. "Did she?"

Debbie nodded. "That way I'd be able to work with the best writers while I was working on my own book."

"Are you working on a book?"

"Not yet. But I would be once I got to New York."

I wondered if my eyes were actually spinning or if it only felt that way. "Well, I can't blame your mom for killing her," I said.

Debbie's expression never changed, and I was relieved to discover I had only thought the words, not said them—sincere though they were. I wondered if Peaches had planned to use Debbie for creative harvesting or if she'd merely carelessly tossed off the advice never thinking—or worrying—of the ramifications if Debbie followed it.

"I guess that's what your mom was upset about that night she argued with Peaches."

Debbie nodded unhappily.

"Well, if it makes you feel any better, your mom thinks you're talented too."

"Yeah, but that's Mom. Peaches *knew*." She gave a little gulp, her eyes tearing as she remembered the tragic loss of Peaches.

"Did J.X. ask you any questions about...anything?"

"He asked me about the glass in Ms. Ving's room. The one that was supposed to have an earring in it." Her eyes met mine. "There was no earring."

"It's okay." I touched my earlobe. "I found it."

"*Oh.*"

"Nothing else? He didn't ask you about Peaches?"

"Well..." She looked vague. "Just if I'd seen anything or had any ideas about who might have hurt her." She darted me a guilty look indicating her suspicions had been focused on me.

So J.X. had either not included Rita or Edgar in his conjectures, or he had kept those conjectures from Debbie.

What was I missing? There had to be something I was overlooking.

Yes, the lodge was a big place, and the grounds were spread out, but the killer would not have limitless time in which to act. The conference guests were jumpy and alert at this point. No one could risk disappearing for hours on end. If J.X. was alive— if he wasn't buried out behind some shed—he had to be nearby. But where?

I stared unseeingly at the pale oak paneling, the black and white photos of the lodge...vineyards and wine vats and grape pickers...

I said slowly, "Is there a wine cellar here?"

"Sure."

"Could I see it?"

She stared at me. "Why?"

I smiled—an effect probably similar to the Grinch trying to reassure Cindy Lou Who that he wasn't stealing Christmas. "I'm a writer. I'm always looking for settings for my stories."

She wasn't buying it.

I abandoned all pretense and hit her with the truth. She wanted to experience life? Well, here was a big slice of it: fear and loss. "The truth is, I'm running out of places to look for J.X., and I'm getting desperate. We didn't search the lodge itself. It's the only place left I can think of."

Debbie bit her lip. "He wouldn't be here in the lodge."

"Did you ever read a story by Poe called 'The Purloined Letter'?"

"No."

My eyes widened. Maybe this higher education thing was a waste of time. What *were* they having these kids read?

"The point of the story is that sometimes the best way to hide something is in plain sight."

She considered this. "But guests aren't supposed to go down to the cellar. It's part of the original structure, and a lot of it isn't used anymore. It's not in good shape."

"I won't tell if you won't."

The law-abiding tyke disapproved of that suggestion. "We should probably ask Mom or Dad."

"Let's not," I said quickly. "Your mom doesn't like me, and your dad already thinks I'm a nut after the thing at the icehouse."

I could see by her expression that Edgar had indeed had colorful things to say about me dragging him down to the icehouse.

"Welllll…"

"If you do this for me, I'll look at your manuscript when it's finished, and I'll give you all the free advice you want."

She looked astonished. "Are *you* published?"

CHAPTER TWENTY-FIVE

"The door is supposed to stay locked when we have people staying at the lodge," Debbie whispered to me, "but we all forget."

We were standing in a rough-hewn stairwell a few feet from the back door leading to the kitchen. The wine cellar entrance was down a short flight of outside steps. The stone stairwell hid us from casual observers, but if anyone came hunting us it would be hard to explain what we were doing lurking outside the wine cellar door.

Debbie clipped the key ring on her belt and pushed the heavy door open, feeling around inside for a light switch. "The cellar runs the full length of the lodge," she said. "It's huge. But we only use the racks nearest the door now. That's plenty of room for us these days."

"You don't use it for general storage?"

"No. It's not convenient to have to run outside every time we need a fresh jug of milk. There are two pantries and a small storeroom inside the lodge. We keep the wine and the rest of the booze down here." Her voice echoed hollowly as she started down the narrow staircase.

I followed slowly. The drop in temperature was noticeable. Fifty-five degrees for storing red wine, wasn't it? And less for white. I wasn't a wine drinker myself, but I'd done quite a bit of research for *Last Call for Miss Butterwith*.

The room immediately below us was lined with redwood racks. It was neatly laid out and carefully organized, the red bottles from the ceiling to the floor on one side, the white on the other end of the room. An additional shelf held a quantity of hard alcohol: whiskies, gins, bourbons, etc. A large empty vat sat in the center of the room. An arched doorway led off to a shadowy interior.

Halfway down the steps, Debbie halted. "What was that?"

"What was what?"

She stood frozen in alarm.

I heard it too—Rita bellowing for her daughter from the kitchen like Demeter trying to recall Persephone from the Underworld.

"Shit," Debbie exclaimed. She started up the stairs again, edging past me. "I'll be right back." She flew up the steps and out the door, easing it shut behind her.

I could hear her muffled yell in response to Rita.

I waited, but there were no further developments, so Debbie must have successfully diverted Rita. Good. Diverting Rita was exactly what I wanted to have happen.

I went the rest of the way down the stairs and looked around. As prisons went, I could think of worse places to be locked up. There was a nice selection of liqueurs too, everything from Campari to X-Rated Fusion. If J.X. was here, he would not be in this part of the cellar, though. He'd be held in one of the unused sections.

"J.X.?" I called.

I didn't really expect an answer, so when I heard an indefinable rustling sound from one of the next rooms, I stopped dead. My heart, however, kept going like the Energizer bunny... going and going and going...

Over the rushing in my ears, I listened feverishly, trying to pinpoint the sound.

"J.X.?" I called more softly. Switching on my flashlight, I started through the arched doorway. Light from the main room spilled into the adjoining room, casting severe drunken shadows over more shelving units half-filled with glinting bottles. Another arched doorway led to yet another room.

Something shone near the doorway. I picked it up. A key. One of those thick, patented Schlage keys. I recognized it because I'd had the house rekeyed after David had exited stage left with Dicky.

I remembered J.X. saying he had dropped a key next to Peaches' body. Of course, it could be anyone's key.

Tucking the key in my pocket, I went through the next arched doorway. The light from the main room did not reach this far, and the darkness was nearly complete. My flashlight beam played over still more shelving units—these were empty. A large wrought iron gate leaned against one wall. There was a quantity of empty fiberglass urns.

I shone my flashlight around. This was not a contained room like the two previous spaces. A long unfinished open stretch was broken only by ugly pillars and open beams. Several yards down I could make out more empty shelving units, old wooden crates, and a pyramid of old-fashioned casks. Cobwebs trailed gracefully from the open beams like gauzy draperies.

I directed my flashlight beam to the stone floor, and time seemed to stand still. There, like fresh tracks in new-fallen snow, was the perfect outline of footprints in the thick velvety dust. Footprints coming and footprints going. More going than coming.

Boot prints, unless I missed my guess. I'd opened my mouth to call out, but now I shut it.

I followed the path of the footprints in the dust straight down the length of the cellar, my heart thudding in a mixture of dread and hope. The only sound was the scrape of my own boots on the stone floor. I paced the rough length of several large rooms, about one hundred and sixty feet.

That odd stirring noise caught my ears once more, and I aimed the beam across from me. The bright white ray caught the gleam of eyes and teeth, and I nearly dropped the light.

I managed to hang on to it, but I think my heart literally stopped while my brain fought to make sense of what it was seeing...

A bear.

A grizzly bear.

A *stuffed* grizzly bear, maybe eight feet tall—taller than me even without the stand it was mounted on. The paws alone were the size of my head. The stained, outstretched claws were bigger than my fingers. The snarling muzzle displayed ferocious yellow teeth; the black eyes seemed to be staring right at me.

"Jesus fucking Christ," I said faintly, and the echo of my voice rolled softly down the empty vault.

Lowering the flashlight beam to the floor, I saw that the footprints turned off to the left and vanished behind another stack of barrels. As I started forward again, I heard the distinct whisper of footsteps. I wheeled, my flashlight playing over the rough coat of the bear and catching movement. I swung the light.

Nothing moved.

I waited, listening over the thunder in my ears.

It could have been a mouse. A rat. But no rat or mouse made those footprints in the dust. Or dropped his house key. I waited more endless seconds.

Not so much as a shadow flickered. A growing unease was creepy-crawling up and down my spine, but I was not turning back until I'd seen what lay behind that stack of barrels.

Illogically, the longer I waited and nothing happened, the more convinced I became that someone was in the cellar with me...standing a few yards away, hiding in the shadows behind the broken shelving. I could *feel* that I was being watched.

I nearly popped a blood vessel at the muffled and eerie moan behind me. I swung the light, the white circle jittering its way over barrels and wall. Out of the corner of my eye I spied movement to my right, but I could only deal with one threat at a time, and the sound to the left indicated the more immediate danger.

It also gave me hope.

I darted a quick look around the wall of barrels. Was there a stirring in the darkness? A pool of shade on the floor still darker than the surrounding shadows?

I shone the light. A pile of tumbled clothes...that resolved itself into dusty boots, rope, filthy jeans, a formerly white shirt...a ghostly face with silver duct tape across the mouth.

"Oh God," someone cried—and dimly I knew it was me. I threw myself down beside J.X., dropping the flashlight as I checked him over with frantic hands. He was warm—he was breathing—he was still alive. But his eyes were closed; he wasn't conscious. I felt gently over his skull and found a sticky patch on the back of his head.

I propped the flashlight on a box so I could see what I was doing, and eased the tape from over J.X.'s mouth, trying not to take too much of his beard or skin with it. And then—God knows what gripped me—I covered his mouth with my own. His lips were dry and chapped, and he tasted terrible. No kiss was ever as sweet. He was breathing, alive, and that was all that mattered then.

His eyelashes stirred and lifted. He blinked at me dazedly.

"You're okay," I said, working the knots at the ropes around his wrists. "You're going to be fine. I just have to get you out of here."

His mouth worked. "Light's...in...my eyes..." he managed huskily.

I rolled the flashlight away, still clumsily plucking at the knotted rope. "God *damn* it. Who the hell tied this?"

"Kit..."

"Don't talk. It's okay. I've almost got it." I was babbling. I don't think I could have shut up to save my life. "I hope to hell you've had your tetanus shots because you've been lying here with an open wound in a pile of dust for—for the longest fucking day of my life." I jumped up and started yelling, "Help! *Help!*"

I never said *I* was the hero of this story. If there was a hero, he was lying at my feet trying to get a word in between my shouts.

"*Kit*...calm...the hell...down," J.X. said faintly, finally managing to make himself heard.

I dropped down beside him again and finished untying his arms. The rope fell away, and he rolled onto his knees, groaning and swearing as circulation returned. I rubbed his arms, yelling frantically all the while.

"Where *are* you?" Debbie's voice reached me.

"*Here*," I cried. "I found him. Go get help."

"Do you mind...not yelling in my ear?" J.X. creaked. He gave up trying to get to his feet and rolled back on his side, ineffectually chafing his wrists.

I crawled down to untie the rope around his legs. "Did you see who hit you?"

He moved his head slightly in the negative. His eyes were closed again. I got the rope off his legs as a dozen flashlight beams stabbed into the darkness and the cellar was flooded with people calling out to me.

"Good God Almighty," Edgar exclaimed, reaching us. Debbie was with him, and the skeleton kitchen staff was right behind, followed by George and an assortment of pink ladies.

"He's alive," I told them—unnecessarily since J.X. was feebly trying to push himself upright again. I got hold of him. "Lie still, will you?"

He subsided against me, his face dropping against my shoulder. He swore indistinctly.

"Well, I guess you were right," Edgar told me, grimly. "I should have thought of this place myself." He cleared his throat. "I have to admit I thought..."

"Yeah." I bent my head to J.X.'s ear. "You'll be interested to hear that you're now everyone's favorite murder suspect."

His eyes, which had been closed—giving him a misleadingly defenseless look—popped open.

There were more than enough helping hands, so I'm not sure why it was impossible for me to let go of J.X. as he was lifted to his feet and then pretty much carried out of the cellar. Granted, it wasn't all one-sided. He was gripping my hand back, but we had to let go in order for them to lug him up the stairs. I followed the rescue party slowly, my legs unsteady with reaction.

It wasn't until we found him that I realized how very much I'd feared J.X. was dead.

Hauling my weary carcass up the stairs, I paused and stared down at the motionless room below. Nothing stirred.

I turned at last and trailed the sound of voices through the kitchen to the bar where J.X. was being tended to by a crowd of ministering angels—and Rita. Granted, Rita's part was mostly to stand there and make acerbic comments about blood being dripped on her clean floor. There was not a lot of blood, though the basin of water on the table was a definite pink. One of the women—an emergency room doctor in real life—was swabbing J.X.'s battered head. "Looks like you need a couple of stitches," she pronounced at last.

"We've got medical supplies," Rita said, and she pushed past Edgar and the rest of us who had formed a giant horseshoe around J.X.

"Did you see who hit you?" Mindy demanded.

"How could he? He was hit on the back of the head," one bright young thing offered.

J.X. gave her a funny look, quickly concealed. "I don't remember a damn thing," he said wearily. "The last thing I remember was…" His gaze fell on me standing at the end of the table. The faintest color rose in his face.

I felt blood warming my own cheeks in response. Not because we'd had sex—well, not entirely—but because of the asinine way I'd behaved afterward.

"…was walking out to the cabins with Christopher," J.X. concluded finally.

As though synchronized, nearly fifty heads turned my way. I held up a hand. "Don't bother to say it. I'll go quietly. I could use a nap about now."

Rita, returning with a professional-looking first-aid kit, said, "What sense does that make? You're the one who found him." To J.X. she said, "You never want to see a fuss like the one this bast—er—guy made over you going missing."

Now I really was red. J.X. studied me soberly while the doctor took the first-aid kit and began sorting through supplies.

"Tell him about the icehouse, Christopher," Espie put in jovially.

"There's nothing to tell."

That brought another round of those annoying giggles.

It was funny how quick everyone was to forget that less than an hour earlier most of them had been convinced J.X. was the killer. Now, in their relief to find him alive and mostly unharmed, not only had their suspicions been discarded, it seemed to me that everyone was well on their way to forgetting two people had died and a murderer was still on the loose.

Rita said dourly, "Your buddy dragged Edgar down to the icehouse and insisted he open it up to make sure you weren't tied up inside."

More laughter from the handful of people who hadn't yet been regaled with my idiotic adventures. J.X. didn't look like he found it all that funny—which I appreciated.

Testily, I said, "Okay, maybe I had the wrong location, but he *was* being held prisoner. I wasn't wrong about that."

"Don't get in a huff. We're teasing you," Espie said, trying to placate. "We're happy."

"Me too," I said. "Never happier. But doesn't anyone wonder why J.X. wasn't killed?"

There was one of those silences that often seemed to greet my comments.

J.X.'s gaze held mine. "Why do *you* think I wasn't killed?"

Suddenly it was the two of us talking—as though we were the only people in the room. "Because you're an ex-cop and everyone knows what happens to cop killers?" He blinked at me, mulling this over. "Or maybe the killer doesn't hate you the same way he or she hated Peaches and Krass? Maybe you were simply put out of the way to stop you from snooping around?"

"Maybe she likes your books," someone suggested.

"Or he," someone else put in.

More laughter. J.X. was still studying me in the owlish way of the semi-concussed.

"You should lie down when we get finished here," the lady doctor told him.

He nodded vaguely and felt the back of his head with cautious fingertips. She waved his fingers aside and began swabbing his scalp.

I really did not want to see J.X.'s head sewn up, but I couldn't seem to make myself walk away.

"Any word from the sheriff's department?" he asked Edgar, who had started to turn away from the crowd in the bar.

Edgar paused, shaking his head. "The good news is the wind blew the fog away. The bad news is the wind makes it impossible to land a helicopter."

There were assorted moans and groans from everyone. Edgar and Rita proceeded to reassure their unwilling guests that there was plenty of food and drink, and that, while they couldn't feed and house everyone for free indefinitely, they could certainly cover one more night gratis.

"We have jobs. We have *lives*," one woman protested.

"So far," someone else muttered.

I wasn't sure what they expected our hosts to do about either of those things. I imagined Edgar and Rita couldn't wait to see the last of us. I listened without really hearing the discussion around me. Abruptly, I felt drained...let down. The adrenaline that had kept me moving while we hunted for J.X. was a memory now. A not very pleasant memory.

For a few more minutes I watched the ladies fussing pleasantly over J.X. Watched him smiling sheepishly, responding as best he could.

Edging back through the crowd, I left the bar. I didn't have a direction in mind, but I knew that I couldn't stand there any longer staring at J.X.

Someone else had the same idea and was walking down the hall ahead of me. I recognized Rachel's distinctive sashay. Hearing footsteps behind her, she turned warily, and then relaxed.

"Oh, it's you." She didn't exactly smile, but her expression was one of grudging approval. "Good work, Christopher."

"Thanks." It seemed an odd thing to take credit for—or maybe I was too tired to view it normally.

"What made you look down in the cellar?"

"Lucky guess. It was the only place I could think of that we hadn't checked yet."

She nodded thoughtfully. "Maybe this trip has been good for you after all."

"Ha. Well, for the record, the next time you ask me to attend any kind of writing conference or convention, the answer is no." I added, "Assuming you're still representing me."

She stiffened. "What does that mean? Are you firing me?"

I'd sort of meant it the other way around, but her attitude intrigued me—and gave me an opening.

"It depends. What exactly did Peaches have on you?"

Expressionless, she stared at me for several seconds. Then she said, "We can't talk about this here. Come up to my room."

CHAPTER TWENTY-SIX

Rachel lit a cigarette and went over to the window, shoving it open. Rain-scented air blew the rust-colored draperies out and sucked them back. She took a couple of nervous puffs and then said, "You're happy with your representation, right? I've never given you cause to doubt my commitment to your career?"

"Are we counting this weekend?"

She gave me a bleak-eyed look. "Yes, we *are* counting this weekend. How could I know it would turn into *Friday the 13th*? I was striving to do what's best for you."

"Okay. I accept that. And, yes, I'm happy with my representation." I added, "Although I think you are seriously deluded when it comes to stories involving either kitten heels or demons. However, I accept that you have my best interests at heart. When it comes to my career at least."

She considered that last reflectively. "They aren't always compatible," she admitted. "I don't think living with David was good for your writing."

"Now you tell me. I don't think living with David was particularly good for me on any level."

I could tell that she wasn't really listening. "What I'm about to tell you will ruin my career if it ever gets out."

I nodded. There seemed to be a lot of that going around this weekend.

Rachel took another nervous puff on her cigarette, before shooting me a sideways glance. "I'm not English. I wasn't born in Hong Kong, British or otherwise."

"I did wonder," I admitted. "Your accent keeps slipping. I never noticed before. Probably because we never spent any real time together before."

"I was actually born in San Francisco. I went to San Francisco State University. That's where I met Patty. Peaches, I mean."

Now things began to make sense—including her enthusiasm for my reinventing myself. "Someone else who made up her history? Is it something in the air up here?" I thought it over. "Okay. I guess I can live with not having an English agent. I mean, it was kind of cool and cosmopolitan, but—"

"That's not the confession," she said painfully. "Or, rather, it is partly the confession, but…" She drew on the cigarette again. "All right. Here it is. After college I got into some trouble. I'm not going to try and make excuses. I was young and stupid."

"Is *that* the confession?" I inquired when she didn't continue. "Because a *lot* of people are young and stupid. Personally, I don't think it's as serious an offense as old and stupid."

"I went to prison for embezzlement."

"Oh." My agent was a former embezzler. Yes, I could see how that might put a crimp in our working relationship.

"It was right after college. I was working as the receptionist at a high-end auto body repair shop. I was responsible for the petty cash and for making bank deposits." She closed her eyes and shook her head. Seconds passed. She opened her eyes and stared right at me. "Anyway. I did my time, and I swear to you, I have never since so much as taken a penny that didn't belong to me. I don't even pick change up off the sidewalk."

"Me either. You don't know *where* it's been…"

She waited for me to get to it, and I was thinking rapidly while my mouth flapped. Because it *was* serious. She was an ex-crook, and I was trusting her with my livelihood. What was left of it.

At last, I said, "Okay, Rachel. I believe you. Everything you've ever sent me matches the publisher's royalty statements to the penny, and as you know, I do pay close attention to these things. You've been my agent for eight years, and you're a hell of a lot better than the first guy I had." I met her gaze, and I could read the strain there. "I'm not going to terminate our relationship."

She relaxed a fraction. "Thank you. But you can see why everyone might not feel the same way?"

"Oh, yeah. It's not information I would share. Is prison where you hooked up with Espie?"

She nodded. "We became friends. We were enrolled in one of those prison writing courses. I figured out right away that as much as I loved books and storytelling, I didn't have what it takes to be a writer. Espie did. And I thought maybe I would be good at the business side of it. And I am. Very good at it."

"You are," I agreed. "For the record, you've never threatened to break anyone's legs, right?"

She grimaced.

"I'm joking. Not that I would have cared if you'd broken Krass's legs."

"I told you the truth," she said quickly. "I went for a walk that morning, and I came on you standing over his body. I had nothing to do with his death."

"I believe you," I said. "I can't quite see you splitting some-one's head open with an axe. I think poison would be more your style. Or maybe a little jeweled dagger between the ribs."

"You have a ghoulish sense of humor."

"I didn't use to. I think it's this weekend." I was silent, considering.

Watching me narrowly, Rachel asked, "What's the matter?"

"Peaches knew the truth about your prison record, obvi-ously. That's what she was blackmailing you with. If you didn't hand Espie's book over, she was going to ruin you by exposing your past."

Rachel stubbed out her cigarette in a drinking glass. "Yes. About a year after I moved to New York, I ran into her." Her smile was caustic. "I was still young enough, naïve enough, to think you could be honest with people."

"You can be honest with some people, Rachel. You have to use discretion."

She flicked me a wry look. "Hm. Well, at least these days I'm better about judging people. Anyway, I ran into Peaches, and it turned out that she was writing a book. I'd managed to sell Espie's novel to Steven Krass at Gardener and Britain, so I thought I was a hot-shot literary agent." She shook her head. "God help me. But you have to understand. Peaches was a world-class manipulator."

"And you had some kind of an affair?"

"I have worse luck than you when it comes to relationships."

Stung, I said, "You know, for the record, I was in a stable relationship for ten years."

"It was only stable because you were too preoccupied with your career to do anything about David's philandering."

"At least he wasn't a blackmailing plagiarist. *Anyway*, you and Peaches came together over cosmopolitans and royalty clauses, and you spilled the beans about your summer at Camp Gotchabadgirl, and when she ripped off Espie's first novel, there wasn't anything you could do about it without wrecking your budding career."

Rachel nodded dully.

"Peaches moved on up the food chain and, I'm guessing, you gave each other a wide berth in the goldfish bowl that is New York publishing—until this weekend when you, Espie, Peaches, and Krass were all thrown together again. Peaches, who had more nerve than sense, decided to replay her greatest hit and rip Espie off again by threatening you with exposure if you didn't give her a peek at this magnum opus. How am I doing so far?"

She said sarcastically, "Did you ever think of writing mysteries?"

"Funny. Funny, funny, girl," I said. "So the question is, what did you tell Peaches? How did you plan to stall her?"

"What I didn't do was kill her."

"I know."

"How do you know?" she asked suspiciously.

I gave her a lopsided grin. "Well, I'm sorry to say it's not my faith in your better nature. You aren't tall enough to have slammed Peaches over the head with a blunt instrument. You could have kneecapped her without problem, but—"

"Most amusing, Christopher." She was glaring.

"There's no way you could carry her, and I don't think you're strong enough to have dragged her any distance. It's possible you could have brained Krass since he was sitting down when he was hit, but no way in hell could you have knocked J.X.

out unless you stood on a stool to do it, and you couldn't have dragged him anywhere."

"I'm touched by your belief in me."

"Hey, I've got plenty of belief in you. I'm not phoning William Morris to pitch my new Regency P.I. demon project, am I?"

She blushed and looked away.

I asked, "Are you sure Espie had no idea what was going on between you and Peaches? Don't you think she could probably put two and two together pretty fast?"

"Espie wouldn't..."

Curiously, I watched her trail into silence. She said, "Espie couldn't have...for the same reasons you think I couldn't have."

"Espie's taller than you—nearly everyone is—and she's a lot stronger than you. Not to mention the fact that she's got the stomach for violence, which I don't think you do."

Rachel was shaking her head, rejecting this. "I know her. She wouldn't commit murder. The other time...was an accident. She was a kid, and she was...enraged. She didn't understand the consequences."

"I think she'd have been pretty enraged if she'd known what Peaches was up to."

"She didn't, though."

"You sound pretty sure."

Rachel's face twisted. "I am. Because she was angry with me the next morning. She thought...Peaches had propositioned me."

"She did kind of."

"Yes, but not that way. Someone was with Peaches that night, and Espie thought it was me because she had heard us arguing."

Ah-ha, Watson. The return of the mysterious gentleman who belonged to the boots Mindy had spied at the foot of Peach's bed. It looked more and more like Mr. XO had been the last person to see Peaches alive.

* * * * *

It really wasn't my problem, was it? Two unpleasant and probably highly deserving people had been violently dispatched. But since I was no longer in the front running for prime suspect, and since J.X. had been found safe and relatively sound, it seemed to me to be a very good time to hang up my deerstalker. Before the killer decided to hang me up.

All I had to do was hole up in my cabin until the rescue teams arrived, and then I could go back to my quiet, dull existence and decide whether I really had it in me to write about demons and whether I should fight David for possession of the player piano currently sitting in our—my—den.

It was, in fact, the course of least resistance—and what was wrong with that? For all those sententious speeches I had Miss B. deliver at the end of each novel, some people deserved killing.

The problem with murder was that it was contagious. Like eating potato chips, it was hard to stop at one—if only because concealing the first murder often led to a second and third murder. And while I sympathized with someone wanting to deliver Peaches her just reward—and maybe even Krass—I didn't appreciate the attempt at sticking me with a murder rap. And I really didn't appreciate someone trying to do away with

J.X. Not that there hadn't been times when I'd considered it myself. Still...

Yeah.

So after I left Rachel's room, I didn't go back to the bar. I didn't want to ask any more questions, I didn't want to see the uneasy way people watched each other, I didn't want to hear any more lies—

I left the lodge and walked back through the silver, shivery rain to my cabin. I locked myself in, shoved the desk against the door, and built up the fire in the grate. I undressed and got into bed and told myself to go to sleep.

The room gradually warmed, and the shadows softened and blurred.

I jerked awake. Someone was pounding hard on the door. Jackknifing up into sitting position, I sat rigid, heart hammering. My gaze fell on the poker conveniently placed beside the bed, and I rolled out of bed, snatching it up.

"Kit? Can you hear me? Kit?"

Poker poised, I paused. Not a line I would have written myself, but rather accurate under the circumstances.

"Kit."

"J.X.?"

"Who do you—? Open the goddamned door," he yelled, sounding uncharacteristically bad-tempered. I went to the window, peered out, and sure enough J.X. was staring up at the stormy skies with an expression that clearly read, *why me?*

I shoved the desk away from the door and unbolted it.

J.X. pushed the door open. "I thought something had happened to you. What the hell are you doing in here? Rearranging the furniture?" He squeezed past the desk and slammed the door shut. Without looking at me, he slid the bolt.

My heart unaccountably sped up. "Do you mind? I was sleeping."

He turned then. "*Again?* Are you sure you don't have sleeping sickness?"

"What do you mean, *again*? Most people do try to schedule a little shut-eye into every twenty-four hours."

We were glaring at each other, and I suddenly wondered why. Was it simply because we didn't know how to relate to each other if we weren't arguing? The silence between us was abrupt and awkward.

J.X. tore his gaze from me and looked at the bed with the rumpled sheets and blankets. His profile was unreasonably grim. Maybe he was in pain. There was a neatly taped square of white gauze on the back of his head. He was certainly pale, and there were shadows beneath his eyes. I probably didn't look much better.

"Aren't you supposed to be lying down?" In case that sounded like maybe I wanted him lying down with *me*, I added aggressively, "What are you doing here?"

"Why did you leave the lodge? It's not safe down here."

"It's not safe up there either."

"It's safer there than it is here."

"I felt perfectly safe until two minutes ago when you woke me out of a peaceful sleep."

"Which goes to show how much you know."

Luckily testosterone is not flammable, so the cabin did not spontaneously combust while we squared off.

Then J.X. had to go and spoil all our fun by saying calmly, "You didn't give me a chance to thank you."

"No thanks necessary," I clipped. "It's all part of the service."

Damn it. He was looking at me in that particular way of his, his dark eyes a little quizzical, his mouth tugging into a reluctant smile. Why did he have to do that? It was so much easier when we were hassling each other.

"I owe you an apology," he said.

"Probably." I added, "But I actually *am* an egotistical, self-centered prick. I just...don't approve of murder. On general principles."

"I understand." He reached a hand out and brushed my bare shoulder. "You're getting goose bumps."

"Fancy that," I exclaimed mockingly. "It must be *you*. It can't possibly have anything to do with the fact that it's forty degrees in he—"

His hand closed on my shoulder, and he drew me forward. He said softly, "Let me warm you up."

CHAPTER TWENTY-SEVEN

"Maybe this isn't such a good idea," I said as he stepped out of his jeans—and I don't think Superman ever shed his clothes as fast or looked as gorgeous naked. "The sex is nice, but we seem to singe our eyebrows on the afterglow."

He glanced up smiling, and the sweetness of that smile literally stopped the breath in my throat. "Don't worry. I'll take good care of you."

My swallow was audible.

He straightened, took my hand, and led me to the disheveled bed. I lay down, and then I sat up again. "Really," I said. "This isn't necessary. It just confuses everything."

"What are you confused about?" He sat next to me and reached out, brushing the hair out of my eyes.

"Well, you know. Various points. Anyway, you probably have a concussion," I told him. "I'm sure you're not up to this."

He chuckled and glanced down meaningfully. Apparently he was up to it.

"Still…"

"Here," he said suddenly brisk. "Let's get under the covers. You're shaking."

I dived gratefully under the covers, wrapping myself modestly up to my chin. He stretched out beside me, brown and muscular against the sheets as he made himself comfortable. He propped his head on his hand. He was still smiling that knowing smile, and it was beginning to alarm the hell out of me.

"When I came to, you were kissing me," he remarked.

"I…uh…thought you weren't breathing. I was giving artificial respiration."

He laughed, his teeth very white. "Debbie said you were crying before you bribed her to let you into the cellar."

"I wasn't *crying*," I returned irritably. "I'm coming down with a head cold."

"No wonder in this weather." His breath tickled my cheek. Reaching over, he hauled me into his arms. I was too nonplussed to object—not that I'd have really wanted to object. His soft-haired chest thrust hard and arrogantly against my own. Every satiny muscular inch of him was shockingly, beautifully hot. "Jesus, you really are half-frozen." He pulled me closer still.

We lay there for long moments. Face pressed into the curve of his neck, I was forced to admit that this was…well, bizarre. I wondered if I was dreaming and reached around him to pinch the back of my hand.

"What are you doing?" he asked drowsily.

I raised my head. "Are you going to sleep?"

"Just closing my eyes for a sec…" He shifted, maneuvering so that my head was comfortably tucked under his chin. I curled one arm beneath the pillow cushioning our heads, cautiously wrapped the other around his lean waist. He moved one leg between my own, capturing my feet between his.

"Cold feet…"

"Warm hands," I whispered. And his hands were very warm, moving against the small of my back in slower and slower circles.

"Should you be sleeping with a concussion?"

"I've already woken up twice since I got hit…"

He let it trail, breathing softly and moistly into my ear. His half-hard cock was nestled into my groin, bare hot limbs twined with my own. The arms holding me slackened as he dropped into sleep.

My own cock was nudging him impolitely, but that was clearly going to have to wait.

I blinked wonderingly into the soft gloom. Obviously he'd been knocked over the head a lot harder than anyone had imagined…

It was one of the nicest dreams I'd had in a very long time. No arguing, no yelling, no David at all. A delightful flush and sense of well-being…a dawning awareness of a pleasure so keen it was almost poignant.

Yep, something felt really, really good…

I opened my eyes to a soft and unthreatening darkness—the shine of eyes and smiling teeth and the pleasurable knowledge that someone's warming, knowing hand was on me, a skimming, tugging, glissade up and down—and I was responding, my cock filling in slow, sweet pulses. To save my life, I couldn't bite back the little moan of gladness as that hard but subtle hand took me right to the edge and held me there, precisely balanced on the knife-edge of joyous release.

J.X.'s mouth came down on mine, the Van Dyke beard as silky soft as a baby's hair. I shuddered, and he murmured gentle indeterminate noises. His tongue flicked my lips, and I opened to him, permitting that delicate exploration of teeth and tongue—unsettlingly, his taste was already well-known to me, a budding addiction.

All the while his hand held me positioned on that dizzying final step, reeling but not allowed to fall. His other hand nestled my balls, squeezing gently, then lightly, lightly scratching with his fingernails, and I bucked a little, making a desperate sound in the back of my throat. That combination of mouth and hands—exquisite torture.

I reached, relieved to find him right there, silky cropped hair, neat ears, strong neck, broad shoulders—my fingers fluttered over hair and skin and muscle, urging, needing—

His hand tightened, increased the tempo, and pressure was building quite unbearably inside me—like giddy laughter, like a little kid on a swing, lilting higher and higher toward the sky, over the treetops, sailing up, giggling irrepressibly at the rush—

"Oh, Christ…" I said against his mouth.

I began to come, white-hot heartbeats spilling over his hand, splashing my belly and tensed thighs. There was a sharp, sweet smell mixed with the scent of rain and naked skin, and all the wires holding me tight snapped, and I was free…floating free, free falling…

I was laughing—and J.X. was laughing too. What the hell were we laughing at? But suddenly everything was light and lovely…and very funny. He dropped back into the sheets beside me, and we lay there panting and chuckling.

"I'm not married," he told me when we had caught our breath and were tangled warmly in each other's arms again.

"No?"

His laughter died. His voice was edged. "You honest to God think I'd *cheat*?"

I could have turned the question on him, but maybe I'd learned something over the past couple of days after all. "It's hard to imagine."

He grunted. Finally he said, "I *was* married, but it wasn't a real marriage. My kid brother, Alex..." He drew a sharp breath, and I turned to study his face. There was a quiet, controlled pain there. "He was killed in Iraq."

"I'm sorry."

He nodded. "Anyway...his girlfriend, Nina, was pregnant. Our families are...very traditional, very conservative. So Nina and I married."

Holy guacamole. I thought that kind of thing only happened in chick flicks and Harlequin romances. "To give the baby a name?"

"That, yes. But for Nina's sake too—and Alex's. He'd have married her if he'd known. Anyway...when Gage—my nephew—turned three, we divorced. I still spend a lot of time with them, but it was never a genuine marriage. It's not like I ever lived there or anything. I can't believe you thought I'd—"

"Hey, first of all, I didn't. Others insisted to me that you were married. Secondly, you *did* marry, so...it's not like everyone was totally off base."

"But if anyone should have known my...my inclinations..."

In an effort to move the conversation away from these awkward channels, I said, "Does your very conservative, very traditional family know you're gay?"

"They know," he said austerely. "It's not something that's ever discussed."

That sounded fairly forbidding. I was mulling it over when he turned his head and kissed my shoulder.

"So why were you scared?" he asked.

"What?"

"The last time I was here, you said the reason you never returned my phone calls or emails—"

"Oh." I met his eyes. "Right. Look…it's not like you're going to like me better after you hear this."

"Tell me anyway."

I sighed. "You already know that the weekend of the conference in DC I was…"

"Vulnerable."

I made a face. "I guess. Anyway—" I met his gaze. His eyes were dark and serious. "That weekend was…I'm not kidding when I say you might have saved my life. But when I got home, David was waiting, and he was distraught, apologetic, willing to do anything to put things right. And…I thought I loved him. I'd thought myself in love with him for three years, so I couldn't believe that just like that it was over for me and I'd…that I could feel that for someone else so quickly…"

He didn't say anything.

I explained painstakingly, "It didn't seem realistic. It didn't seem practical. I thought I was mistaking lust for…something else." It was very hard to hold his gaze. "I panicked, lost my nerve."

"You should have told me."

"Yeah, I should have. But I wasn't sure if I saw you again, spoke to you again, that I could break it off with you."

He smiled faintly, derisively. "And what happened with David?"

"He ran off with my PA. And if you laugh at me, I'll kill you."

"It's not particularly funny," he said. "We lost ten years."

I said carefully, "When you say we lost ten years, are you implying—or am I inferring—that there might be some years left?"

"I don't know. We still have to survive the rest of the weekend." He didn't appear to be entirely kidding.

"The weekend is over," I protested. "All we have to do is wait until the relief arrives. That can't be many more hours."

"You think we're going to be permitted to hide out here till the sheriffs show up?"

"Yes."

"Kit."

"Well, why not?"

"You know why not. Because the killer knows that you know."

"I don't know *anything*."

He was eyeing me steadily.

"I don't know for sure," I said weakly.

"But you've narrowed the possibilities down to what... two? Three suspects?"

I said evasively, "That's not the same as being able to prove it."

"The killer is not going to want you trotting to the sheriffs with your suspicions. Nor is he or she going to necessarily believe that I don't remember anything about when I got hit."

"Do you remember anything?"

"Some. More than I let on at the lodge."

"Do you know who hit you?"

"I've got a pretty good idea."

I sighed. "I think we should leave it alone."

"You're talking to the wrong person. I'm not in the leave-it-alone business."

"You're not a cop anymore. You could leave it alone. It's not like either of them were a great loss to humanity."

"Is that really the point?"

"Isn't it?"

He said, "Do we discourage vigilantism to protect the bad guys or for the sake of the good guys?"

"I'm not endorsing vigilantism. I'm saying this isn't something I necessarily want to stick my neck out for."

"What would Miss Butterwith do?"

"Call Inspector Appleby."

He was amused. "Okay. What would Inspector Appleby do?"

I sighed. "Gather all the suspects in a conveniently located drawing room…"

"Will a conveniently located meeting room do?"

I closed my eyes. "I guess it will have to."

CHAPTER TWENTY-EIGHT

"I want you to know that I think this is a bad idea," I called over the sound of the shower. "And, furthermore, I don't think you should get that bandage wet."

"You can glue it on for me if it falls off."

"Funny," I said around a mouth full of toothpaste. "I faint at the sight of blood."

"You haven't fainted so far."

I spat and bent down to rinse my mouth. When I straightened, J.X. had turned off the taps and was shoving back the grisly shower curtain, stepping out of the tub.

I tried not to stare, but he was...hard to ignore. It was a fairly small bathroom. And talk about a man in his prime. Tall, lean, cleanly defined muscles beneath satiny brown skin. Sable hair bisected his pecs and arrowed down to the straight and unequivocal statement of his returned interest. Forcing my gaze to his face, I said, "I really don't think we have time for that."

"You know that, and I know that, but *he* doesn't believe it."

"Believe it," I told *him*.

J.X.'s mouth tugged into one of those heart-stopping smiles. "Maybe you should whisper in his ear."

And, insanity though it was—and at my age, no less—I got down on my knees in that small and steamy room and took his hard, jutting length in my mouth. Soap and warm, damp skin...

the salt-sweet taste of his excitement. Was there a greater aphro-disiac in the entire world?

I steadied him—and myself—hands on his lean hips, thumbs tracing ethereal circles on slick skin. J.X.'s breath caught raggedly, and he let his head fall back, gasping for air as I sucked him.

His hand brushed my head, fingers twisting in my hair. "Oh God," he said throatily. "I can't believe this…"

Me neither. But here I was putting my experience, if not wisdom, to good use, massaging his cock with my tongue while he blinked wetly down at me, bemused as little jerks of light-ning shot through his nerves. Nice to be able to do this to him—for him. I lowered one hand to cradle his balls, and he groaned.

I hummed, teasing, and he laughed unsteadily, his fin-gers twining restlessly in my hair. It didn't take long and he was coming, sperm slinging from his cock and sliding down my throat, and I was lapping the fountain up like mother's milk, gasping and swallowing. His knees gave, and he was kneeling with me on the little damp square of rug, holding me tight, kissing my mouth.

* * * * *

"Do you still live in L.A.?" he asked as we trudged once more across the field separating the guest cabins from the main lodge.

"Chatsworth Hills," I agreed. "Are you still in San Francisco?"

He nodded.

The rain had lessened to a fine mist, and for the first time in days, the sun had slunk out from behind the clouds. It had immediately retreated—and I couldn't blame it—but I thought it was a promising sign that the storm was finally passing. The wind had stopped too.

"Do you get down to Los Angeles much?" I asked casually.

"No." He glanced at me. "But I didn't have a reason before."

I smiled twitchily. Our shoulders and arms brushed as we walked. He was right there in my personal space, and I liked it. But where was this heading? I had failed at one relationship; jumping into another didn't seem like the smartest move.

"Don't look so worried," J.X. said. "We're just going to talk to them. It's better to handle these things directly."

"It is?"

"In this case it is. We don't want anyone having time to brood and maybe coming down to the cabins with a shotgun."

My expression must have said it all. He reassured quickly, "That's not going to happen, but it's best to keep them together and talking till the sheriffs show up. Better for everyone—and safer."

I was still fretting over the "safer" comment as we reached the lodge entrance. J.X. banged on the door, and after a time, it swung open cautiously. Rita glared out at us.

And maybe the door hadn't opened cautiously so much as reluctantly, because Rita couldn't have missed the fact that, whoever the killer was, he was inside the lodge.

"Let's get everyone together in the meeting room," J.X. instructed as we stepped inside the lobby.

"Right away, sir," Rita snarled. "Lord knows I've got nothing else to do today."

"Are you sure about this?" I asked him in an undertone as we followed Rita down the hallway.

"It always works in your books," he said innocently.

I shot him a narrow-eyed glance. "Well, I can see why you don't want to try to wrap things up the way you do in *your* stories. It might be hard to explain fifteen people killed in a shoot-out."

He laughed, not in the least offended. But then why should he be with everything he wrote hitting the bestseller charts? I didn't use to be touchy either.

"How long is this meeting supposed to last?" Rita questioned, leading us into the room. A lot of the conference attendees were already there, killing time chatting at the tables placed around the room.

"Hard to say," J.X. replied. "Can you make sure everyone is down here? Kitchen staff, everyone."

Rita expelled an affronted breath and stalked out of the room.

J.X. and I waited while the room slowly filled. He leaned against the wall, relaxed and alert while I wandered to and from the windows. Outside, the rain had stopped.

I walked back to J.X. and said quietly, "You're doing this to keep them together, aren't you? You're trying to keep someone from making a break for it. That's what this is about."

"Maybe."

"You don't *really* expect me to solve this or anything?"

"Stage fright, Mr. Holmes?"

"No, I don't have stage fright. I don't think of this as a play. Or a game."

"Good, because neither do I." He added honestly, "And I really am interested in hearing how you figure it all went down. I think *you* think you know what happened."

By now the room was filled, and everyone was looking our way. Edgar approached and said, "What's going on, boys?"

"Kit is going to share his theories on the murders," J.X. said. "I think everyone is going to find them as interesting as I did."

Edgar looked taken aback, but he nodded and went over to the fireplace, tossing wood into the grate and then taking a seat on the raised hearth.

I looked around the packed room. Rita and Debbie were standing near the doorway with most of the staff. Rachel and Espie were at a table with the remaining Wheaton & Woodhouse contingent including Mindy and George.

A sea of curious and critical faces turned my way.

J.X. said, "Excuse the disruption to the day's festivities, folks. Christopher Holmes has been sharing some of his theories about the murders with me, and I think some of you will be very surprised to hear what he has to say." He nodded to me.

I threw him an ungrateful look. Miss Butterwith always had Inspector Appleby and the redoubtable Mr. Pinkerton on hand for these scenes. Not that I wouldn't take J.X. over Inspector Appleby and Mr. Pinkerton both, but I was so far out of my comfort zone I could have been lying on a bed of nails.

"Go on, Christopher," Rachel said. I could practically see the dollar signs in her eyes as she envisioned a new direction for my writing career. True crime stories.

I cleared my throat. "I think in order to understand this crime, we need to examine the character of the first victim, Peaches Sadler."

"The victim is not—and cannot be—placed on trial," a voice called out stridently. I recognized a new up-and-coming legal thriller writer.

J.X. said, "We're not holding a trial."

"Is it an inquest?" a fresh-faced newbie inquired. She was holding a notebook, under the impression this was now part of the conference's program.

"Uh…no." J.X. gave me another of those encouraging nods.

I said, "Okay, so back to Peaches. I never had a chance to meet her, but…" My gaze fell on Debbie's face, and I changed what I'd been about to say. "I understand that she was the kind of person you either loved or hated."

"Mostly hated," Espie put in, and there was an uneasy titter of laughter from the Wheaton & Woodhouse table.

"I don't know a lot about her background. I know she grew up locally and that she had a wild reputation. I'm not sure if that was something she later felt she needed to live down, but when she moved to New York and sold her first book, she changed her name to Peaches Sadler."

The legal thriller writer chipped in, "The use of pen names is well-established and—"

"This wasn't a pen name, though. According to her former agent, she legally changed her name. I don't know if that was indicative of other problems, but it seems to me that Peaches—or Patty as she was formerly known—had a chip on her shoulder and the sense that other people owed her. Her professional and personal philosophy seems to have been *Do unto others before they do you.*"

"That's not true," Debbie cried. "She was wonderful to me. She was generous and encouraging."

Rita patted her arm, pacifyingly. Her black gaze drilled into me.

I said, "I think she liked you, Debbie. But generally speaking, she was not very nice to people. She was also not a very good writer, although writing seems to have been her burning ambition. When her first novel didn't sell, she successfully plagiarized a much more talented author to launch her career."

Espie's face was flushed.

"That seems to have been a pattern through her professional life, stealing other people's work and passing it off as her own. What Peaches was very good at was the personality side of it. She might have been a pill to those closest to her, but she knew how to turn on the charm for readers and booksellers. She was pretty, she could be charming, and she was very smart. Her career flourished. I don't know about her personal life. Steven Krass obviously knew her pretty well, and he seemed genuinely broken up over her. But there were other people close to her who she betrayed. Betrayed with unnecessary cruelty, which is what I think got her killed."

J.X. tipped his head to me in that...*keep it rolling* fashion. His eyes were on the room, watching the faces turned and listening.

"For whatever reason, she liked hurting people," I said. "She went out of her way to hurt people, and the people who she seemed to have the biggest grudge against were the people who knew her when she was transitioning from Patty to Peaches. I don't know what that was about, but this weekend she found herself sharing airspace with some of her oldest and most bitter enemies. And being Peaches—or Patty—instead of trying to mend some broken karma, or ignoring those folks, she turned her hand to a little more mischief-making."

"Meaning what?" George asked warily.

"Well, to start with, trying to seduce you. Seduction was pretty much her default setting, so I don't think it was about you so much as trying to get at Mindy who probably didn't try and hide the fact that she thought Peaches was an ignorant and talentless slut."

"Oh my God," Mindy exclaimed, looking around. "He's trying to do the drawing room denouement. I *knew* this felt familiar." She was chuckling.

George stood. "If you think *I* killed that bitch, you're out of your mind."

"Sit down," J.X. warned, pushing away from the wall.

Mindy tugged his arm. "Sit down, silly. The guilty party is never one of the first people mentioned." To me, she said, "Go on, Christopher. This is fascinating. So you *do* know who did it."

"I don't think you killed her, George. I think you're pretty experienced in the ways of the…heart, and you aren't about to jeopardize your…" at the last instant I substituted *meal ticket* for "…happy relationship with Mindy." I glanced at Mindy. "And Mindy alibied you, which I believe is true because I don't think Mindy lets you out of her sight long enough to get into trouble."

Espie hooted with laughter at that one. "What about Mindy? She could have killed Peaches. I heard them arguing that night."

Mindy gasped indignantly.

I said, "If George wasn't having an affair with Peaches, and I don't think he was, then Mindy doesn't have a real motive. On top of that, we have the nature of the second crime to consider. Peaches was struck with a piece of firewood—probably in this very room—which indicates rage and impulse. But Steven was killed out back with an axe. I can't see Mindy using an axe to take someone out. But even if that grandmotherly exterior hides the heart of a Lizzie Borden, we come to the problem of moving Peaches' body. Whoever killed her had to be strong enough to carry or drag her out to one of the vehicles, probably the truck, and then get her from the truck to the shrine in the woods. If you've ever tried to move a deadweight, you'll understand why that eliminates almost everybody here, including me."

"Maybe Krass and Peaches weren't killed by the same person," Rachel suggested.

"I thought of that."

Mindy said, "What about the man who was in her bedroom the night she was killed?"

"Ah." I glanced at J.X. He was watching me curiously. "Yes. We had two accounts of this mysterious man belonging to the pair of boots Mindy saw sitting at the foot of Peaches' bed." My gaze lowered instinctively to J.X.'s boots. He crossed his ankles casually.

"Of the remaining men here at the lodge, both Edgar and J.X. are physically strong enough to have carried Peaches down to the garage and into the woods. And I think they're both strong enough—and mentally tough enough—to wield an axe and kill someone. I don't think either of them are killers by nature, but they're both the manly man type who're willing to use violence to protect themselves and the things they value."

"What makes you think it was a man with Peaches that night?" Espie asked. "She swung both ways."

"I don't know that she really swung both ways or whether she occasionally used sexual favors with same-sex partners to get what she wanted."

"Who *was* in the room with Peaches that night?" Mindy asked, shooting distrustful looks from Edgar to J.X.

"Oh, that's easy," I said. "That was J.X."

CHAPTER TWENTY-NINE

"Huh?" J.X. said, straightening.

"Yeah, you're the killer," I said. "Didn't you know?"

"What are you talking about?" He was staring at me in bewilderment. So was everyone else.

Rachel said uncertainly, "But...but J.X. was hit over the head and thrown in the cellar."

"He faked that."

"I...*w-what*?" J.X. stammered.

"Sure," I said.

"How the hell would I do that?"

"You're a cop. You know all kinds of ways to do stuff."

He was staring at me as though I'd gone insane. It was very satisfying.

"So what's my motive?"

"Peaches was your first wife. You married her when you were both attending San Francisco State University. When you tried to divorce her to marry your brother's girlfriend, she threatened to take half of everything you owned."

You could have heard a pen drop. In fact, several pens did drop from the hands that had been busily scribbling notes.

I met J.X.'s wide gaze steadily. After a long stunned silence, he said quietly, "You shit."

I shrugged.

"What happened to this isn't a play, this isn't a game?"

"I told you I didn't want to do this."

"So you accuse *me* of murder?"

"You accused me."

"I didn't accuse you. I locked you up for your own protection. I should have killed you myself."

"Ha!"

"What the hell is going on?" Edgar asked grimly, rising. He looked from J.X. to me.

"Kit is trying to be funny," J.X. said.

"No one's laughing," Edgar pointed out.

"No. Sorry." I looked at him. "And I mean that. I am sorry, Edgar."

He blinked, then lost color. "What's that supposed to mean?"

"It means, I can't prove it, but I'm pretty sure you killed both Peaches and Steven Krass."

Debbie gave a little scream. Her mother grabbed her, hugging her. Rita's bleak gaze met mine over her daughter's blonde head.

I said to her, "And I think if you didn't know all about it, you suspected it."

Her lips folded. She held Debbie closer.

The room was dead silent except for Debbie's hysterical cries. I said to Edgar, "This is what I think happened. I think a long time ago, you and Peaches knew each other very well. I think she came back here, and there was still a certain amount of chemistry between you, and I think you allowed yourself to be seduced."

And who the hell could blame him married to the unlovely and unpersonable Rita? But while Miss Butterwith could have said that aloud, I could not. Instead I said, "And I think Peaches, with her socio-pathological streak, threatened to go to Rita." My gaze was drawn again to Debbie sobbing on her mother's shoulder. "I think maybe Peaches had a particular ace up her sleeve—"

"Don't," Edgar said roughly. Rita was shaking her head back and forth over Debbie's.

I stopped. So I *was* on the right track. I said, "And I think that knowing how jealous Rita is, you tried to reason with Peaches. But I don't get the impression that Peaches was a very reasonable person, and at some point you lost control and hit her with a piece of firewood from that basket over there."

Edgar looked at the basket on the hearth beside him.

"When you saw what you'd done, you carried Peaches down to the truck. Then you either told Rita—"

"Leave Rita out of it."

"Or you went upstairs yourself and packed up Peaches' belongings and carried her suitcases down to the truck. You or Rita are about the only two people who could move about the lodge at any hour without anyone questioning it, and naturally you have keys to every room and every cabin and every vehicle."

He said nothing.

"I think you drove down to the shrine and dumped Peaches. I don't think you had time for more than that, and I don't think you had decided what to do yet. For obvious reasons you didn't want her found on your property."

Tentative sunlight was gilding the faces of everyone in the room. The storm had finally moved past.

"I think maybe I did hear a truck that night," one of the pink ladies chimed in.

J.X. said, "And Steven saw what happened?"

I was watching Edgar's face. "I don't think so. I think if Krass knew for sure what had happened, he would have spoken up. But I think he knew what Peaches… I think he knew a fair bit of Peaches' history, and I think he was drawing some natural conclusions. Did he arrange to meet you that night?"

Edgar said nothing. His eyes moved to Debbie and Rita. He looked at me.

I said, "If you tell me what happened, I won't offer my theory on motive."

When he spoke, Edgar's voice was hoarse. "I didn't arrange to meet him. I waited for him to go to bed that night, but he didn't. He couldn't sleep, I guess. He paced in his room for hours and then, finally, when the rain stopped for a little while, he went outside to smoke. I followed him to the patio, and I… shut him up once and for all."

There were a number of winces and shivers from our spell-bound audience.

"How did you get hold of my earring?"

His eyes met mine unwaveringly. "It was in the folds of her clothing. It must have fallen out of your ear when you bent over her body. It dropped on the truck bed when we lifted her in." He shrugged. "I didn't have anything against you, but you'd had a run-in with Krass that night, so I thought I'd use it."

"Why did you attack J.X.?"

"I was snooping in the cellar," J.X. said. His eyes met mine. "That much I do remember."

Edgar nodded reluctantly. "You were snooping everywhere."

"Why didn't you kill him?" I asked.

Edgar scrubbed his face wearily. "Because I wasn't sure we—I—was going to get away with it, and I didn't want to make things worse for myself. Things were unraveling too fast, and there was no point killing a cop if I was going to be arrested anyway. I thought I'd wait and see what happened. If I could have made someone believe that he'd killed Patty, but..." He looked at me. "You kept insisting on all the reasons he couldn't have."

He could have killed me, of course, but that was veering into mass murderer territory, and Edgar wasn't that kind of a killer, although as frightened and desperate as he was, he must have at least considered it while I was bending over that black pool in the icehouse. A shudder rippled through me as I remembered—

"There's a plane coming," George spoke suddenly, pointing at the long picture windows. "Helicopter, I mean."

We all turned and stared out. Sure enough a sheriff's copter was hovering over the vineyard, making its slow approach, scanning for a good place to land.

"I don't think I should say anything more," Edgar said.

I tended to agree with him.

Everyone was rising, crowding out through the meeting room doors, going to greet the sheriffs. Edgar went to Rita and put his arms around her and Debbie. The three of them stood there in a small huddle, holding tight.

There was a hand on my shoulder. I turned, and J.X. was behind me. Having to look up to meet his eyes gave me that funny fluttering feeling in my belly. He was shaking his head, but he was smiling too—wryly.

"Nice going, Holmes. Even if you did get sidetracked and accuse me of murder."

"Elementary, my dear—"

He kissed me.

ACKNOWLEDGMENTS

Thank you to the book's original editor, Sasha Knight. Thank you to Keren Reed for additional edits.

Keep reading! Here's an excerpt from
the next book in the *Holmes & Moriarity* series:

ALL SHE WROTE

HOLMES & MORIARITY II

JOSH LANYON

CHAPTER ONE

"I knew it," J.X. said. "I knew you'd do this."

I held onto my temper, although that's a comment guaranteed to fry anyone's fuse—and mine isn't the longest to start with. My fuse, I mean.

"No, you didn't. *I* didn't know I'd do this. How could I have known this would happen? Anna didn't know this would happen. If Anna *had* known this would happen, I'm sure she'd have done her best to avoid falling down those twenty-two flagstone steps in her garden."

"And if your old former mentor hadn't taken a tumble down the garden path and needed you to fill in for her with this writing seminar in the Berkshires, you'd have come up with some other excuse for why we couldn't get together this weekend."

I think it was more annoying because J.X. was using that vastly reasonable tone of voice on me. Like my predictability was *almost* amusing. But the main reason it was annoying was because deep down inside I knew he was right. I had been thinking of possible reasons for canceling before Anna's phone call.

I said vehemently, "Bullshit."

"No, it's not." No trace of amusement now. "I wish it was."

"Anna needs my help. She's got a broken ankle and busted ribs. What was I supposed to tell her? No can do. I've got a hot date?"

"Kit..."

"What?"

"In three months we've seen each other three times—two of which times you had to cut the weekend short. It's pretty obvious that this...relationship isn't something you want to pursue."

My heart sank like a stone. I could almost hear the lonely little plop.

"That's not true," I protested. "You're not being fair. I'm just out of one relationship. Of course I'm proceeding cautiously."

"*That* I could understand. The problem is, you're *not* proceeding. Three times in three months is not proceeding. Your brakes are locked and your transmission is stuck in park. I think it's bad timing, Kit. Again."

J.X. didn't sound angry. He didn't sound hurt. He sounded resigned. A little wry. And I knew he'd been thinking about this—as he waited for me to cancel yet again—and that his mind was already made up.

And that was probably for the best, right? Because it *was* bad timing. It was too soon after David. I wasn't ready to start up again—let alone with a guy five years my junior. It was doubtless a good thing that one of us had the presence of mind to see that it was not going to work between us. We'd had our shot and it hadn't taken. That was that.

So why did my heart keep foundering in that arctic bath, trying vainly to gain some kind of purchase on the icy walls?

"What are you saying?" I asked. "I'm off your Christmas card list?"

"I'm saying…" J.X. took a deep breath and I understood that it wasn't as easy for him as I'd thought. "I'm saying that if you ever…change your mind, give me a call."

I opened my mouth, but the words didn't come. Not because I didn't want to say them, but I wasn't sure I would be saying them for the right reason—and whatever J.X. thought, I cared too much for him to say them for the wrong reason. I was trying to make my mind up when he disconnected.

Like fine wine, I do not travel well. Sure, when I was young, fresh, low in acidity and not so tannic, I was a more adventurous spirit. But at forty, divorced—or as good as—and my career having been through the shredder and back, well, let's say I had developed a taste for home and hearth. My own home and hearth.

Especially after being involved in a homicide investigation three months earlier. Of course every cloud has its silver lining, and the bright side of my being suspected of murder was that my books, featuring intrepid spinster sleuth Miss Butterwith and her ingenious cat Mr. Pinkerton, were once again hitting the bestseller lists. Well, some of the bestseller lists. As my agent Rachel kept reminding me, platform is everything in publishing these days, and my wobbly new platform was apparently that of amateur sleuth. Which was still an improvement over my previous platform of crotchety reclusive has-been. *That* platform had more closely resembled a scaffold.

Anna Hitchcock was one of the few people in the world I would break my no-travel rule for. Way back when I was a student in the MFA program at UC Irvine, Anna, already touted as the American Agatha Christie, had been my professor and my advisor. She had been more. She had been a mentor and a friend. I owed my writing career—and it had been a highly successful career until recently—to Anna. So when she had called to say she desperately needed my help, even I—famous for my lack of, er, helpfulness—could hardly refuse.

Even if I'd wanted to. And I hadn't—not least because it gave me an excellent excuse to avoid another awkward weekend with J.X.

Which was something I didn't want to think about as I staggered off the plane at Bradley International Airport in Windsor Locks, Connecticut. Anna's estate was in the Berkshires. Nitchfield, to be exact.

From what I remembered, Nitchfield was a historic small town right there at the intersection of Routes 202 and 63. It was in the heart of a region that referred to itself as "America's Premier Cultural Resort". The Berkshires were popular for hiking, biking, skiing, fishing, white-water rafting, antiquing, wine tasting…you-name-iting. In the fall the area was famous for its gorgeous autumn foliage.

But this wasn't the fall. This was dead winter. February. And Nitchfield was buried under a scenic blanket of snow. Did I mention I hate driving in snow? It should go without saying. I picked up a car at Budget Rent-A-Car and proceeded north to the Asquith Estate.

I'd been there once before, more than ten years earlier. The house, designed in 1908 by noted architect Wilson Eyre, was a registered historic place. Ten thousand square feet of hand-carved chestnut wood paneling, marble staircases, limestone fireplaces, hardwood floors, and French doors opening onto fifty acres of garden and landscaped woodland. It was an authentic classic English country estate complete with tennis court, pool, garden house and a guest cottage where the writing seminars were held.

In short, the Asquith Estate was proof that some people did still earn a nice living from writing fiction. All that it lacked was someone named Bunty and a corpse in the drawing room.

I felt qualified to apply for the part of corpse after I arrived shortly before dinner. What the idea is behind combining the serving of salty packets of dry snacks and overpriced alcohol might be, other than trying to turn airline customers into desiccated fossils, I can't imagine.

"We haven't met." A tall, serious-looking young blonde woman greeted me as I stood studying the stately life-sized portrait of Anna which hung over the enormous fireplace in the entry hall. She offered a cool hand. "I'm Sara Mason. Anna's PA."

"Lucky Anna."

I meant lucky Anna to be able to afford a PA, but Sara gave a weary smile as though she was getting rather tired of predatory men hitting on her day in and day out. "How was your trip, Mr. Holmes?"

My trips are always horrible. That's why I strenuously avoid traveling. I spared Sara the gruesome details, restraining myself to a mild, "I don't think any of the passengers will actually sue. And they did eventually find my luggage."

Sara gave me another of those polite and automatic smiles. She was taller than me, and probably about my age—it's hard to tell with women who take care of themselves. She looked younger than I felt at the moment. Her eyes were a steely gray and her hair was that shade of blonde that is closer to white. A snow princess. I half expected to hear the tinkling sound effects for ice crystals as she beckoned me to follow her.

"Anna is upstairs. She's anxious to see you."

"How is she?"

"Lucky."

"What exactly happened?"

Sara's direct gaze faltered. "An accident. She was on her way back from the guest cottage and she slipped on the garden steps. They're icy this time of year." She added huskily, "It was a miracle she wasn't killed."

My luggage had already been whisked upstairs by well-trained minions, but I wished I had time to splash water on my face, freshen up before I faced Anna. Not that I would dare demur once the chilly Sara had given me my marching orders.

I followed her across shining parquet floors and up a marble staircase past a gallery of oil-painted nobles who I happened to know for a fact were not related to Anna. We came at last to a walnut door in the private wing of the house.

Sara tapped politely, and I recognized Anna's rich, cultured tones bidding us enter.

The room was furnished in soft grays and muted creams. At the far end were three banks of diamond-paned bay windows half veiled by gold and cream brocade shades and valences. The windows looked out over a frozen ornamental lake. There was a seating arrangement of chairs and loveseats in front of the windows. Against another wall was a large fireplace and across from that was a king-sized bed. Anna was ensconced in the bed. She was wearing some kind of lacy, sage-green peignoir, and she reclined against a mountain of satiny pearl-gray pillows. There was a tea tray on one side of her and a computer table on the other. But she wasn't drinking tea and she wasn't working at her laptop. In fact, she was staring moodily up at the delicate vines and flowers of the plaster ceiling overhead.

As Sara and I walked in, she turned to face us and a bright smile lit her tired face.

"Christopher, *darling*. Look at you, all grown up and sophisticated. I always thought they'd bury you in jeans and a flannel shirt." She held out a hand in greeting. Of course I'd have had to climb on top of the giant bed to take it, so I settled for circling around and bending to kiss her cheek.

"Anna. It's been too long."

"And it would have been longer if I hadn't played the guilt card." She was chuckling, and I felt the old irresistible tug of her charm. Anna would be in her sixties by now, but you'd never guess it. Her hair was still that incredible shade of fiery copper, her eyes—always her best feature—were still wide and green and striking. Her hands and face and feet were meticulously cared for—I could tell because I could see her perfectly polished toes sticking out of the cast on her left ankle.

"How did it happen?" I asked, nodding at the cast—it had several signatures scrawled on its hard shell.

"*So* fucking ridiculous," Anna murmured. I'd forgotten about her potty mouth. Anna always did swear like a sailor. The rumor was the irate student reports used to send shivers through the UCI administration. It takes a lot to offend the sensibilities of your average college English major. "But never mind that. How was your trip? Did the plane have to make an emergency landing? Was your luggage lost again?"

"They found it. And our takeoff was only delayed about an hour."

Anna said to Sara, "Christopher has the most horrendous luck traveling of anyone I know. The only way it could be worse is if the plane actually crashed." She gave that delightful chuckle again. "Do you still have to get plastered before boarding, darling?"

"I'm much more disciplined. I wait for in-flight service now."

"Did you need anything, Anna?" Sara inquired.

"No, darling." Anna waved her away. As the door closed behind Sara, Anna said, "That girl is a fucking *jewel*. My ciggies are on the table, darling. Would you?"

I retrieved her cigarettes from the low table in front of the gray velvet loveseat by the window. There were white roses on the table and more of them in a crystal vase next to the bed. I handed Anna her gold cigarette case.

"Lighter." She nodded to the gilt table beside the bed.

I opened the drawer and blinked at the sight of a pistol nestled beside a couple of paperbacks—all Anna's own—an enamel pill box and a tube of AHAVA hand lotion. The pistol was a Browning Hi-Power, which I recognized from my research for *Open Season on Miss Butterwith.*

"Is that thing real?" I asked.

"Absolutely. Guaranteed or your money back. Straight from the laboratories by the Dead Sea in Israel. The bath salts are amazing. My skin is as soft as a baby's behind."

"I mean the gun."

"Oh. Yes. It's real. Don't worry. I have a permit."

I handed Anna her lighter. "I don't remember you packing heat before."

"Things change. How's David?"

"We're not together."

She raised her eyebrows, lit her cigarette and flicked shut the lighter. "Don't tell me you finally left him? No. Of course not. Well, I can't say I'm surprised." She took a long drag on her cigarette and expelled a blue stream of smoke. "Let me guess. He ran off with your neighbor."

"My PA."

She laughed. I laughed too, although I didn't really find it funny. I doubted if I would ever find it really funny.

"Seeing anyone new?"

I thought of J.X. "No."

"Poor you. But you've still got Miss Butterwith. Although I'm surprised, frankly. I'd heard through the grapevine you'd been dropped by Wheaton & Woodhouse." Her green eyes studied me shrewdly. It was the look that used to make it impossible to come up with a good excuse for handing papers in late.

"We took the series to Millbrook House's Crime Time line."

"Oh, they'll do a lovely job. Such adorable covers. What kind of advertising budget are you getting?"

I shrugged. "It's not extravagant, but it's better than we were getting at Wheaton & Woodhouse."

A sudden silence fell between us. I could feel something was wrong, but I couldn't put my finger on what or why. Anna was still smiling through the veil of cigarette smoke, still watching me.

"What's wrong?" I asked.

"Wrong?" She gestured with her cigarette for me to pull one of the white velvet side chairs over to the bed.

I slid the chair across the glossy floor and sat down. "Not that I'm not flattered by your faith in me, but I don't have any teaching experience, and you know plenty of mystery writers a lot more successful and well-known than me. Why did you call me?"

Anna smiled. "Perhaps I thought it would be good for you."

"That's flattering, but I can't imagine you've given me more than the occasional passing thought in the last decade."

"You don't make it easy, Christopher. You've cut yourself off from everyone. You don't do signings, you don't do conferences, you don't do book tours. You were the best and brightest of my students, and you've lived up to that promise to some degree—"

I snorted.

Anna shrugged, then winced in pain at the unwise move. "Do you deny it? Do you deny cutting yourself off from the old crowd?"

"No. I've been focused on building my career."

"Haven't we all." Anna's voice was bitter. "Listen, Christopher, I know what I'm talking about. My own ambition cost me my first two marriages."

Third time's the charm?"

"There is someone again, yes."

"Congratulations," I said, surprised, although I guess there was no real reason for surprise. It's not like Anna was in her dotage. Sixty is the new fifty, right? And fifty is the new forty, and forty is the new thirty. By the way, how come I didn't *feel* thirty?

"Thank you." She seemed preoccupied.

"I'm still not sure what I'm doing here."

Anna sighed. "All right. The truth is, I read an article in *People* magazine about what happened to you at that writing conference in Northern California. How you solved that murder."

"Wait a minute. You're not saying—"

She gave a funny laugh. "I think I am, actually. That is, I'm not absolutely positive, but I think someone might be trying to kill me."

ABOUT THE AUTHOR

Author of over sixty titles of classic Male/Male fiction featuring twisty mystery, kickass adventure, and unapologetic man-on-man romance, **JOSH LANYON**'s work has been translated into eleven languages. Her FBI thriller *Fair Game* was the first Male/Male title to be published by Harlequin Mondadori, then the largest romance publisher in Italy. *Stranger on the Shore* (Harper Collins Italia) was the first M/M title to be published in print. In 2016 *Fatal Shadows* placed #5 in Japan's annual Boy Love novel list (the first and only title by a foreign author to place on the list). The Adrien English series was awarded the All Time Favorite Couple by the Goodreads M/M Romance Group.

She is an Eppie Award winner, a four-time Lambda Literary Award finalist (twice for Gay Mystery), an Edgar nominee and the first ever recipient of the Goodreads All Time Favorite M/M Author award.

Josh is married and lives in Southern California.

Find other Josh Lanyon titles at www.joshlanyon.com, and follow her on Twitter, Facebook, Goodreads, Instagram and Tumblr.

For extras and other exclusives, please join Josh on Patreon at https://www.patreon.com/joshlanyon.

ALSO BY JOSH LANYON

NOVELS

The ADRIEN ENGLISH Mysteries

Fatal Shadows • A Dangerous Thing • The Hell You Say
Death of a Pirate King • The Dark Tide
So This is Christmas • Stranger Things Have Happened

The HOLMES & MORIARITY Mysteries

Somebody Killed His Editor • All She Wrote
The Boy with the Painful Tattoo • In Other Words...Murder

The ALL'S FAIR Series

Fair Game • Fair Play • Fair Chance

The ART OF MURDER Series

The Mermaid Murders •The Monet Murders
The Magician Murders • The Monuments Men Murders

OTHER NOVELS

The Ghost Wore Yellow Socks
Mexican Heat (with Laura Baumbach)
Strange Fortune • Come Unto These Yellow Sands
This Rough Magic • Stranger on the Shore • Winter Kill
Murder in Pastel • Jefferson Blythe, Esquire
The Curse of the Blue Scarab • Murder Takes the High Road
Séance on a Summer's Night • The Ghost Had an Early Check-Out

NOVELLAS

The DANGEROUS GROUND Series

Dangerous Ground • Old Poison • Blood Heat
Dead Run • Kick Start

The I SPY Series

I Spy Something Bloody • I Spy Something Wicked
I Spy Something Christmas

The IN A DARK WOOD Series

In a Dark Wood • The Parting Glass

The DARK HORSE Series

The Dark Horse • The White Knight

The DOYLE & SPAIN Series

Snowball in Hell

The HAUNTED HEART Series

Haunted Heart Winter

The XOXO FILES Series

Mummie Dearest

OTHER NOVELLAS

Cards on the Table • The Dark Farewell • The Darkling Thrush
The Dickens with Love • Don't Look Back • A Ghost of a Chance
Lovers and Other Strangers • Out of the Blue • A Vintage Affair
Lone Star (in Men Under the Mistletoe)
Green Glass Beads (in Irregulars)
Blood Red Butterfly • Everything I Know • Baby, It's Cold
A Case of Christmas • Murder Between the Pages
Slay Ride

SHORT STORIES

A Limited Engagement • The French Have a Word for It
In Sunshine or In Shadow • Until We Meet Once More
Icecapade (in His for the Holidays) • Perfect Day • Heart Trouble
In Plain Sight • Wedding Favors • Wizard's Moon
Fade to Black • Night Watch • Plenty of Fish
The Boy Next Door • Halloween is Murder

COLLECTIONS

Stories (Vol. 1) • Sweet Spot (the Petit Morts)
Merry Christmas, Darling (Holiday Codas)
Christmas Waltz (Holiday Codas 2)
I Spy...Three Novellas
Point Blank (Five Dangerous Ground Novellas)
Dark Horse, White Knight (Two Novellas)
The Adrien English Mysteries
The Adrien English Mysteries 2

CPSIA information can be obtained
at www.ICGtesting.com
Printed in the USA
LVHW080328020721
691578LV00013BA/2165

9 781945 802867